I0662325

THE FULL CIRCLE:
A SAGA OF UNREQUITED LOVE

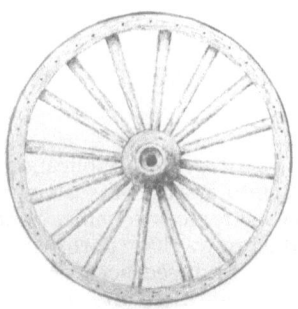

Ratan Kaul

"Life is a full circle, widening until it joins the circle motions of the infinite."

— *Anaïs Nin*

FROG BOOKS

ISBN 978-93-52019-39-7
Copyright © Ratan Kaul, 2017

First published in India in 2017 by Frog Books
An imprint of Leadstart Publishing Pvt. Ltd.

Sales Office:
Unit No. 25, Building No. A/1,
Near Wadala RTO,
Wadala (East), Mumbai – 400037, India
Phone: +91 96 99933000
Email: info@leadstartcorp.com
www.leadstartcorp.com

US Office:
Axis Corp, 7845 E, Oakbrook Circle,
Madison, WI 53717, USA

All rights reserved. No part of this publication may be reproduced, stored in or introduced into a retrieval system, or transmitted, in any form, or by any means (electronic, mechanical, photocopying, recording or otherwise) without the prior written permission of the publisher. Any person who does any unauthorised act in relation to this publication may be liable to criminal prosecution and civil claims for damages.

Disclaimer: This book is a work of pure fiction. Names, characters, organizations, entities, places and events referred to in this book are either a product of the author's imagination or are used fictitiously. Resemblance, if any, to actual people, living or dead, events or locales is purely coincidental and not intentional. Some names, dates, locations, events and technological developments have been used to aid in storytelling and providing a historical backdrop, without any intention to imply anything else. No representation is made as to the completeness or the accuracy of information herein. This book does not purport to promote or criticize any specific country, organization, management system, political thought, philosophy, religion, traditions or cultures.

Editor: Sanjeev Mathur
Cover: Tina
Layouts: Chandravadan R. Shiroorkar

Typeset in Palatino Linotype
Printed at Repro

ABOUT THE AUTHOR

RATAN KAUL'S background includes many years of top-level corporate management and arbitration practice. He is the author of *Wings of Freedom*, a published historical romance novel and a co-author of an anthology on *Arbitration: Procedure and Practice*, published by LexisNexis Butterworth Wadhwa. He is presently working as a management consultant in the information technology sector and other fields and also as an arbitrator.

He loves writing fiction to give an expression to the stories emanating in his mind from the day-to-day incidents in life. He finds it challenging and exciting, constantly discovering new thoughts and ideas and at the same times providing entertainment value to the readers.

He lives in New Delhi, India. More information about him can be viewed on his website http://www.ratankaul.in and he can be reached at email@ratankaul.in

***

By the same author

Wings of Freedom, *a historical romance novel that received wide critical acclaim:*

The book keeps the reader glued with how the protagonists overcome the many hurdles they face to be with each other for ever.

– Hindustan Times HT City

One realized how many layers exist in our diverse society for a simple emotion like love....... It takes you through the freedom movement and blends with it a bit of suspense and adventures.

– The Hindu

A Wonderful Read...Kaul is a fabulous writer, engrossing the reader in his story as the beautiful descriptions, the gripping action, and the sweeping romance all come together to create a wonderful novel that I couldn't put down.

–A reviewer from USA on goodreads.com

The tone of the book is indeed pleasing and the major character is a driven and ingenious man in more ways than one who faces up to many challenges in an honourable fashion. An enjoyable, well-researched read.

– A reviewer from UK on amazon.co.uk

Ratan Kaul's dramatic opening to Wings of Freedom captured my attention immediately. I wanted to turn the page and keep turning. The story flows with the ease of cleverly descriptive language.

– A reviewer from Australia on amazon.com

"Wings of Freedom" is a beautiful love story...The plot captured my attention and held me hostage to the last page... It is with great honor that I highly recommend this book.

– Review by 'Readers' Favorite', USA

***

ACKNOWLEDGEMENTS

To Leadstart Publications and their management team, Sanjeev Mathur, editor of the book, and the design executives.

To my readers for their love and encouraging response that keeps me inspired in my writing journey.

To my wife, Usha, for bearing with me during my literary pursuits that involve long hours before the computer.

***

CONTENTS

CHAPTER 1

Pipra (A tribal forest area in Central India)
December 1982

'Oh hell! Was this a mistake?' Rohit wondered, staring at the film of dust covering his baggage that stood on the edge of the dirt road.

He looked around. Not a single soul was to be seen and there was a stunning silence, except for the rustle of teak tree leaves by the wind, or the occasional distant howl of a jackal. It was the strangest feeling he had ever had.

His friend, Sachin, sat wearily on a stone slab, holding his head in his hands. Soon, his melancholic voice broke the eerie silence as he stood up flailing his arms. "*Yaar*, I'm pissed off. This place appears to be farther away from civilization than we'd anticipated...two hundred kilometers from a city...seven hours of tortuous, rattling journey...deep into ravines and forests. I'm not sure if it'd figure anywhere on a geographical map."

The two of them had been waiting for over an hour near a road sign with an arrow reading 'Udyog Nagar-12 Km'on a desolate forest road, where their state roadways bus had dropped them. A company vehicle from their new employers, Udyog Steel, was supposed to take them from that T-junction to the construction site at Udyog Nagar, where they had to report for their first job. But not even a bullock cart was in sight and dusk was approaching fast.

Soon, it started getting dark and the clouds became thicker. "Oh god, it's making the night even more threatening," Rohit thought with creased eyebrows as he looked up at the sky.

He was now praying for the miraculous appearance of some transport, even just a horse-cart or a rickshaw. His thoughts snapped as he saw twin gleaming rays of lights from a distant road curve piercing the darkness on the road, and then heard the whirring sound of an automobile, both getting amplified slowly.

In a few moments a car reached them and came to a screeching halt. Rohit's legs jerked impulsively and he quickly scanned the passenger in the back seat. Before he spoke, the rear car door opened and a man in his forties, wearing a blue suit, came out.

"Hello, boys, can I help you?" The man asked in a gruff voice.

"Sir, we are new engineers from Delhi proceeding to Udyog Steel, and as luck would have it, we're stranded here. The vehicle promised by the head office did not turn up. Can you please give us a lift to the factory?" Rohit pleaded.

"Oh, sure. Come on inside," the man said comfortingly.

Rohit's face lit up. "Sir, it's a great help."

The man had a friendly smile. "I'm Shyamal Bose from LT Constructions, contractors for the steel project."

"Good to meet you. I'm Rohit Kapoor and this is my friend, Sachin Malhotra," Rohit said, extending his hand.

They dumped the baggage hurriedly in the boot and jumped into the car. As they drove on the bumpy dirt road, Rohit could discern the vast expanse of the factory area and the mass of undeveloped land with valleys and ridges adjoining it despite the darkness.

"Do they have a guesthouse here?" He asked, turning to Shyamal.

"Yes," Shyamal replied briefly.

The thoughts in Rohit's mind now centered on a nice shower followed by the gastronomical delights of *tandoori* chicken washed down with chilled beer in the air-conditioned dining room of the company guesthouse.

Shyamal stopped in front of a building that looked like a large, unplastered, ramshackle cabin with a projected asbestos roof. "Boys, this is the administrative office. You're lucky, the lights are on. It seems Mr. Divakar, the chief administrator, is working late hours," he said.

"Such a clumsy, inelegant building," Rohit thought disappointedly, but "Thanks for your help," he and Sachin said in unison, as they hurriedly took out their baggage, covered with layers of dust, from the car boot.

Divakar Srivastava, the Chief, wearing heavy moustaches and crew-cut hair streaked with grey, narrowed his eyebrows as he looked up with a frown and glanced at their dusty clothes. Rohit could guess a blend of annoyance in his eyes at being intruded upon at the late hour and a bit of amusement at seeing two men in their sweaty, dust-covered shirts and disheveled hair.

His heart raced. "Good evening, sir," he started and explained to the Chief about the bus leaving them at the road junction and then their rescue.

"I am sorry for that." The Chief's voice had softened and his face now reflected a blend of apology and sympathy. "Anyway, welcome to Udyog Steel. Please meet the admin manager, Rajiv Verma, tomorrow morning and he'll give further instructions to you."

"And, as for your stay," he added, "my secretary, Manik, will right away escort you to the guesthouse in my car."

At the guesthouse, which had the appearance of shoddy barracks, Rohit's thoughts of sleeping in a cosy air-conditioned room and eating a sumptuous dinner vanished. All they got to eat was a sandwich with lukewarm coffee. Was that the reason Shyamal was so brief and cryptic when asked about the guesthouse? Rohit wondered.

The room that he was guided to later was clammy and it reeked of a musty smell. A bed with unkempt bedding under an antiquated fan stared at him. But by that time, he was too tired to think of anything else than to jump in it.

***

Rohit and Sachin woke up to a warm sunny day with the anguish of the earlier night largely dissipated. With a renewed enthusiasm, they had proceeded to meet Rajiv Verma in the admin department to present their joining papers.

"Ah! Engineers from Delhi, coming all the way to this remote area," Rajiv remarked as they produced their appointment letters.

"You may proceed to the conference room for your first briefing and orientation meet," he added hurriedly.

As Rohit left the room with his friend he had a strange feeling that that Rajiv's behavior was a bit cold... no words of welcome that the new engineers would have expected... perhaps he was beset with his own problems.

***

'UDYOG STEEL PLANT' was the heading on the layout map hanging in the conference room located in the factory.

About a dozen other trainee-engineers were already seated there.The din of 'hellos' reverberated in the room, but was interrupted when a person, around fifty, entered and walked towards a chair on the dais. His receding hairline and weathered skin indicated the long innings he must have had in industrial construction.

The man wore a welcome smile. "Gentlemen, my name is Prasad and I'm the project manager as well as the training head here. Now, you may also introduce yourselves."

Rohit and Sachin stood up to introduce themselves as the engineers from Delhi, and the others too followed suit. As the introductions continued, it was revealed that that there were two engineers each from the metro cities of Delhi, Calcutta, Bombay and Madras; the rest came from other cities.

Sachin nudged Rohit. "Did you see the arrogant airs of those two from the BIT, particularly the one towering over others and with a surly face--perhaps his name is Vikrant--thinking they're superior, being graduates from an elitist college?"

"Don't worry, we'll take care of them later," Rohit whispered as all settled down on their seats and Prasad called them to attention.

"It's good to have you all here. Now, as for your training, we've planned that in the morning hours you'll observe the construction work in various sections allocated to you and in the afternoons you'll have the training classes. After every quarter, there'll be a performance evaluation, and the grades that you get will determine your departments and the salary structure."

Ashok from Bombay hissed, "Oh, no sir! Not again! We've already had enough of these classes, assignments and evaluations in the last five years in our college." Voices rose in support of Ashok's remark, but the din increased gradually, becoming reminiscent of uproars in a college lecture room.

Prasad raised his hand in a pacifying gesture. "Don't worry; you'll find this to be quite an enjoyable period." He then proceeded towards the whiteboard and continued, "Now, I'll draw a chart to explain various sections in the factory. Please have patience in the meantime."

As Prasad's back was turned toward the trainees, whispers erupted again in the room.

"Hey, Rohit! It seems we're back in our engineering college with another semester of academics. Imagine this to be Prof. Karunakaran teaching industrial chemistry. Prasad just resembles him," Sachin said and then added looking toward a window, "except that we can't see any girls here."

Rohit's mind was working in another direction though. He was pondering how these evaluations might lead to a fierce regional competition with the trainees from different states. "Sachin, get ready for the heat. You're the one who can put Delhi on top. As for me, you know I'll be taking it easy with lots of trekking trips in these ravines," he teased his scholarly colleague.

Sachin mock-punched Rohit's arm. "You're always up to some mischief! I know you're going to explore these areas for semi-clad tribal girls, like the ones we saw at the bus-stops on our way here."

While Rohit's lips extended in a faint, silent smile, Sachin was unstoppable. "And I do remember your crush on Shalini and the love poems you used to send to her."

Rohit didn't reply but a current of happiness surged from his heart. For a moment, his mind went back to Shalini and his meetings with her in college. "You creep!" He blurted, his voice a bit loud this time.

A stony voice came from the back. "Hey, you two. Don't think this is your college in Delhi!" Vikrant, in the back row, shouted, grimacing coldly. "Better be quiet for a while."

Rohit's face tightened for a moment, but then eased gradually. *Seems, there are going to be bullies here too, like in college.*

Meanwhile, Prasad turned toward the trainees and his voice now had a lecturer's tone. "Well, boys, let's have silence, so we can talk business now. Just to refresh your memory--the basic steps in steel melting are conversion to steel of various grades in a converter, and then rolling it to various forms like bars and billets in rolling mills. This is the first phase of the project. But the company has plans to set up an integrated steel plant here in the second phase. The main raw materials for that—iron ore and coal— are available in plenty in this region and that's the reason this plant has been located here in this remote area."

"Sir, what technology is being used for these processes in the first phase?" Dipankar from Calcutta shot a question.

"We've imported the technology from Steelco of USA in most of the sections," Prasad was quick to reply.

Sachin was up on his feet. "Sir, I'm just wondering why the US technology has been used and not the Russian technology. We already have the Bhilai steel plant where the Russian technology is working well."

Rohit, who was listening intently to all this, chuckled internally. *Sachin, a scholar as he is, seems to be right. Perhaps, we can have an interesting ideological bout here between people having leftist and rightist leanings.*

"Yes, that seems to be quite an important question," he said emphatically.

"What's the big use of this comparison when the technology supplier is already finalized?"Vikrant retorted, raising his voice.

"These people from Delhi always think themselves to be super intelligent."

Prasad raised his hand. "Please be quiet," and added, brushing his chin, "Well, Vikrant, I think that is a relevant question and I'd surely like to answer it myself to demonstrate the special features of the Steelco technology. But presently, we are short of time, so, let's keep it for our next session."

As Vikrant threw angry glances at the two friends, Prasad walked up again to the whiteboard and explained the location of various plants and facilities, starting from the storage areas for raw materials to the warehouses for finished steel.

"Now, boys, if you don't have any further questions, may we proceed to the construction site and see what's happening there practically?" Prasad asked. "Please put on the steel helmets, lying on the table outside."

There were no questions and he led the group to the site. Rohit curiously watched the area humming with a lot of activity with the cacophonic sounds of construction. Suddenly, a massive red-painted excavator rushed in with a roar threateningly from a side road.

"Watch out!" Rohit shouted. The group dodged sideways and then moved on amidst the clank of treads, grinding of gears and the roars, whirring and vibrations of tractors, loaders and bulldozers.

Questions swirled in Rohit's mind as he cast a curious, wandering gaze on the huge sprawling area—a blend of completed buildings, sheds under construction with concrete and steel bars butting out and half-finished walls, and excavation going on at other places with mounds of earth lying aside, clouds of dust flying over. He turned to Sachin. "This job of execution of a green field project has its thrills, but will it prove to be more satisfying than the lucrative management jobs we had been offered in Delhi?"

Sachin looked up at the sky. "I'm sweating even on a winter afternoon," he said with skeptical laughter. "Well, we'll be missing the air-conditioned cubicle environment here, but let's see how it goes."

Soon, a convoy of dumpers and loaders carrying sand, cement and bricks drove past under the blazing sun, after which his ears pricked to the resonant shouts of *haisa, haisa*. As he turned, he saw half a dozen sweating Khalasis–the manual construction workers, with sweat trickling down their faces, pulling a large tank with a rope. Another group maneuvred strenuously to place a piece of equipment on its foundation with wedges, pry bars, jacks and a chain.

He scanned the scene pensively for a few moments and then nudged Sachin. "Do you see the blend of mechanization and human labour here? On the one side, you can see the up-down movement of pile drivers and the swiveling of gantry cranes, and on the other side, there are these men moving the heavy machinery manually by ropes."

Sachin nodded. "Of course. Quite a new experience."

When they reached the end of factory area, Rohit stood still for a few moments as he caught a glimpse of a large number of huts with thatched roofs. "That's the colony where most of the construction workers live. Beyond that is a cluster of villages," Prasad pointed out

"Why is it that the company has not made proper residential quarters for these workers?" Rohit was on the brink of asking, when the emptying out of stone aggregate in the storage yards by the dumpers raised a heavy mass of white dust, forcing the group to halt. It was also the end of day and time to return to the guesthouse.

On way, Rohit remained engrossed in his thoughts about his college days and the good time he had with Shalini. He was still unsure whether he had taken the right decision to join this factory.

***

Rohit and Sachin had a quiet dinner, barring the only words from Rohit, "The food is so bland here. I wonder if they'll change the menu."

Back in his room, Rohit slumped on his bed, but sleep evaded him. His stomach churned, and suddenly, he felt homesick as memories of his hometown haunted him. He got up and gazed out the window at the star clusters. He fondly recalled the words Sachin had said about Shalini during the day in the training class and his mind went back to days in his college, which he had entered as a seventeen year old.

Shalini, his first crush and first love...

His college, housed in an old British-style building with octagonal turrets, included both engineering and fine art departments. While there were no girls in Rohit's class, there were quite a few of them in the arts department. During free hours and breaks, the students of both departments occupied the domed pavilions or the lawns, but they rarely mixed with each other.

 Rohit was particularly fascinated by a girl of the same age, who used to sit on the far side of the lawn during the break and remain busy with her sketches. He never had the courage to speak to her, but during lunch, his eyes always wandered towards the arched corridors and the circular staircases from where the arts students would exit. On a few days, he would see her coming out with her drawing board in hand, wearing a *salwar* and *kameez* dress, her hair hanging loose. But he had never ventured to approach her.

One afternoon, he was passing the corridor, his mind engaged in his physics assignment, when he heard a thud. As he halted and turned, he saw the same girl, a few thin lines etched into her forehead, standing near a colonnade of the building. She had an easel in her hand and she looked down at a palette-box and a rolled drawing sheet at her feet. "May I help you?" He said spontaneously and with sudden animation, he leaned over, picked up the strewn things and handed them over to the girl.

"Thank you," she said effusively. "I have seen you sometimes in the campus here. You seem to be an engineering student."

He nodded shyly, as his heart raced. "And obviously, you're in the fine arts department."

A smile spread across her face. "Oh yes. I'm in the first year."

Rohit stood bewitched by her charming, innocent face and melodious voice.They had become friendly...

His train of thought broke as there was a roar of thunder and thick, dark clouds hovered in the sky. A prickly feeling enveloped his heart. He was sure he would never be able to meet her again. Restlessly, he returned to his bed.

***

The training sessions continued and Rohit was assigned to the the rolling mill construction, whereas Sachin got the design department.

"You'll be comfortably working on the drawing boards while I will be toiling in the sun," Rohit had said laughingly after the assignments had been announced."But you are the ingenious type and quite suited for the design work. I'm a misfit for that."

Sachin's face showed a flush of excitement. "Yeah! I do like the design work and I'm looking forward to use the recently developed computer-aided design systems."

"Ah! I read somewhere that that the US company Apple will soon introduce personal computers too. 80's are going to be exciting with all these innovative things coming in."

A few days later, Rohit sat on a rickety chair and looked keenly at the nearby dust-layered black signboard that read: "Site For Steel Rolling Mill 2," and then his eyes moved to the row of construction workers' huts close to the metal grilled gate of the factory with the sign "Gate no. 2" painted on it. Far beyond, was a ridge with a dense cluster of trees.

"Balu, how long have you been working here?" He turned to his junior, an overseer, who had been deputed to carry out the site survey and preparation of site plans.

Rohit had started visiting the site of the shed, the supervision of which had been assigned to him temporarily, as the civil engineer in charge was away on emergency leave. The site was in a green field and excavation had just started. Rohit became fond of peering through the theodolite, a kind of telescope, rotating it in various directions over the tripod and looking at the people working there. In between he would spend time conversing with Balu to learn as much as he could about the place, the local tribal people and their culture.

Balu shifted his chair and turned to Rohit. "I have been in this factory for only three months, but I have lived and worked in this region for quite a long time." His short stature, light brown skin and wavy hair testified his local habitation in the tribal area.

Rohit curiously watched the female labourers employed at the site, digging or carrying materials from one place to another. Most of them had tattoos on their arms and they wore bell metal earrings, beaded necklaces and thick silver anklets that produced musical sounds.

"That's the traditional jewelry of this place," Balu pointed out.

"By the way, what have these people been doing for their livelihood?"

"These people had small agricultural farms, fully dependant on rains. That's how they managed to sustain themselves, though it was quite hard for them."

Rohit straightened up in his chair. "But why are they now working here in the factory and not on their agricultural lands?" He noticed Balu's forehead getting thin lines with furrows on his forehead as he replied, "They are in a big mess. Their lands got submerged when the government built a dam and a hydro-electric power station here. Rehabilitation was promised by the government–land at other locations and compensation money. But then, not much was given and they were forced to take up employment as labourers. If you like, someday, I will take you to the shanties where they live. They are very poor."

"Yes, this seems to be a great problem," Rohit said as his lips turned down in anguish.

Meanwhile, it was lunchtime and all the workers went for their break. Balu also followed them. Rohit stayed on, juggling with the survey instrument. Suddenly, he saw a female form entering into the frame of the telescope and then disappearing.

Simultaneously, a high-pitch shriek pierced the calmness of the site. It was from the direction of an excavated pit around which a mound of earth was lying. He rushed to the spot, and his body stiffened with a momentary shock. A girl had fallen down the pit and was now struggling to get up.

"Oh god," he shouted and sprinted toward the gate, looking for some help from the shanties located outside. "Hey, anybody there? A girl has fallen in a pit. Help!"

The gate was locked and no one was around to help. He would have to do something himself. Rubbing his temples for a moment, he sprinted back and jumped into the pit.

The girl lay there in a semi-dazed state, sobbing hysterically. Blood dripped from her ankles and elbows, spotting her *lehnga and choli* dress. A current of alarm rushed through his body and he hurriedly tied shredded strips from his handkerchief to stanch the flow. Then, he lifted the girl in his arms and carried her slowly up the scaffolding materials lying nearby.

"Are you okay?" Rohit asked, wiping the sweat on his forehead. His hands shook as he put her on the level ground.

There was no reply.

Soon after, the girl started opening her eyes and the wrinkles on her face smoothed out slowly. The corners of her lips stretched to a faintly smiling expression, with dimples forming in her cheeks. But soon, her lips retracted and the dimples faded away. She brushed her hand over her face, got up slowly and swept off the dirt from her clothes.

"Thank you," she said slowly in a tribal accent, her gaze still averted. Her soft voice went straight to Rohit's heart. But before he could respond, she hastily tucked back the loose strands of her long, black hair and limped off, her gaze cast on the ground.

Rohit's palpitation subsided as he saw Balu running in. "What happened?" Balu asked with alarm. "That girl seems to have been hurt."

"She had an accident–fell into a pit. She needs help. Perhaps, you know her?"

"She is Jhilmil, the daughter of Ramesar, one of our local excavation contractors," Balu explained.

Rohit's forehead was creased. "She needs immediate first aid and a tetanus shot. I'm not sure if they've emergency medical facilities here. You better go and escort her."

After Balu left, Rohit returned to his chair and stretched himself under the sun. Warmth surged in his body. "Jhilmil is a nice name–means twinkling, like the stars do. And she does have charming features– a tribal beauty with dimples," he thought, as a smile crossed his face.

***

As Jhilmil reached home, her younger sister, Barli, met her near the doorstep. Barli's eyes grew wide seeing her limp and downcast face. Then, her eyes darted to the bloodstained clothing and her face grew tense. "*Didi*, what has happened to you?"

Jhilmil looked down, evading her sister's eyes. "Nothing. Just fell down and had some bruises."

As she entered her cottage slowly, her face weary, Barli followed her quietly. "Sit down and let me wash your wound and apply some herbal ointment."

"Barli is so affectionate and cares for me a lot," Jhilmil thought gratefully as she watched her sister grinding a few leaves with a pestle in a mortar. With an age difference of only two years, they had been like friends and confidantes since their childhood.

As Barli applied the thick green paste on her ankles and elbows, Jhilmil swung her two plaits back and forth, leaning back on the chair. Thoughts about the accident in the factory pervaded her. Her family–her father, she and her sister–were new to this place, and she had not met many people. But she had been a regular visitor to the areas near the factory site, climbing up the hillocks and picking berries. Sometimes, she would scurry down the rocky slopes, but this was the first time that such a mishap had taken place.

"Grow up, Jhilmil, you're eighteen now," Barli used to tease her. Though she had reached adulthood, she always acted like a small schoolgirl, sometimes wearing a short *saree* reaching up to her knees or the usual *choli and ghagra* dress.

Barli covered the ointment with a leaf and tied a strip of cloth over it. "Okay, now tell me what actually happened."

When Jhilmil related details of the incident, Barli's lips moved into a half-smile. "*Didi*, it's so strange, you're injured but you have a glow rising on your face," she teased.

"Please keep quiet," she commanded, but she couldn't control her thoughts. *It was a strange experience as it was for the first time that she had felt the tingling warmth of touch of a young man. She had shivered all the while he had carried her from the pit on his arms.*

She felt too shy to relate all these events to her sister. "Barli, I'll tell you some other day. Leave me alone for some time," were the only words she spoke. She didn't know who he was. Perhaps, an engineer. "Are you okay?" He'd asked, and these words kept ringing in her ears.

The memory of his touch shot waves of warmth in her body. She envisioned meeting him again...soon.

***

"Appears we have company! This duo hailing from the great engineering college of Delhi." A taunting voice called out as Rohit and Sachin appeared at the entrance gate of the bachelors' quarters, a plain unpainted two-storey structure, where rooms were allocated to them.

After a week's stay in the guesthouse, they'd arrived at the lobby of the quarters, where the residents sat on chairs in a circle and gossiped. When the duo entered, some whispers, chatter, and intermittent loud voices announced their arrival.

Rohit ignored them and went up the stairs, key in hand, followed by Sachin. As they tried to enter one of the rooms allotted to them, Vikrant, whom they had met earlier in the training class, came up and stood at the door of Room No. 21, tugging his *lungi* dress.

"Hey, rooms twenty-one and twenty-two are already reserved for me and my friend, Shekhar," said Vikrant curtly, his gait a bit unstable and there was smell of alcohol in the air.

"But we've been given the keys of these rooms by the admin manager. And I was told these are the only two rooms available for now," retorted Rohit.

"And Vikrant, you're already staying in Room 10," said another trainee, Dipankar, passing by.

Vikrant was defiant. "Hey, you. Don't come between us!"

"And you two, go and ask Rajiv," he turned to Rohit.

In a sudden move, he picked up a hockey stick and stepped menacingly toward Sachin. "And better behave properly with me in future!"

Rohit grimaced and his muscles flared. Taking a swift leap, he slammed a kick square in Vikrant's abdomen. Emitting a high pitched shriek, Vikrant fell to one side but steadied himself holding a window bar while Rohit grabbed his hockey stick and hurled it into the corridor.

Only one in the group, Karan, the senior engineer stepped forward to moderate the situation. "Hey, what's this commotion here? These are newcomers and they need to be welcomed and not put to this kind of treatment." He checked the room allotment papers of the two. "And they have valid papers for these two rooms."

Vikrant stepped back on hearing the words from his senior. But his eyes fired up as he edged his head back momentarily. "All right, I'll see you some other time."

He picked up his hockey stick and walked away. The crowd dispersed with murmurs.

"Things are going to be tough here," Rohit mumbled as he picked up his baggage and entered his room. "Sachin, get settled in your room. I'll see you soon," he called over his shoulder.

***

"*Yaar*, it's impossible to sleep here," Rohit said as he stood in his shorts and vest at the door of his buddy, Sachin's adjoining room.

Sachin, who was in similar dress, switched on the light and scratching his arms, said, "I've been bitten on both arms by mosquitoes. At least, they could have provided protection nets. This place is surrounded by shrubs and plants and these menacing creatures are bound to be there."

"We'll talk to Rajiv and, if necessary, the Chief," Rohit consoled Sachin.

Next day, in the dining room, Rohit saw Vikrant sitting at the next table. But soon, he averted his eyes from the hung-over guy. "Have we come here to build a career or to get into brawls? Somehow, this place isn't to my liking," he ruminated.

Sachin's voice broke into his thoughts. "Hey, let's go and serve our food."

The two moved to the food table, where the trainees queued up for a buffet-style service.

Frown lines appeared on Rohit's face as he silently scanned the dishes laid on the table, but he couldn't resist complaining when he peered at one of the dishes, a pool of thin watery liquid with a few brown potato pieces floating in it.

"What kind of food is this?" He scowled at the kitchen attendant. "And what is that black stuff? Burnt *rotis*?"

The next in the queue, Dipankar also joined. "What to do? The kitchen is being managed a contractor and it's turned out to be a dismal affair."

The tablecloth was soiled with curry spots of yellow and red. "And see how dirty it looks," Rohit said, wrinkling his nose.

The attendant looked away, ignoring Rohit's observations. "This is all that is available today. Please be quick as other people are waiting."

After they took their seats at the table, Rohit finished his food reluctantly and whispered to Sachin, "Nothing works here, not even the food."

Sachin, who sat with his head down, seemingly in contemplation, shuffled in his seat. His brows wrinkled and he pushed aside his plate. "But you know, it was your idea to come here. You and your ideologies...blah blah!"

Anger rose up Rohit's spine and he thumped the table. "That's just rubbish. Don't put the entire blame on me. You too were a party to it."

After a while, he softened. "Let's give it a couple of months, and then we'll see whether to stay on or quit."

Sachin's face reddened and he got up. "For god's sake, let me take my own decision this time."

Rohit was speechless, wondering about Sachin's sudden reaction. Was something else bothering him? A sigh arose in his chest as he saw his friend walk away.

***

A month passed during which Rohit and Sachin remained busy in their respective departments, though continuing to struggle with the poor living conditions. After the dining room incident, they spent less time with each other, and built up their own set of friends.

Though, Rohit was keen to make it up with Sachin, he didn't get much success for his efforts.

One Sunday noon, he stepped into Sachin's room. "Hey, it's time to go for lunch and you're still in bed with your night dress, unshaven."

Sachin didn't get up. "I'd like to skip my lunch today. I'm feeling somewhat tired and I'd like to take a rest. Also, I've to write some important letters."

"Are you sure?"

"Yeah. Please carry on."

Rohit moved back reluctantly. "Okay, as you wish. I'll catch up with you later. Take care in the meantime."

Halfway to the dining room, Rohit stalled. *Let me go and find some other place to eat. I've heard there is a roadside food stall nearby, run by a guy called Dholakia.*

He turned to the main road and soon entered the dirt track and then a narrow dusty stretch, where a small shack appeared. *"Dholkia's Dhaba"* announced a dust-littered wooden name plate in front of the rustic, open-air eating section. Another hanging board announced the food items: *tandoori* chicken, mutton dishes, vegetarian and non-vegetarian curries and 'speciality of the day' *saag paneer*—all mouth-watering for Rohit.

He drew nearer and hungrily eyed the row of pots on a mud-coated hearth, and *parathas* being baked in an oven. "Hello, I believe you're Dholakia. I'd like to have lunch here today," Rohit announced to the pot-bellied man with a few strands of white hair strewn on his head, sitting behind the counter.

The man looked up and smiled. "Ah yes, I'm the one. You seem to be a newcomer. I know many factory employees who come here regularly, as they don't like the food in the kitchen there. Have a seat. I'll join you soon to take your order."

In the name of furniture, there were a few string cots alongside half a dozen tattered tables and chairs. Rohit walked to a cot that lay side by side with the tables and chairs. "Ah! Finally, I'll have a food to my liking," he exclaimed to himself.

He rested himself with his arms stretched behind him on the cot. Huge stacks of oven fresh breads and curries, being served by the bearers to other customers, whetted his appetite.

"Our factory area is a very dull place, but here it seems to be quite lively," Rohit thought as the mingled voices rose from the groups of customers on other tables. "This should be a good place for gossip, particularly about goings on in the factory."

He ate voraciously and eagerly as if he had been starving. When he had finished, a faint smile rose on his face. That was a hearty meal after a long time.

As Dholakia came over with the bill, Rohit gestured him to sit next to him. "I'm Rohit from Delhi and I joined the steel factory recently. I've another colleague from Delhi, but he didn't join me today. He'd also be happy to know about you and this place that is like an oasis in a desert."

Dholakia's lips curled slowly into a hearty smile. "Thanks. I've started liking you; you seem to be quit an amicable person."

Soon, he was pensive, rubbing his fingers on his chin. "Delhi, you said, isn't it?"

Rohit edged towards him and laughed. "That's right. You seem to have some experience of people from Delhi."

"It's not that..." Dholakia said and paused for a while.

"C'mon, it seems you want to share something with me."

"Well, the truth is that I need to warn you."

Rohit squirmed in his seat. "Warn me? Now, what's that? We met only an hour ago and you seem to sound mysterious."

"Let me explain. There is a group of people from your factory, who come to my place frequently and spend a lot of time here..." Dholakia broke off as he was hailed by a guest sitting on another table. "Sorry, I'll be back in a few minutes."

As Dholakia paced away, tucking in his *lungi* dress, Rohit wondered about what the man wanted him to know. For a moment, he turned his eyes to the two buffaloes tied to a tree trunk. "Ah! He has a dairy here, too. I should try the butter-milk also."

When the man returned, he said hastily, "Well, now more people are pouring in, so I'll be quick."

Rohit's eyes narrowed and he sat upright.

Dholakia's voice was low. "I've heard some people saying they won't allow the engineers from Delhi to continue here, even if they have to use muscle power for driving the two away."

A spasm ripped through Rohit's body momentarily. "I don't believe it," he gasped. "What could be the motive behind this?"

"I heard Vikrant, the leader of their group, saying that you've insulted him," Dholakia said. "I've heard that he is a big bully. And he has the support of Rajiv, the manager. I've been told that they come from the same town."

Rohit's jaws stiffened as the other man continued, "In fact, I feel there is going to be a big problem in the factory. Rajiv is involved in some kind of a dirty game and he's keen to recruit people only from his own town to help him in that."

He sat there, his fingers grazing his temples, trying to assimilate all what Dholakia had said, after the man walked away to attend to other customers.

***

Various strands of vitriolic thoughts swirled in Rohit's mind as he walked back home. Had he chosen this factory for his first job for a progression in his career or to fight the bullies…or to counter the intrigues of the crafty people? He had never capitulated before his rivals and he had the strength and the courage to face all this. But that would deflect him from his career, which was his prime motive. He had his cherished career dreams and he had to realize them at any cost. No, things were not working out there. Perhaps, he should return to Delhi and look for another job.

***

"How are you feeling now?" Rohit asked as he returned and stepped into Sachin's room.

Sachin sat silently, rubbing his eyes. Rohit pulled a chair near him. "You seem to be annoyed because I went out alone to eat."

"No, it's not that. Actually, I've been thinking a bit in your absence." Sachin started but broke off. He then cupped his arms on his pillow and went on in a subdued voice. "I don't like this job and this place. I want to go back to Delhi."

Rohit straightened up and a faint smile crossed his face. "Ah! What a coincidence! That thought has come into my mind too. But what is your reason for quitting?"

There was no answer. As he looked at his friend's sullen face, his eyes fell on a photograph peeking out from behind a pillow. "May I have a look at this?" He stretched his hand and picked it without waiting for an answer. "Ah! Now, I know why you didn't join me for lunch. And your reason for quitting this job is clear too. You're missing your girlfriend, Kavita."

"Yes..." Sachin faltered and then his voice rose to the level of a shout. "Yes, I do. And this time, my decision is final. I've received a letter from her. She has recently got a journalist's job with the *News of India* and now she is keen that we get married and settled down by next year." After a brief pause, he added, "You said you too have been pondering it. What's your reason?"

Rohit's shoulders sagged and his voice was laced with frustration. "Things don't seem to be working out here, the way we wanted."

"But tell me if anything particular happened today that set you thinking about it?"

"Yes, a lot happened." Rohit stoked his chin and narrated the details of his visit to the *dhaba,* the dialogue he had with Dholakia and the thoughts that pervaded him since then. Both sat still until Sachin got down from the bed and moved to his desk animatedly. He picked up a writing pad and a pen. "If you agree, let's hand in our resignation papers tomorrow to the Chief and plan to leave for Delhi, may be a day later, after clearing the release formalities."

Rohit nodded, "Okay, carry on."

Sachin scribbled the letters, signed one and handed them over to Rohit. "Here, sign the other one and take them both to the Chief first thing tomorrow morning. Meanwhile, I'll pack the baggage, make arrangements for the tickets and send telegrams home informing everyone of our arrival."

***

CHAPTER 2

Next morning, Rohit carried the letters to the admin building, a sense of relief enveloping him.

He recalled the words of his father Vineet, a couple of months back as he was packing up to to leave for Udyog Nagar. "I know that you're an adventurous person and you don't mind taking up a job in a remote place. But, Kamla and I would have very much liked you to be in Delhi."

He'd watched his mother's moist eyes and said. "Don't worry, Ma. I'll be back soon, maybe after just a year. I'll be visiting in-between."

He envisioned the happiness on his parents faces, when they'd know about his return.

"Mr. Srivastava is out of town today," the Chief's secretary, Manik, said as Rohit went up to office to hand over the letters. "He'll return tomorrow."

A muscle twitched in Rohit's jaw, but he soon composed himself and walked away. *Doesn't matter. It's just a matter of one day. I don't feel like going to work today. Let me have a cup of tea to relax.* He strolled lazily to the factory canteen and winced as he saw the "CLOSED" sign.

"First time I've found it closed," he mused. "Perhaps, I have to look for some other place to get tea."

Strolling to the periphery of the factory area, he reached Gate 2, near which he had spent quite some for excavation work. "Ah! The workers' hutments. There is a village beyond too. There must be a tea stall somewhere."

The guard opened the gate for him and after a short walk to a lane in the worker's colony, he found a small tea kiosk. As he waited his turn on a worn-out bench, he looked keenly at the brown, boiling tea brewing in a discolored pan and was reminded of the tea sessions with his friends in the high-end Delhi restaurants.

Then, turning his head, he watched people walking hurriedly on the narrow brick-paved street in both directions. The hustle of cycles and the din of rickshaw bells in the narrow street made it quite lively. He wondered what kind of errands these people would be running in such a great hurry.

He was distracted as there was a sudden commotion with an increase in the rush of people amid raised voices, shrieks and wailings of some men and women piercing through the air.

Soon, he spotted a man pacing up briskly from the opposite direction, his hair ruffled and face pale. "Ah! He is the excavation contractor, Ramesar. He seems to be disturbed," he murmured and got up. "Ramesar! Do you live here?"

The man folded his hands and bowed slightly. "Yes, Engineer *Sahib*. But how come you're ..." He broke as his eyes misted.

Rohit's eyes were quizzical. "I just came to have tea here as the factory canteen is closed today. But you seem to be worried."

Ramesar pulled the red cloth that he wore around his neck and wiped his face with it. "There has been a very sad incident here. One of the residents, Banbasi, and his wife committed suicide together ten days back, jumping in the dam reservoir. I and other people here are just returning from the final rituals and prayer meeting."

"Oh god! That's tragic," Rohit's face turned somber. "That probably was the reason why I didn't see you in the factory for a few days. But why did they commit suicide?"

"All due to the building of this cursed dam here," Ramesar sighed.

Rohit stiffened. "Dam? Suicide? What's the connection?"

A cycle rickshaw passed by, touching Ramesar's shoulders. He looked around. "It's getting crowded here. Can you come over to my residence, where we can talk freely? It's not far off, just in the adjacent village."

Rohit hesitated. He'll be soon leaving this place. Why should he get involved in all this? "Thank you. I'll come some other day. I have to return to the factory for some work."

"Won't you like to hear the story of these unfortunate people? Please do come; you can also have a look at the place I live," Ramesar pleaded.

Rohit looked into Ramesar's pleading eyes. *I don't have to go the factory. I don't have anything else to do either. So, I might as well accompany him to his village. Maybe, just to pass the time.* "Okay, let's go," he said tepidly.

The two walked through the forest area amidst mounds and valleys with the sunrays peeping through the trees. Rohit was romping over the cushy bed of strewn leaves, when a few squirrels crossed his path. He stilled for a moment and mumbled, "I have been here for several days, but never visited these scenic spots."

Soon, some rickety houses appeared, with tiled roofs and cow dung cakes drying on their walls. "Have you been living here for long?" Rohit asked.

"No. Actually, I come from Bilaspur. After I got a contract here for earth excavation, I moved to this place temporarily," Ramesar clarified as he entered a narrow lane with smelly open drains on either side, and then stopped before a door.

They passed through a hanging clothesline near the entrance, wriggling through still wet *sarees*, blouses and shirts near the entrance.

Rohit stilled for a while as his gaze turned to a girl standing in the verandah.

He tried to recall the face, now partly hidden by long, shining hair. "Ah, the girl who fell into the pit!" He recalled and the scene of that incident in the factory flashed before his eyes. He had gotten busy with his work and forgotten the girl, whom he had rescued some time back.

Now, his lips creased into a smile and for a moment, he caught a glimpse of the large eyes outlined on a face with high jaws.

Ramesar's voice distracted him. "She is my daughter. Seems, she has seen you before...perhaps in the factory. She is quite fond of watching the machinery and construction work in the factory."

"Yes, it seems so," he nodded. He edged his eyes again toward her, but the girl had perhaps moved inside.

"Jhilmil, we have a guest," Ramesar called as he led Rohit to his sitting room and offered him a chair.

The girl appeared, her cheeks blushing and her head now covered with a blue scarf. *"Namaste,"* she said, folding her hands. Rohit smiled and looked at her round face radiating girlish-innocence. Waves of pleasure rose from his chest and suffused his body.

Ramesar turned to her. "Get some tea for him," he said and then to Rohit, "Well, I'm happy you came here and graced our small place. I live here with two of my daughters--the younger one's name is Barli. My wife passed away a few years back. Jhilmil finished her high school examinations this year from Bilaspur."

Rohit sneaked another look at the corner where Jhilmil was standing, his heartbeat accelerating, as Ramesar said. "I was telling you about these suicides..."

Rohit's manner was now grave. "Yes, please let me know about it. It looks to be a serious situation."

"These were the people who were doing well till about five years back, sustaining themselves on their agricultural land. But when this dam was planned, their entire land came under the area earmarked for the dam reservoir. Like Banbasi, there were thousands of other people whose lands were to be submerged," Ramesar lamented.

Rohit sighed deeply. "This is quite distressing. But they must have been informed by the government about this and arrangements made for their resettlement before starting construction work for the dam."

"Yes, some political leaders and government officers came and made announcements about the dam and alluring proposals for rehabilitation of the evacuees. But when it came to actual execution, there was a hell let loose. Their lands were scooped up by the government and they were evacuated. Initially, they lived in tent camps provided by the government, and they were given token amounts, with promises that it would be followed by alternate lands, houses and full monetary compensation. But that hasn't materialized so far."

There was a knock on the gate with some voices calling for Ramesar. He got up hurriedly. "Seems, *Panchayat*–the village council–members have come to meet me. I'll speak to them and return in a few minutes. Meanwhile, make yourself comfortable. My daughter should be here soon with the tea."

Uneasiness crept into Rohit's mind as he found himself alone in a strange place. But the thoughts of spending some time with Jhilmil warmed him up.

She entered holding a cup of tea and some snacks and placed them on a small table. Then, sitting a distance away, she looked down, twisting and untwisting the corners of her scarf.

"This is the first time that I'm in this situation, facing a girl I don't know much about," Rohit thought. The two exchanged quick, sneaky glances as he sipped the tea.

At times, he saw her lips moving. He guessed she wanted to say something but was too shy to utter a word. He too didn't find words to utter, either.

He finally broke the silence. "How are you?"

Jhilmil raised her face slowly. "I'm okay. Thank you for your help that day. It was really a bad accident." Her words were accented but having been in Balu's company for sometime now, he had become somewhat familiar with the language in that area.

There was silence for sometime as her face came alive looking at Rohit with a faint smile.

His attention got diverted as Ramesar returned. "I had a discussion with the people from *Panchayat* about these suicides and the need to do something to prevent it." He sat on an adjoining chair and went on, "Now, they want to meet you."

Rohit straightened. "Me! They want to meet me! But why?" He asked in an incredulous tone.

"As soon as I told them that I have a guest in the house, who is an engineer from Delhi, they felt you could help them by guiding them in finding a solution to their problems."

Rohit threw up his arms. He could not fathom what was expected of him. "That's ridiculous! How can I help?"

"*Sahib*, they are innocent and uneducated people. They can't even write a letter. They feel that if someone guides them as to how they should take up their case with the government officers in Delhi, they can at least make a start," Ramesar pleaded. "I know, it'd need some resourceful people with political connections who could do this job and your field is totally different. But if you meet them even for a few minutes, it may give them some consolation, maybe only temporary."

Rohit cupped his cheeks in his hands. No harm in meeting the people. At least, he can speak a few words to comfort them.

He got up reluctantly. "Okay. Let's meet them."

When he came out with Ramesar, he looked keenly at the somber faces of people in the group. One of them was holding a sickly-looking child, about five, in his arms.

"*Namaste, sahib*. This child has been orphaned after the suicide of Banbasi and his wife. His debts had mounted and he was unable to repay. That led them to end their lives. All of us are in deep distress as we're in a similar situation." The man holding the child patted the wailing child. "We want help in getting the compensation for our lands. But all that depends on the government in Delhi. We don't know any one there. Also we are uneducated and cannot even write our representations to the authorities. Can you please help us?"

There was a twinge in Rohit's heart as he looked at the men in the group, wrinkles spreading over their prematurely-aged faces.

Ratan Kaul

His mind churned with conflict. They did need some help. But what could he, just a young engineer starting his career in a factory, do? And he had decided to quit that job too. His gaze turned to Jhilmil standing at the gate of her house and watching the proceedings. Innocent. Unblemished. She was also one of them.

Suddenly, her eyes flickered and then her gaze dropped. *Was she trying to convey something to me?* But she soon rushed back inside her house.

Rohit's mind was in turmoil and he stood still for some time steepling his fingers. Not Many words had been spoken between him and Jhilmil. But, her charm and a feeling of some affinity with her possessed him. Soon, a decisive pattern started building up in his mind. "It'd be good to support these people and pool the resources to help them. After all, any person in the society, in any profession, must also think of taking up some social responsibility."

He pondered some remote possibilities. His uncle was a government officer in Delhi—there could be other people who could help. Perhaps, some support could be garnered through the media.

He cleared his throat. "I'll see what can be done, but I can't promise anything."

As the people dispersed after thanking him, he turned to Ramesar. "I'm not sure whether I can be of any help to them, but I'll definitely try. I must leave now. I will talk to you later."

Gratitude was writ large in Ramesar's eyes. "I don't have words to thank you. I'll look forward to meeting you soon."

When Rohit had gone a few steps away, Ramesar caught up with him. "Oh! I forgot. You may have some difficulty finding back the way. I'll ask Jhilmil to escort you to the end of this village. She is quite accustomed to this area."

As they left, Jhilmil stayed ahead for some time, Rohit following her. His hands shook with the closing and opening of his fists as the web of thoughts about this sudden development in Ramesar's village agitated his mind. Gradually, the distance between them narrowed. And they were now walking alongside.

Rohit did not look at her, but he could sense the closeness between them.

His thoughts dissolved as he heard her feeble voice. "Thank you, again."

"For what?"

"For helping our people. My father. Our community."

"Ah! I thought you're too young to understand all these problems. But you seem to be of quite a mature mind."

"I understand some of them. But, unfortunately, I can't do anything about it. I'm glad you've agreed to help."

She stopped as they reached a banyan tree with its aerial roots spread widely.

"I'll have to leave now. I think from here you can find your way. That's the factory area," she said, pointing toward the silhouette of a tall crane at a distance.

He was just about to say his words of thanks, when she startled him with a question. "Do you like banyan trees?"

He had seen only few banyan trees. "I don't know much about them. But I remember one I saw during my visit to the botanical gardens in Calcutta. That's a huge one. People say its canopy is the biggest in the world, and it's about twelve hundred years old!"

Jhilmil's eyes grew large. "Ah! So big! But this tree, though much smaller, is special for me. It provides a kind of umbrella to me. Whenever I've a problem, I come here and spend time reading and writing."

His hand went up to his mouth. "Writing? What do you write?"

"Oh! Nothing much. Sometimes, I try to write some lines to express my thoughts and preserve them..." She stopped short and thrust the corner of her scarf in to her mouth shyly.

Rohit's eyes flickered. He couldn't imagine a tribal girl, with perhaps just elementary education, keeping a kind of a diary. "Ah! Some day, I would like to see what you write?"

She had a mischievous smile. "*Baba* must be waiting for me; I should leave now."

As she turned to walk away, she shouted over her shoulder, "When we meet next, I'll tell you about it."

Rohit stood transfixed for a moment under the tree. It's so strange. This girl, whom he considered a rustic tribal girl, seems to have some intellectual traits.

He started for the factory with the jumbled thoughts of his decision to quit, the suicide of the couple, the severe hardships the people in these regions were facing, his promise to the community members, and most of all, Jhilmil's words crisscrossing his mind.

***

Jhilmil walked slowly toward her home, sneaking glances backwards every few seconds. When she was sure Rohit could no longer see her, she started hopping, jumping, and romping through the forest. A sense of joy swept over her body as she recalled fondly the moments of togetherness with Rohit under the canopy of her favorite banyan tree. With her writing instincts, she began looking for appropriate words to compose a few lines describing her state of mind while humming them simultaneously.

She had crossed the forest area immersed in her thoughts and entered the lane leading toward her home, when she bumped into her sister, playing hopscotch with some girls in the lane, holding a milk can in one hand. "Barli, where have you been all this time?" She asked in an admonishing tone.

"Why? You know I'd gone to the dairy to fetch milk. You've started forgetting things," Barli teased.

An apologetic smile crossed jhilmil's face. "Anyway, leave that game and come with me."

When they were in a less crowded area, Jhilmil stopped in her tracks and tapped her sister's arm playfully. "While you were having the company of buffaloes and cows in the dairy, there were important things happenings here–Engineer *sahib* came to our home."

Barli laughed heartily. "Ah, you mean the man with the telescope instrument for looking at girls? Did he follow you here? He seems to be the reason why your cheeks are flushed pink today."

Jhilmil pulled Barli's blue-ribboned plait. "Shut up and be serious. He came here with *Baba* to discuss about villagers' problems. He has agreed to support them in getting help from the government."

"Ah! In that case, I really missed meeting him today. Maybe, later. But now, tell me everything in detail."

"Okay, let's go over to the well, where there may not be many people at this time of the day," Jhilmil suggested.

They walked toward the well at the end of the lane, where a woman was drawing water with a bucket, pulling a rope over the pulley. After she left, the sisters settled down on the platform near the well.

Jhilmil ran her fingers through her dark hair and let them sway loosely in front of her. "He is a very caring person…" she started, as her heart throbbed with pleasure.

***

"Sir, you didn't come for work today?" Rohit heard a familiar voice as he re-entered the factory gate after returning from Ramesar's village and walked through the construction areas, his mind again getting beset with the villagers' problems. That was Balu, his colleague.

Rohit halted momentarily and forced a smile on his lips. "Just not feeling well today; I'll see you later."

After meeting Balu, his streaming thoughts about the villagers broke. He stopped and looked at the two letters protruding out from his shirt pocket.

"Oh god! I'd forgotten about these resignation letters," he ruminated as he fidgeted with them for a few moments and then returned them to his pocket. His mind went back to his and Sachin's decision to quit the job.

When he reached his quarters, the enormity of the day's events weighed him down. He paced across the room several times, hands held behind his back. Finally, he threw the letters on his writing table and walked to his rocking chair. His train of thoughts swung like a pendulum. On one side was his earlier resolve to quit because of the poor living conditions, the aggression he had experienced, and intrigues about which he had come to know from Dholakia. On the other hand, were his feelings for the severe hardships of the village...the suicide and an orphaned child of five years. Perhaps, there were some latent feelings too that Jhilmil had evoked in his youthful mind, he surmised.

Sachin burst into the room and his exuberant voice startled Rohit. "Hey, good news! I've packed my bags. You better keep your baggage ready, too."

Rohit sat in grave silence, his chair still rocking. Sachin's tone was now subdued as he added, "By the way, what was Chief's reaction to our..."

Rohit didn't answer but he saw Sachin moving to the table and picking up the folded letters. "Oh god! You didn't deliver the letters. And you're silent. Is something wrong?"

Rohit stilled the movement of his chair and grimaced. "Please sit down. I need to talk to you."

Sachin scowled. He took a chair near the table and looked keenly at Rohit. "Okay, carry on."

"The Chief is away on a tour. He will be back tomorrow. But..." Rohit started, his head downcast.

Sachin was impatient. "But what?"

"There is something else, which puts me in a dilemma as to whether I should quit this job."

Sachin shuffled his feet with disgust, as Rohit spoke about his visit to the village and the happenings there. His fists thumped the chair hand rests, and his face reddened. "Look, your arguments are crossing the level of idiocy. We're not social workers. We have to build our careers and in a congenial atmosphere. This is not the place where we should be. We have had a long discussion about that. In fact, you yourself were keen to leave this damned place."

Rohit rubbed his chin and spoke slowly. "I can understand your views. But we cannot completely wash our hands off the social problems. Nobody is helping these people and these suicides will continue. I think we should start a signature campaign and bring it to the notice of the higher authorities."

"This is absurd. I don't want to take part in any of your campaigns. I told you about my personal reasons, the letter from Kavita, and her desire that I return to Delhi...and they weigh heavily for me. Nothing can come between me and her–neither you, nor this factory and most of all not the social work."

Rohit sat motionless for some time and then rose. "Of course, it is your decision and I can't force you to stay on. You're free to tear up your quit letter. I leave it to you."

As he started to exit, he stalled for a moment and turned back. "Wait. I've an idea."

"You and your ideas! No more of them," Sachin remonstrated.

Rohit knew his friend was agitated. But he wanted to make another try. "I know you're missing Kavita. You said she's joined the *News of India*. Let's invite her here to report the distress of these dam-displaced persons and their demands. That will give a great boost to them."

Sachin's face was grim as Rohit continued pleading, "And it will give Kavita a good platform to boost her journalistic stature by bringing up such an important issue affecting this entire region--rather a scoop, as they call it. She may even get a promotion and be picked up by the editor to cover more such important causes in future."

Sachin's face softened though he still looked weary. He moved toward the window, holding his head in his hands.

Minutes passed by, during which Rohit watched his friend standing still. He continued with his pitch, now more vigorously. "And don't forget that she'll be grateful to you for getting this big break and getting into the media limelight because of you."

Finally, Sachin stirred and he spoke, though in a tone laced with uncertainty. "That seems to make some sense, but there is a hitch. What about other problems like the poor living conditions, office intrigues and Vikrant's threats?"

Rohit patted Sachin's arms. "We are two and we'll fight it out. We'll get help from the Chief. And the social cause we are fighting for will give us the strength. Let's draw up a plan."

A faint smile crossed Sachin's face, "Okay, let me think about it." A few moments later, he picked up the letters, looked at them sharply for a moment and then tore them up. "I'll write to Kavita, but I'm sure it'll take a few weeks before she can manage her visit here. Meanwhile, we can explore other resources in Delhi as well as here."

Soon, he set an inquisitive glance at Rohit. "All this is okay, but I'm wondering about the transformation taking place in you. Till now, you have been a happy-go-lucky man; not at all an emotional type. How come now you feel distressed by the villagers' plight, and want to go out of the way to help them? Nothing short of a miracle."

Rohit was tight lipped for a while. He was not sure of the answer. Was it because of Jhilmil? He laughed heartily. "*Yaar*, all that later. I'm feeling starved. Let's have a gourmet dinner at Dholakia's *dhaba.*"

An emphatic high–five clinched the issue.

***

CHAPTER 3

Both friends had settled down again into their regular routine in their different departments, while their training and construction job schedules went on simultaneously.

In the first quarterly evaluation, Rohit scored 9.1 points, surpassing all others. His seniors, particularly the training-head, Prasad, had been quite impressed with his ingenuity and hard work and good reports had been sent about him to the Chief. Sachin was at times envious of him, but he took it in his stride.

One day, Rohit got summons from the boss. As he entered the office, the Chief raised his head from the pile of files in front of him and said, "I have a special assignment for you."

Rohit's eyes sparkled. "Thanks, sir."

"You know we're setting up this plant with US technical collaboration—Steelco of USA is the collaborator. One of its senior engineers, Daniel Armstrong, is coming here to supervise the erection of machinery."

"It would be good to interact with engineers from the US. And out of all the peers here, I have been chosen for this task," Rohit thought cheerfully, as the Chief continued, "Daniel is coming next Monday and I want you to go and pick him up at the Varanasi airport. The flight comes in at ten in the morning, so you have to start early as it is a four hour drive. I'll leave instructions for the driver to pick you up."

Rohit's heart throbbed with joy. "Sure, sir. I'll be there in time."

***

Vikrant met him on way to the factory gate. "It looks you're becoming the Chief's favorite. He calls you quite often," said Vikrant wistfully.

Rohit was silent and didn't want to argue with Vikrant. In fact, after Dholakia had warned him about Vikrant's intentions, Rohit had started avoiding him.

"Anyway, Rajiv Verma has been looking for you," Vikrant blurted. "Something urgent, it appears."

From day one, Rohit had not found the admin manager amiable and he wondered why he had been called.

Rajiv rolled his eyes as he saw Rohit entering his chamber. "Where have you been? You are never to be found on the job. And you have not filled in your performance evaluation report for the last month."

Rohit was still contemplating the answer to Rajiv's queries, when Rajiv continued to growl, "Also, I've been told you and your friend, Sachin, are getting into brawls with people here."

Rohit peered keenly at Rajiv's cunning-looking face. He was not absent from his work but had just gone to meet the Chief. There was still a day left for the deadline to submit the report. And it was not Rohit, but Vikrant who had started the trouble and that too long back. But Rohit did not want to argue. What Dholakia had said about the vicious office politics and intrigues was coming true. But now that he'd decided to continue with the job here, he needed to handle it diplomatically and find out what kind of dirty games those people were into.

He put on a faint smile. "Sir, I'll surely put in the report by the deadline… today itself. And these minor scuffles do happen among colleagues on personal basis–nothing serious."

"Okay," Rajiv muttered as he moved away with a strange cryptic expression.

***

Rohit was deputed to assist Daniel in getting acquainted with the progress of construction and also be a member of the machinery installation team.

One day, during the mid-day break, they strolled along periphery of the factory. As they crossed the site for raw material handling plants, Rohit spotted a few urchins standing behind the boundary fence.

Rohit walked up to them and asked their names.

"Hey, Rohit, you seem to have got busy into something else," Daniel said.

He followed Rohit and looked beyond the barbed wires. "There seems to be some habitation around here. But as I have observed for the last few days, the workers here seem to have facial features different from others and they don't have proper houses to live in."

"You are right. This is a tribal region and people have been living segregated from the mainstream population. Due to genetic differences they have different features. Also, these areas have remained backward for ages but now efforts are being made to develop them."

Daniel smiled weakly. "That's interesting. You see, I also come from a backward area in USA."

"A backward area in USA!" Rohit exclaimed with widening eyes. "Never heard of it."

Daniel corrected, "The place where I come from is in the Appalachian region. Perhaps you may not be aware of the US geography, but this area runs from southern New York to Mississippi."

Rohit listened with inquisitive attention while Daniel continued, "My dad worked in a mine there. There were not many facilities available at that time–wages were low, not all the houses had power, there were no colleges..."

Daniel had a faraway look on his face. He fell silent for a while and then went on, "He used to tell me stories of his childhood — with a limited income and seven kids, his family always had problems getting food, medicines and clothes. When there were protests, the government woke up and appointed Appalachian Commission to improve the facilities there."

Rohit was curious to know more. "I'm sure things would have changed for the good by now."

"Yes, of course, but the area is still not as affluent as the other regions are," Daniel clarified. "Anyway, someday, I'd like to visit the colony of workers here."

"All right." Rohit was cautious. Actually, he was not sure whether he should expose the poverty of the workers to an engineer from USA and whether the Chief would like it. "We will go there someday. Meanwhile, I'll tell you about the problems they've been facing."

The conversation halted momentarily as the hooter blew a siren. "They're just testing the system," Rohit said as he led Daniel to sit on a concrete slab.

"Dan, there seem to be some similarities here with the Appalachia. This region was almost in oblivion, till they decided to build a dam here about five years back. The objective was to produce hydroelectric power that could lead to setting up industries that would in turn provide jobs to the locals," he explained. "The Prime Minister had declared that this belt would become one of the most prosperous regions of India."

Both looked intently at a crane carrying a crated machine and a man shouting instructions to the crane driver.

"The concept appears to be logical, because industries are needed to wipe out poverty," Daniel commented, after the crane had passed.

"Yes," Rohit rubbed his chin. "But there has to be a balance between industry, ecology and agriculture. It seems the planners here did not take into consideration the problems the inhabitants would face when their villages were submerged in the reservoir area. That's what has happened here."

The pitch of his voice increased as he added grimly. "See, now these people don't have a place to live. There are no sources of livelihood as they are neither educated nor skilled in any trade. Agriculture, which has been their traditional source of livelihood, no longer exists for them."

"Perhaps, they need help for rehabilitation," Daniel observed gravely.

"I'm trying to help these people. I'd like to have your advice too, about how best we can help them, based on your experiences in Appalachia."

Daniel was silent for a while and then he edged toward Rohit. "Well, first you need to understand that you can't do it alone. I suggest you approach a few more like-minded people. Get a petition signed by the people in the entire belt here and submit it to the top authorities. Also, invite the media so that the matter comes to a limelight. You need some political lobbying, too."

After a short pause, he continued, "There are things you can do on personal basis, too. For example, start a small school to educate their children. This was also done in our area by social activists."

Rohit listened intently and Daniel's words about starting a school struck a chord. A plan appeared to be crystallizing in his mind.

Warmth suffused Rohit's voice. "Thanks a lot, Dan."

***

With the end of spring, it was still warm when Rohit plodded back from the factory late one evening. He wiped the sweat on his forehead as he still struggled to find solutions to the technical problems in machinery alignment that he had encountered that day. But as he neared his quarters, his train of thought broke and he stiffened for a moment—there had not been much headway in the plans for getting relief to the villagers.

He stomped to Sachin's room and tossed his hard hat aside. "Hey, any news from…" he started, but stopped instantly as he looked at Sachin, peering over a large drawing spread over the table, a pencil dangling in his fingers.

Bending forward, he whistled. "*Yaar*, what is this? This reminds me of the engineering drawings you used to secretly copy from others in the college for submitting your assignments. Whose layout plans are you plagiarizing now?"

Sachin lifted his head and flung a chair cushion at Rohit. "You big mean nasty devil! Was I the only one copying in the college? The entire class, including you, did it."

"Okay, truce!" Rohit guffawed, throwing the cushion back. "I just came to ask whether you received Kavita's reply."

Sachin rolled back the drawing sheet. "I was just compiling the bill of materials that I have to submit tomorrow morning to the boss. Come, have a seat and we'll discuss Kavita's visit." He leaned his head back on the chair as he went on, "Yes. I got the letter only today. She says she's talked to her bosses about the assignment and they've approved her proposal to visit this place and interview people here."

Rohit brightened up. "Superb! Now things will start moving."

Sachin ran his fingers through his hair. "But there are a few things she's pointed out. One is that she can get here only in about a month, after she has finished her current assignments. Also, she feels the campaign would be more effective if we have also the support of some political leaders."

Rohit weighed what Sachin said. Things were progressing, but still there were question marks. Getting the support of local political leaders appeared to be difficult. No one would be interested in taking up such local social causes that wouldn't increase their voter response significantly. But these were the pieces of puzzle he had to put together. "Looks quite workable. But I'm doubtful about the political support. I've written to my uncle in Delhi. But all that will take some time."

Sachin looked again at Kavita's letter and he was now in a light-hearted mood. "Hey, you are forgetting the most important thing. Kavita will be here next month. What plans do you have in mind for her stay here? May be we can go for long drives to the scenic spots nearby."

"Hey! If you are thinking that arrangements have to be made for your and Kavita's secret rendezvous here, forget about it.

She'd be coming here for an important assignment and she won't have any time for amorous activities with you," Rohit replied jovially.

Sachin stepped forward playfully with a tightened fist, while Rohit bent down to avert the blow. "Rohit, you are a devil. Don't forget the college lectures that you used to bunk to chase your girl friend, Shalini, on the buses and later, the secret bike trips you had with her," Sachin blurted.

The friendly repartee between the two continued till it was time for them to retire to their rooms.

***

Next day, at lunch break, strands of thoughts about the villagers' problems began agitating him again. There were other things also that could be done even before Kavita came. Daniel had suggested starting a school for the children. But who would manage that? He didn't have any experience in running a school. And who would be the teachers?

An idea struck him as he gulped the last bit of sandwich with a sip of tea. He could get advice from the Chief, who should surely be willing to help in this social cause. He'll meet the Chief one of these days. As for teaching, one could start with just one teacher. Would Jhilmil be able to help in that? As he reclined on his chair in the canteen, her sweet, charming face flashed before him and his heart beat wildly at the memory of the glowing intensity in her eyes. She had promised she'd tell him about her writing when they met again. He closed his eyes reliving those moments and looked forward to another meeting with Jhilmil under the banyan tree.

***

"Sir, Sinha *sahib* has sent for you. He said it's urgent," said chief engineer, Jayant Sinha's assistant.

Rohit had just crossed the factory gate, walking along a cavalcade of truck-trailers carrying 20-ft and 40-ft containers, enveloped in a great cloud of dust, rising from sand trucks. His eyes were set at the signs "NEW YORK TO CALCUTTA" on the containers, when the assistant hailed him.

What could be so pressing? Rohit speculated, while pacing toward Sinha's office.

There was desperation in Jayant's voice. "There is an urgent job for you. Water supply to the factory has stopped suddenly. Seems, there is a problem with the main water pump at Dongi *nullah*. The construction work is at standstill. Please proceed immediately to see what's happening there."

Rohit picked up two technicians with their toolboxes from the workshop and jumped into a jeep. The vehicle wobbled violently as he changed the gears fast, traversing the rocky terrain and then came to a screeching stop when he applied the brakes near the water intake point on the nullah, upstream of the dam.

As he bent down to examine the two pumps with rusted panels, he found that the terminal boxes of motors were covered with mud, and electric wiring and bearings had been damaged.

He turned to the technicians. "Seems, the water level had increased in the nullah, seeping into the pumps. That caused this damage. For a permanent solution, we need to relocate them to a higher level. I'll discuss it with Mr. Sinha when I get back."

His eyes focused for some time at the long stretch of the water-body and the steep earthen embankment and then he added, "For the time being, please replace the wires and bearings and get the pump running so that water supply to the factory is resumed soon. Meanwhile, I'll search for a better place for a permanent pump location."

He had just started to walk up the embankment when he heard some giggles. Angling his eyes, he noticed a group of girls standing and talking near his jeep. One of them, wearing a sky-blue *saree* dress, and carrying a small sling bag on her shoulders, had her back toward him and she was talking to three other girls. He watched them with raised eyebrows for a while and then walked slowly toward them.

"Ah! That's something interesting. Never thought there would be girls guarding our pumping station," he chuckled on the inside.

When he was near the group, the girl in the *saree* turned toward him. Her laughter stopped and she stilled. Fear swept the faces of other girls and they started walking away.

"Jhilmil!" Rohit exclaimed. "What are you doing here?"

She cast her gaze downwards. "Sorry, *sahib*. We came here to pick berries, and saw this jeep. We were curious to know whose vehicle it could be."

Rohit edged closer to see her lips red-tinted with berries, while her eyes turned to the two technicians at work, a little distance off. "Ah! I see you came to check your machines here."

"Yes, you're right. Actually, I came up the embankment to check if we can shift the pumps to another location at a higher level. Would you like to accompany me and show the way, as I am new to this place?" He said and then added with a hearty laugh, "On the way, I can help you pick more berries."

After some silent moments, she said, "I will accompany you for some more distance, but you have to promise you'll drop me home on your return, as my friends seem to have ditched me."

"Sure," Rohit nodded.

When they reached a broad, rocky slab, Rohit stopped. "Ah! This could be a good place for installing the pumps. A firm foundation and at a secure level," he muttered to himself. "Let's rest here for some time."

He looked curiously at the nullah merging into the vast expanse of water reservoir of the dam. There was no habitation for miles, he gauged. Relaxed, peaceful feelings enveloped his mind as he experienced deep proximity with virgin, unblemished nature.

But soon, he twitched. Scores of villages must have been submerged in that water-body. It must have been be so calamitous for them to get uprooted from the places where they and their forefathers had been living for ages.

There was a rustling sound and soon he saw Jhilmil shifting the bag to her lap. "Ah! What's in the bag? Berries?"

"Yes, would you like to taste some? I don't know if you've tasted such red jungle berries before."

Rohit looked warmly at her innocent face, her slanted part and black hair loosely gathered in the front. The black kohl liner accentuated her eyes. *She is so tender, so simple, so unblemished, and so divine. I shouldn't break her heart.* "Yes, of course. I like them."

Jhilmil picked out a few berries from the bag and placed them in Rohit's extended palms. As he put one in his mouth, his gaze fell on a piece of paper protruding from her bag.

"What's that?"

Jhilmil's face turned shy. "Nothing," she mumbled and tried to put back the paper quickly. But in that hurry, it dropped from her hand. Rohit picked it up quickly from the ground.

"Please don't read it," she pleaded.

But Rohit moved some distance away and peered at the lines scribbled on the paper. "Ah, it looks good with emotional thoughts," he said with excitement, as he read it with a quick English translation of the tribal dialect in his mind. "Some words seem to be rhyming with each other. If you like we can try to make some kind of a poem out of it."

He suggested some changes in the words and after some crisscrossing, it finally read:

When I sit under the banyan tree,
I look keenly at the blue sky;
I feel very relaxed and free,
Watching the babblers fly,
A bird of multi-hued feather
Circles and glides above me;
Is that a message from my mother
Showering her love on me?

"You seem to miss your mother a lot," he said solemnly.

Jhilmil's eyes moistened and she was silent for a while. Finally, she nodded. "Yes, I do. I lost her at a very young age."

Rohit put his hand hesitatingly on her arm as Jhilmil wiped the wetness under her eyes.

"Anyway, this poem has turned out to be wonderful!" She exclaimed. "I have a notebook in which I have been writing my thoughts. If you find time, I will bring it next time and we can together make some poems out of it."

"Sure, but I myself am a novice. Anyway, it would be quite an interesting hobby for both of us, " Rohit said.

He was thoughtful for a while, as he threw a pebble into the nallah. Soon, he turned to her. "Actually, how did you pick up this writing skill?"

"Well... one of the teachers in my school in Bilaspur was also a writer and she had written a book about the life in tribal areas. I learnt to write a few lines from her. In fact, she had asked me to note down my thoughts whenever I felt depressed."

"I'm happy you have this talent. It's god's gift," Rohit said. "That reminds me of something that I've been thinking of sharing with you for some time."

Jhilmil lifted her eyebrows. "Please tell me."

"Last time, you said you've studied up to high school. Why don't you continue your education now?"

A huge, skeptical smile crossed Jhilmil's face. "There is no college here. How can I study further?"

"I don't think that would be a problem. You can study by distance education programs. Some universities allow that now."

"Really?"

"Yes, and if you want I'll help you," Rohit offered. "In fact, I've another idea too."

Gulping a berry, he continued, "A school is needed for the small children in your village.When I visited your home last, I saw lots of them just loitering around. I'm sure none of them has ever gone to a school."

Jhilmil nodded. "You're right. There are no schools here, not even a primary one. And even if there was one, people don't have enough money to spend on educating their children."

"Let's start a school near your house. There will be no fees and we'll give the books and stationary free," Rohit said excitedly.

Jhilmil played with her bangles, passing them up and down her wrist. "But won't money be required for the building and the furniture?"

Rohit felt charmed by the melodious tinkling sound of her bangles, but he soon realized the seriousness of the plan they were discussing. "We don't need a lot of funds. There will be no buildings. It'll be an open-air school amidst a cluster of trees like the one at Tagore's school at *Shantiniketan*. Children will sit on mats on the ground. Whatever funds are required, they will be provided by me and my friends," he explained and then added humorously, pointing his finger toward the tree where they had met earlier. "We can have the school under your favourite banyan tree."

"Ah, everything worked out already! But where would you get the teachers from?" Jhilmil's eyes widened on her cheerful face.

Rohit's lips extended to a hearty grin. "One teacher is sitting here right in front of me. Along with your studies, I want you to be a teacher too."

"No, but..." Jhilmil started, when Rohit broke in, "You can't refuse that. You'll look a great teacher in a *saree* with a red dot *bindi* on your forehead. And you have to take charge of persuading the parents of the children to send them to our mini-version of *shantiniketan*. Will you?"

Jhilmil nodded and Rohit noticed the warmth and gratitude in her eyes,

His glance shifted to his watch and he stood up hurriedly. "Oh god! I must get back now and check whether the pumps have been repaired. Let's meet here next week and we'll finalize the plans."

A heavenly smile spread on her lips. "Thank you. Now you needn't drop me home, as you're in a hurry," she said in a mellow, sweet voice and extended her hand. Tiny sparks exploded in Rohit's heart as he pressed it fondly. He sensed tremors in Jhilmil's hand too, and he looked warmly at her cheeks turning crimson. Though he had held her in his arms while rescuing her from the excavation pit, he hadn't experienced that kind of sensuous touch. Lingering warmth swept over his body.

She withdrew her hand slowly, gathered her bag and walked away.

"Don't forget to recite some more poetry when we meet next." Rohit's voice resonated in the forest behind her.

***

"Sir, the problem has been resolved," Rohit broke the news enthusiastically when he met Jayant after returning to the factory.

Jayant put up his hand warmly. "That's a good job done, Rohit. The water supply resumed sometime back. I knew I could depend on you. Of course, I got worried as you were delayed."

"Thank you, sir." A feeling of achievement surged through Rohit's body. "I'll discuss with you the technical problems at the pump-station tomorrow."

It was a pretty good day, he thought smugly. Pump job had been successfully done. And he had a good time with Jhilmil. That called for a celebration.

As he turned to leave, Jayant's voice stalled him. "Wait a minute. Another urgent assignment has come up. I had thought of deputing another engineer for that but now I think you'll be the right person to do it."

Rohit's eyebrows arched momentarily with thoughts of having to attend to another errand. *What now? Is there something to be done in the night?* But he put on a brave a smile. "Thanks. Of course, I'd do it gladly."

"I got a call an hour ago from the general manager of Apex Engineering that is fabricating some equipment for us. He asked me to depute an engineer to Allahabad for testing the equipment prior to dispatch. I'd like you to go there and do the checks."

Ah! First, the appreciation of his work by the boss, and now a chance to be in Allahabad, a city he had been aspiring to visit for long. Good things are happening.

His voice was lilted with excitement. "When do I have to go?"

"Be prepared to leave tomorrow afternoon. Before that, I'll brief you about the equipment and the checks to be done. I expect you to be back in two days. Keep in touch from there."

As Rohit walked home, there were several reasons for him to be buoyant. It was his first off-station tour, when he could be in a place closer to civilization—away from that desolate jungle. He'd heard there were lots of things to see in Allahabad, like Sangam, the great mythological confluence of Rivers Yamuna, Ganga and Saraswati; the colonial heritage buildings and the prominent 'Civil Lines' area with its famous shopping centers and restaurants. And it was an assignment that would test his engineering skills.

He increased his pace, keen to share the happenings of the day with Sachin.

***

The two days of equipment testing was a great experience for Rohit. "Mission completed as desired by the boss. The only thing that remains is to make a call to him," mumbled Rohit as he exited the Apex factory gate late evening on the second day.

Next morning, he visited *Sangam* where, sitting in a boat nearby, he looked at the confluence of matronly Ganga and the youthful Yamuna rivers, and the blending stream gurgling along on its onward journey to the east, as it had been doing for centuries. He folded his hands in prayer and his eyes rose reverently skywards. The last few days had been lucky for him. Getting into Daniels's team, meeting Jhilmil and then, some good assignments.

He packed his bags and took a rickshaw to the bus terminus for the return journey. Just as he was entering the building, baggage in hand, he heard a loud cautionary voice from a man standing near the gate. "*Sahib,* buses are not running today. The drivers of this station are on strike for a day."

Rohit winced and his forehead tensed. He put down the baggage on the platform under a tree and sat down alongside it, drumming his fingers on the suitcase. That bus was the only means to reach the factory. He'd have to wait till the next day.

Soon, his gaze turned to a swift movement of people in a building, a few blocks away. A tall man, around thirty, dressed in white *kurta, chudidar pyjamas* and a white cap, stepped out of the building gate flanked by two people. There was a flutter of flags outside as scores of people standing outside raised slogans in his honour, "Jaidev *zindabad*".

Must be some political leader. He paced through the crowd inquisitively to learn who the person was and what the occasion was. A car waited nearby, the chauffeur in grey uniform alertly holding the rear door of the car with blue beacon light on its roof.

"Who is this *sahib*?" He enquired softly of the chauffeur.

The man snapped. "Why? Don't you know? He is Jaidev Singh, the MP, a very popular leader from this region. A very fine person. He is on a tour of various towns around here as the elections are nearing."

Rohit rubbed his ears. "Ah! Such a young person as the parliament member. Must be from one of the youth wings of the ruling party. And he looks decent and an educated person. So different from other political leaders. It's unbelievable, but here he is."

A thought flashed in his mind. "There is a chance, though remote, of my talking to him about the dam-effected villager's problems and I must try that. But that's possible only if I get into the car and get an opportunity to speak to him in detail during the journey."

Jaidev was now approaching the car, when Rohit took a step forward and ventured to say, "Sir, the bus drivers here are on a strike. Can I get a lift to the next town, from where I can take another transport? I'm an engineer and I have to reach my factory in Udyog Nagar urgently but I'm stranded here."

The MP's security officer extended his arm hurriedly, barricading Rohit's advance. But Jaidev raised his hand and stepped ahead. "Let him come. I'll also have a chance to get firsthand news about that area."

Rohit felt out of place and he sat cramped in his seat in the back alongside the MP, when he heard Jaidev's comforting voice, "You said you're an engineer? When did you join the factory?"

After faltering for a few moments, Rohit's voice had a confident tone as he spoke to Jaidev about his job in the steel factory.

"What a coincidence! I too am a mechanical engineer, from BHU. But I chose politics as my career."

Rohit craned his neck to have a better look at the engineer-turned-politician, while Jaidev went on, "The entire dam area and Udyog Nagar fall in my constituency."

Rohit's mind went into a spin. *This is the right time to pitch my case.* He shifted closer toward the man. "Jaidev *ji*, since Udyog Nagar area is in your constituency, I wish to discuss something about the problems of villagers there."

"Now, that's something unusual. A young engineer from Delhi, working in a steel factory, discussing villagers' problems," Jaidev quipped. He kept turning the pages of a magazine he was holding, his eyes focused on it, as he continued, "Okay, tell me."

"Their problems are very severe. There have been two suicides in the last month. Earlier also, some people took their lives. It's really a tragic situation."

Jaidev flinched on his seat and tossed the magazine aside. "What did you say? Suicide? Who were the people? What was the reason?"

"It was very unfortunate. A couple killed themselves together because they lost their means of livelihood after the building of the dam. Their only child was orphaned."

"It's unbelievable. I'm sure they would have got due compensation from the government." Jaidev's tone was serious and grimness spread on his face.

First impact has been made. Some more deft articulation and the MP will be convinced. He is the right person who can help. He was quick to clarify, "No, they haven't got it so far." Then, he went on fervently to explain the promise of compensation, bureaucratic delays and the resulting distress of villagers.

Jaidev's jaw dropped. "I'm sorry that has happened. I'll raise the matter in the parliament and also take up the matter with the concerned departments here in the state as well as in the centre."

"Thank you. But I think the feelings of the people would be assuaged if you visit the area personally and speak to them. You can realize they're quite agitated."

After a brief silence, Jaidev took out a diary from his pocket. "You're right. I'll plan to visit that area in two weeks and I'll inform you of my exact program. Here is my business card. You can also contact me. But how come you got involved in all this?" He added after a moment.

The knots in Rohit's mind had released by now. He folded his arms and explained how he had met Ramesar and the *Panchayat* people and how they had extracted the promise from him.

***

When Rohit returned from his tour, he briefed Sachin about his meeting with Jaidev.

Sachin picked a pad and a pen. "All right. Seems, all is set now. Let's plan out the entire operation. First item on the list would be to look for the place where Kavita and her crew will stay when they're here. There will be at least three of them: her, a camera man and another freelance journalist, as she said. We have to make arrangements for their lodging and boarding. As for Jaidev, I think he'll make his own arrangement."

"Yes. Let's contact the government guesthouse at the power station. And we also need to make arrangements for the rally as thousands of villagers are likely to assemble," Rohit suggested.

"Okay, I'll do that," Sachin confirmed.

"Well, now the next thing we have to do is to write out a petition and get the signatures of as many villagers as possible. I'll take charge of that."

"You mean thumb prints," Sachin snapped. "You know most of them would be illiterate."

***

It was two weeks later that Sachin whistled and flashed the telegram before Rohit. "Finally, the good news! Kavita reaches Varanasi tomorrow morning."

He had been too impatient to wait for the closing time and he had rushed to the workshop to share the news with his friend.

Rohit was standing near a welder, when Sachin approached him breathlessly and handed the telegram to him. Heavy sparks flew as the technician fused the electrode on the joint of two steel pipes. He looked amusedly at the two seniors and removed the welding rod from the joint. Shortly thereafter, he switched off the machine and moved away.

"Great. Things are moving ahead as planned," Rohit shouted over the whizzing sound of lathe machines at the back. "Let me finish this work and I'll join you… say at about five in the canteen. We've to give finishing touches to the the arrangements for the rally. I'll ask Ramesar also to be there."

***

Rohit walked past the factory gate, his heart swelling with joy, as he started to return to his quarters in the evening. Everything was going on as planned. Jaidev, the influential MP, had promised to attend the meet the villagers and get the relief for them. Kavita and other media crew would be there. Also, villagers in thousands would attend the rally. Ultimately, they will get their relief.

He slowed down as he saw a messenger approaching him. A phone call from Delhi awaited him in the admin office. "Must be from home," he speculated.

But a wave of disappointment swept over him as he received the call. "Mr. Jaidev won't be able to attend the rally for the present, as some other jopbs have come up. He will be busy for at least a month," was the brief message he got from the MPs secretary.

Rohit slid into a chair for a few minutes, his head hung down. "Oh god! What to do now. All the arrangements would have to be cancelled.

Back in the quarters, he straightaway proceeded to Sachin's room."There is an anti-climax," he shouted. "These politicians! They can't be relied upon."

"Hey, cool down," Sachin said raising his head. "What's happened?"

Rohit sank into a chair holding his head in his hands. "Got a call from Delhi. Jaidev has cancelled his visit."

"Oh god. This is shocking…after all the preparations," Sachin blurted. "Kavita will be furious as all her preparations for the event will go waste."

"We need to call her and ask her to postpone the visit. Also, we need to meet Ramesar and inform him about the developments, so that he can inform the villagers that the rally will be held after sometime,"Rohit said.

Sachin was in contemplation for sometime. Now, his face grew grim and stern. "Postponement? It's a cancellation. There are no chances of organizing it again."

But the creases on Rohit's face had smoothened by now "Oh no. We have to try again. We can't leave the villagers to their fate. Remember, we are committed to get relief to them."

"What commitment? Take it from me; I am not going to waste a minute on this work from now."

"Listen, Sachin," Rohit said entreatingly, "we'll go together to meet Jaidev, wherever he is, Allahabad or Delhi or any other place and persuade him to schedule another visit within two weeks or a month."

"That's a no-no from my side. Life is not meant for such struggles all the time. There are other finer things to do…I need to plan my marriage to Kavita and you are dragging me into all this…I'm fed up with your notions of social service," Sachin said and got up.

Sachin's jaws dropped. "My philosophy of life is different from yours. Helping others gives me a pleasure."
Sachin was silent as Rohit continued. "Anyway, now I'll not bother you but do it alone. But at least for now, let's go together and inform Kavita and also Ramesar and the villagers about the change in plans."

"Don't bug me. Go and do it yourself. I'm not a part of it anymore."

Rohit left in a huff, promising to himself that he would get justice for the villagers at any cost, even if he has to do it alone. He walked to the factory to phone Kavita and talk to Ramesar, uneasy thoughts pervading his mind.

*****

CHAPTER 4

In the coming days, construction work continued as usual in the factory, though Rohit spent a part of his time in sending letters to Jaidev and other government authorities about the resolution of villagers' problems.

In June, a wave of enthusiasm spread among the cricket fans as the World Cup final match between India and West Indies was being played at the Lord's, London.

As they started leaving for the factory, Sachin turned to Rohit, "I'm keen to listen to the running commentary of the match. I know you can't use the Walkman radio in your department. So, I'll borrow it as I can manage to play it secretly for short intervals in my design office. If you like, I'll relay the scores to you on the intercom."

Rohit was game for this arrangement because he was busy with the installation work with Daniel.

Rohit got the scores periodically, but the process was interrupted after sometime as Daniel came up to Rohit with a paper in his hand. "This is the list of bearings I require. Can you get them from the stockroom?"

Rohit got up sluggishly and mumbled, "Of course."

How will he manage to get updates on the scores? Ah! The materials manager, Ranjan, has a pocket radio in his room, so he won't miss much, he thought, as he raced to the building.

"You'll have to wait for some time; there is an inventory going on," the stock-keeper, Prakash, said. "You can wait in Ranjan *sahib's* office in the meantime."

A smile curled up Rohit's lips. Prakash had always been quite friendly with him. "Okay," he said and moved away briskly.

The radio on the manager's table was on and he listened to the commentary, with more runs being added to the Indian score.

Soon, his eyes roved to the window, overlooking the large yard, where the bigger items of machinery, some packed and some unpacked were lying alongside steel beams, girders and rods. There stood three people, almost hidden by the machinery packing cases.

He walked toward the window till the faces became clearer. There huddled together were Ranjan, Vikrant and Rajiv, in discussion. In between, they would stop, look around and then resume their talk. Soon, the civil contractor, Bhiku, walked in stealthily and joined them. Some packets were exchanged between him and Vikrant.

A thought crossed Rohit's mind. "Something doesn't sound good here. It's not lunch time, when people usually form groups and gossip. And Rajiv, being the admin man, is rarely seen in the factory area. Vikrant, a civil engineer, and Ranjan from the materials department don't have much in common, either. And the way the contractor sneaked in didn't appear to be normal."

He returned to his chair but his mind was not focused on the commentary now. His mind was swirling with the thoughts of something strange and conspiratorial in the manner Ranjan, Vikrant and Rajeev were huddled together in the middle of the yard.

Soon, Prakash came over. "The items you asked for are ready. Please come and pick them up from the counter. By the way, who do you think will win today's match?"

Rohit's mind was still trying to solve the mystery of the trio huddled together. "India is playing well," he said absent-mindedly. "By the way, does the admin manager, Rajiv, come to the store often? There appears to be some meeting going on in the yard."

Prakash tensed and remained silent for a while. Finally he tapped Rohit's arm. "You're my friend, but I must caution you. One should mind one's own business."

Before Rohit could ask him why he was so evasive, Prakash had already left the counter and was lost in the long labyrinth of shelves in the stock-room.

Rohit picked up the heavy packet of bearings half-heartedly and walked to the installation area, puzzled by Prakash's unexpected behavior.

***

That night, a party was held to celebrate the declaration of Indian team as World Cup champions after they defeated the mighty West Indies team.

There was a huge smile on Sachin's face. "Ah! It was wonderful to hear the commentator announcing the lifting of the finger by the umpire for the last West Indies wicket after Kapil's marvelous catch of Richards, running backward. Absolutely amazing."

Corners of Rohit's lips jumped. "Oh yes, it was a great win." But soon his extended lips retracted. The scene in the store yard where he had seen the three company executives with the contractor haunted him.

When they returned to their quarters, Rohit narrated the incident to Sachin. But Sachin didn't seem to be in a mood to engage in the discussion. "*Yaar*, today is a day of rejoicing. Let's forget the Sherlock Holmes act for today. We'll discuss it in the morning."

But when Rohit went to bed, the incident and Prakash's cryptic words in the store, 'one should mind one's own business,' loomed large in his head. Was there something fishy going on in the store yard?

***

Prakash's words and their possible implications kept lingering on in his mind, but there were some promising developments that diverted him from those anxious thoughts. By his continued persuasive efforts that included two quick trips to Allahabad, Jaidev had finally set a date for meeting the villagers. Sachin had also agreed to help, though reluctantly, and Kavita too had informed her willingness to cover the rally.

***

The day in the first week of July had started with a pleasant morning, cool and clear, but it soon changed with small clusters of clouds forming in the sky.

"Soon, it may rain," Rohit pointed out to Sachin in a sullen voice. "In that case, the entire arrangement would get disturbed."

As planned, MP Jaidev, Kavita's press crew and the crew from local radio station arrived the same day at the guesthouse. The petition, with about one thousand thumb prints of the villagers, had already been sent to Kavita and the MP. Nervousness was creeping over Rohit, though outwardly he was calm. Would this campaign go through as planned? Would all this effort bring the desired results?

From early morning on, villagers, men and women, many of them mere skin and bone, with weary and solemn faces, poured over the hilly route that overlooked the dam and settled gradually in at the lawns of the guesthouse. Ramesar led the people carrying the placards, "We want compensation" and "Prevent suicides."

Rohit winced as he saw large posse of armed policemen taking positions outside the building. "Sachin, we hadn't considered that the district administration would take these precautions to prevent these people getting violent. Anyway, let's see," he said with a frown.

A drizzle started, but the stream of people didn't stop. Sachin hurried over to Kavita and the photographer, Avinash, who were now setting their equipment in place. "We may have to wait till the rain stops. Meanwhile, be prepared to film the presentation of the petition by the villagers to the MP and then his speech."

"Don't worry. Besides covering this event, we'll also make a short documentary." Kavita's voice was professional.

The space on the lawns fell short and the villagers began squatting in the open area beyond the premises. Rohit went around the crowd and urged them to be patient till the MP made his appearance. They sat grimly, silently braving the rain, perhaps in keen anticipation of some relief.

The drizzle stopped in half an hour. Soon, there was a flutter among the people, as Jaidev in his usual spotless white dress came out of the building. He pulled Rohit along to stand beside him.

Ramesar's face was grim as he came up to present the petition. "*Sarkar*, we're thankful to you for being here in our midst today. People here are in deep trouble. This dam has deprived them of their livelihood. The distress is now so acute that people are resorting to suicide. Therefore, we wish to present this petition to you with our demands. You're the only one who can help us."

As Jaidev held the document in his hand and turned the pages, his forehead wrinkled deeply. Meanwhile, some villagers at the back raised slogans and there were angry voices from some parts of the gathering.

He raised his hands. "Please calm down. I'll try to help you." When silence fell, he went on, "First, I must clarify that the dams and power plants are for your own good. They're important for the development of these areas, which have remained backward for centuries. Besides, the generation of power is important for industries, which in turn bring employment on a large scale. Also, in these projects, a large water resource is created for irrigation in the agricultural areas."

There were whispers and mutterings among the neighboring people in the crowd. Soon, voices of protest, "We don't want hollow speeches," rose to a crescendo. Many people got up angrily waving their arms.

Two villagers in the front row, their eyes full of fury, advanced menacingly toward the MP. "But you can't sacrifice the lives of people here in the name of development."

Rohit's eyebrows contracted in deep consternation. He paced forward and persuaded them to move back. He was able to hold them back, but there was a downward, frowning turn to his mouth as he thought aloud, "These villagers don't understand this high-sounding theory of development and they are getting impatient and tense. Will the MP continue with his political rhetoric or offer some practical solution to these poor people?

People in the crowd grew more restless, their eyes now reddening with fury. Many got up agitatedly, waving banners and demanding justice. Suddenly, half a dozen of them threw stones directed at the MP, but they grazed Rohit's shoulders instead. Sachin sprung up toward the scene. However, Rohit waved his hand frantically stopping him midway. "It's nothing... just missed me."

Two policemen came up, grabbed the persons by the arm and led them away.

Rohit's legs shook. The situation could worsen and there could be chaos. There had been instances in such situations of baton-charge by the police to bring people under control.

But he steadied as Kavita, wearing her press badge, walked up to the MP and confronted him. "Sir, I think the crowd is looking for some concrete solution to their problem."

Shouts resounded in all directions. "Yes, she's right. We want immediate action."

Jaidev looked dazed for a moment. He glanced at the press crew keenly and then turned to scan the audience. His voice was now louder, pacifying. "I understand your problem. It has happened because of the officers' delay in managing your resettlement process and payment of compensation to you. And I'm here to resolve your issues."

The villagers clapped and cheered, after which Jaidev continued, "I'll raise this question in the parliament and also follow up the matter with the other concerned authorities. I promise you'll get your due within five to six months. It'll take this much time as many government departments are involved."

Resounding slogans of "Jaidev *zindabad*" filled the air.

When the applause subsided, Kavita took the mike. "I've a question. There have been some earthquakes in this area in the past. Have the experts taken that into account while building this dam?"

"Oh, yes. Before coming here, I looked into the documents relating to the dam construction and I found a report certifying that adequate precautions had been taken against earthquakes."

There was a cacophony of voices as Jaidev left with his entourage and the crowd started drifting away, raising a cloud of dust.

Rohit's heart swelled for a moment. The event had passed off successfully. But still there were uncertainties. "Five to six months, Jaidev has said. I hope he keeps his word."

As he rejoined Ramesar, Sachin and Kavita, there was a cry of jubilation. "Hurray!" They exclaimed in unison, as the crowd cheered them heartily.

***

After the people had departed, the guesthouse lawns looked like they had been hit by a storm, with a lot of trash left behind, abandoned banners and trampled grass. While other members of the crew were trying to pack up, Sachin and Kavita stood chatting behind a column of the building, holding hands.

A smile lit up Rohit's face as he watched the couple. He walked up to them. "Hey, guys. Now you're free to have some fun. Why don't you walk up the hill further to the rose garden that has recently been opened to the public by the dam authorities? Not many people know about it and you can have privacy."

After Sachin and Kavita left, he saw Manik, the Chief's assistant, approaching him. "I'm also from the local tribal community. You've done a wonderful job for the benefit of people here. They will remain obliged to you."

"Oh, no. There is no question of any obligation. I took it as my duty."

"You are being too modest," Manik said, folding his hands. "In any case, if I can be of any help to you in future, please do let me know."

"Sure, I will," Rohit said, tapping Manik's shoulder.

Rohit returned to his quarters, his mind suffused with the blend of satisfaction and euphoria after the successful completion of his cherished task.

***

"Hey, Kavita has done the job!" Sachin shouted exuberantly amidst the voices of factory staff and food servers in the canteen as he neared Rohit's table.

Rohit had just had his first nibble of the fried eggs from the plate in his front. His hands shook and he dropped his fork as Sachin thrust himself into the seat beside him.

"Got a copy of the press coverage in the *News of India* from Kavita by today's post." Sachin unfolded and spread a newspaper on the table.

Rohit pulled the paper to his side. He gazed with sparkling eyes at the full page article and several photographs interspersed in the text.

A mischievous smile rose on Sachin's lips and he picked another fork. "Keep reading till I finish the rest of your food."

The paper had it all. A collage of villagers, old and young; some with anger and others with grief writ on their faces; the crying orphan whose parents had committed suicide. Jaidev on the mike. The promises made.

Rohit thumped his friend's back. "This is superb! More than I expected."

He rubbed his chin thoughtfully for a moment and then added,

"But this is only the means, not the end. Most important is whether Jaidev will be able to fulfill his promise of getting the relief package from the government."

Sachin nodded. "Why don't you send a reminder to him?" He suggested. "Now, order another dish for yourself, otherwise you'll go hungry."

***

"The factory construction is progressing generally as per schedule, except for some deviations, which are not critical," reflected the Chief, Divakar, while reviewing the progress report of the factory for the month of September, when he received an unexpected call from Varanasi.

"There has been no news from you, so I thought I'll call you," said the voice from the other end.

Yes, he had not been in touch with his younger brother, Sreedhar, for quite some time. He put the report aside and straightened in his seat. "Sorry, I've been busy. So, how's everything?"

"I called for an important matter. Anita and I have been discussing Sunita's marriage."

"That's a good thought. But don't you think it is a bit too early. She is in the fourth year of her medical course–one more year to go and then the internship."

There was a short pause on the other end. He could overhear his sister-in-law talking to his brother. "Anita says, it takes time to find good boys, so we should start being on the lookout for a suitable match now." Sreedhar's voice was mingled with laughter.

Divakar beamed. "Okay. Ask her about the qualities she's looking for in her future son-in-law."

"Better speak to her directly. I'm handing over the receiver to her."

There was a short break after which Anita was on the line. "You know better, *bhai sahib*. But one thing is clear. Sunita has no particular inclination to marry a doctor, as is the usual norm nowadays. So, we can look for other professionals from decent families. If you find any young engineer from your company, you may consider him also."

Divakar was doodling on a piece of paper and he put back his pen. "All right, I'll keep that in view. By the way, what is your program for the *Durga Puja* festival? Why don't you come here with the entire family and celebrate the event with us? You may ask Sunita also to join. She'd also be having a break in the college during that period."

"Seems to be a good idea. We'll let you know."

After he replaced the receiver on the cradle, the chief fiddled contemplatively with a paperweight on his table. Sunita was his favorite niece and as good as his own daughter. He should look for a decent match for her. His mind tried to sift through the possibilities of suitable match among the families of his friends and relatives, when a name flashed in his mind. Rohit. Yes, he could be a good partner for Sunita, he thought. He was handsome, smart, besides being a promising engineer. And he belonged to a decent family from Delhi. This was good lead, requiring some planning…some smart planning.

His face lit up as he reached for his phone to talk to his brother again.

***

"Hey, do you know *Puja* celebrations will take place in the second week of October?" Rohit's colleague, Dipankar, queried during the lunch break.

Rohit's face glowed. "Oh great. Let's talk to the Chief and plan a get-together…"

Sachin, who had been sitting at a distance in the canteen, butted in, "Guys, it shouldn't be just a get together. You know, the social environment here is as cold as the concrete and steel structures of the construction site. And most of the time, we're thinking about machines. So, let's plan something big, like a big festival, as we have in Calcutta."

Then, he turned to Dipankar. "You should take over the entire planning as you are from Calcutta and you know best how this festival is celebrated there."

***

Dipankar was on the job. A whiff of festive air started blowing and gained further momentum when the Chief announced that *Puja* would be celebrated in the traditional style and all the expenses would be borne by the company.

"Guys, all is set. The celebrations will last five days. An idol of the goddess *Durga* has been commissioned from Varanasi. Arrangements for tents, ornamental *shamiana* canopies, floral decorations and festoons have been assigned to contractors. There will be stalls and kiosks for food, as well as arrangements for dance and music performances. It's going to be a big show," Dipankar announced to the residents of the bachelor quarters. "Be prepared for a lot of fun."

But not for Rohit. He had to rush out as he'd gotten a message from the boss to meet him urgently.

The Chief sat with a sagged jaw in the office. "There is a message from Calcutta headquarters that the construction bills sent to the finance department were all messed up and there were substantial discrepancies."

Rohit was silent, curious about how that concerned him. The Chief continued, "I have a great trust in you, so I want you to verify all the bills relating to earth excavation, foundations, brickwork and concreting. And this needs to be completed within a week. I'm taking you off the machinery installation for the time being."

This meant that Rohit had to abstain from participating in the arrangements for *puja* festivities though he had been eagerly looking forward to it. But he could not ignore the Chief's orders. He put up a faint smile.

"Yes, sir."

***

Finally, the big day arrived. Below the clear, azure autumn sky, a huge pavilion with tented canopy had been set up, leveling a vacant tract of land near the factory, and decorated with jasmine flowers. On one side was a raised platform with a large idol of goddess *Durga,* which looked quite majestic in a sparkling silver *saree.* Two priests had been called specially from Calcutta and they were engaged in religious chanting in a part of the pavilion, lit by clay-oil lamps and enveloped in the fragrance of incense.

Though Rohit had been watching the preparations, he had actually been busy completing the Chief's assignment. He now walked toward the pavilion, a file in hand, pondering its contents somberly.

But his heart cheered as he heard the resounding beat of drums that enlivened the festivities. Nearing the canopy, he had a whiff of the aromas of freshly cooked patties, cutlets and other savouries from the stalls decorated with red and violet festoons. He was tempted to enjoy some of those but the urgency of his work prodded him on.

From a distance, he spotted the Chief sitting in the front rows. He halted for a moment and thought if it would be appropriate to talk on a sensitive matter to the boss at a time when he was busy with the festivities. But the Chief would also be concerned as he had set that day as the deadline for submission of report.

He heard Dipankar's sharp-pitched voice. "Rohit, where have you been all this time?

"Will join you soon." Rohit waved back.

He waded through the people, with occasional hellos and smiles and reached near the Chief's seat.

"Sir, I'm sorry to disturb you at this time. But there is some matter on which I'd like to speak to you now."

"Can't it wait?"

"No, it's urgent," Rohit pleaded.

The Chief's face was now masked with anxiety. He got up and the two walked out of the canopy. Rohit raised his voice over the din of songs from the loudspeakers. "You asked me to handover the report to you by today."

"Ah! Yes. How does it look like?"

Rohit took the papers out of the file as the Chief led him farther away.

"Wait a minute..." The Chief pulled Rohit's arm slightly as his eyes shifted towards the two women getting out a car and stepping toward the canopy "My family guests have come. We'll discuss this matter after today's function. Give the file to Manik tomorrow."

A woman in her mid-forties, wearing a red-bordered *saree*, decked heavily with jewelry, approached them, accompanied by another twenty plus woman, brilliant and coy in her turquoise blue dress.

A spell of warmth passed through Rohit's body as he silently sneaked glances at the two women. The elder one's face twisted into a half smile as she turned to the Chief. "Even today, you can't get away from your official work—always busy with files."

There was a broad smile on the Chief's face. "They go together, you know, dear. By the way, you're quite late. I've been waiting for you for quite some time." Then, turning to Rohit, he said with a smile spreading on his face, "Meet my wife, Smriti... and my niece, Sunita, who has come from Varanasi to join the celebrations here. She is studying in the medical college there."

After a pause, he patted Rohit's shoulder fondly. "And here is Rohit, the most promising engineer we have here."

"*Namaste*," Rohit said bowed politely to the mother and daughter.

While Sunita returned his greeting with a 'Hello' and a shy smile that accentuated her sharp nose and high cheek bones, the mother gestured warmly. "My husband has been keen that we celebrate this *puja* with full festivities. It'll also give the entire staff and their families a chance to become familiar with each other."

Rohit was facing Smriti, but he could guess that Sunita was sneaking glances at him. "Thank you, ma'am," he said heartily. "Your presence will add grace to the occasion."

"Rohit, Sunita will be here for a week, but she will feel bored with nothing much to do," the Chief said. "So, I'd like that one day you take my wife and her around to see some scenic areas near here."

Sunita edged toward her uncle and whispered a few words.

"Ah! Sunita says she'd be happy if she can play some games here, particularly badminton, as she is quite fond of that. I too can play, though I'm out of practice. Can you arrange that?"

The thrill of playing with Sunita surged in Rohit's body. "Yes, of course, it can be done. As you know, we've already started a small club here with a makeshift badminton court and table-tennis tables. We play there sometimes. She can join us gladly as soon as the celebrations are over here tomorrow afternoon. And, it'd be nice to see you also playing."

Sunita's lips stretched into a bright smile. "That'll be wonderful," she said as they proceeded to join the festivities amid the sounds of beating of drums, blowing of conch shells and the chorus of prayers.

***

A large crowd watched as the festivities ended with the idol of goddess being carried on a flower-decked carriage and taken for immersion in the river, as was the tradition.

When the crowd dispersed after the departure of the carriage, Rohit and Sachin appeared with rackets and a net. "Hello,"

Rohit hailed Sunita cheerfully. "This is my friend, Sachin. We can proceed to the badminton court whenever you like."

Sunita beamed with joy. "Thank you. I'll go home and change. Meanwhile, you may proceed to the court. I will join you there in a few minutes."

***

"Sunita looks so pretty and poised in the white shirt and shorts, her black luxuriant hair tied in a bun," Rohit surmised, as she got out from the jeep and approached the court. Soon, a vivid image of Jhilmil crossed his mind. How contrasting were the two. Jhilmil, with her girlish innocence and divine radiance on her face definitely scored over this girl.

As he returned to the present, he nudged Sachin. "After a long time, a city maiden is to be seen in this desolate place."

The two men installed the net over the poles and put chalk powder over the faded marker lines, while Sunita looked around, twitching her nose at the unleveled ground and the shrubs and trees among which the makeshift court had been laid out. Rohit guessed she was not impressed with the setting of the court.

"Let the match begin!" Sachin, who had opted to be the referee, made a high-pitched announcement imitating a professional. "Let's have an 11-point rally. Best of three. First, let's decide who'll serve first. I'll flip a coin."

"No toss. Let Sunita start with the first serve," Rohit shouted.

She walked briskly to the edge of the serving line, flipping her hair aside.

The match proceeded and a few points were scored, Sunita being in the lead. At one point, there was a fault on her serve as the shuttle caught on the net and remained suspended there.

Rohit walked up to the net. "You're an accomplished player," he remarked, as Sunita stood across retrieving the shuttle.

He himself had been a member of his college team. So, he played in a relaxed manner, without much movement around the court, to allow Sunita to score points. When the game reached ten-all, he became a bit alert, but she volleyed the shot over the net.

Rohit and Sachin clapped as Sunita jumped joyfully, raising her racket. However, the next game changed everyone's mood.

Sunita was leading in the second game too, when Sachin shouted, "Fault!" In Sunita's serve, the shuttle had lightly tapped Rohit's head.

She stilled, lines of anger rising on her face. Suddenly, she stomped out of the court and dropped onto a bench nearby, tying the laces of her shoes. "That's cheating," she yelled. "I should have got that point. On two occasions earlier also you decided in his favor."

Rohit's eyes grew wide, puzzled by Sunita's behavior.

"C'mon, Sunita, this is a friendly game." Sachin pleaded, "Okay, you got that point. Let's resume the play."

But Sunita sat in a cold, defiant manner. Shortly afterwards, she slammed her racket on the ground and scurried away toward the jeep, bellowing, "You tried to favour your friend who was losing the game. I don't want to play anymore. Driver, take me home…fast."

Rohit' forehead creased and he slumped on the nearby bench. His reading of this girl had turned out to be so wrong. She was so haughty and stubborn. He tapped Sachin's arm resignedly. "Come, let's go," he said with a sullen, dry voice.

The two walked back toward their quarters. Rohit was unusually quiet, wondering about the unexpected happening.

***

"Sachin, you were busy with the festivities, so I didn't disturb you, but something is bothering me," Rohit said gravely as they were having lunch in the *dhaba*.

Sachin finished the bite of roast chicken. *"Yaar,* what is it now? You're always hassled with problems. Everything seems to be going on well!" He said in a disinterested tone.

"No. Trust me, all is not well. Actually, some suspicious activities seem to be taking place here. Vikrant, Rajiv, Ranjan and Bhiku contractor seem to be conspiring to dupe the company of crores of rupees in purchase of materials. I hinted this to you a few days back, after I saw them in the stockyard. Now, I am getting surer of it."

Sachin wiped his hands with the napkin. "Okay. Carry on. I am all ears now."

"A few days before the Puja celebrations, the boss called me. He said the head office had found some discrepancies in the civil work bills. So, he asked me to check them."

Sachin straightened up. "Oh! That looks something serious."

"Yes, it is. When I reviewed the bills, I reckoned that there were serious issues with the quantity and rates of cement and other construction materials…I mean they were substantially inflated."

"But how do we come into this? Let the Chief handle it the way he wants."

"The problem is that I have got involuntarily involved in all this. I have submitted my report to the Chief, and I am sure he will call Vikrant and other people and call for explanations. That is bound to provoke them to be revengeful against me and maybe you too, as they will be deprived of the illegal gains."

Sachin crossed his arms in front of his chest. "You are right. We need to be careful about their maneuvers. For that it is necessary that we have someone who can keep us tipped about the goings on the Chief's office as well as in the factory. That will help us in planning our further strategy."

"Great idea," Rohit said, shedding his grave composure. "I know a person who can help—Manik, the Chief's secretary. He met me during the MP's visit and offered help when needed by me. I know he has some friends in the factory too. I'll talk to him and ask for his support."

***

The Chief had been busy attending to his relatives from Varanasi. But after they left, he sat in his seat briskly scanning the pending files.

He picked up the file that Rohit had given to him about civil contactors' bills and a frown creased his brows as he flipped the pages. Rohit was right. There were discrepancies in the bills. He needed to get clarifications from all the persons who had verified and approved the bills. Vikrant, the civil engineer, should be the first one to be interrogated.

He watched keenly the tall man entering the office with his usual lumbering style. He knew Vikrant had been recruited on the recommendation of Rajiv Kumar, the admin manager, who had some connections in the headquarters. And the two were close. So, he had to elicit information sensitively.

"Vikrant, I've not been able to correlate some figures of cement consumption in this file. Can you help me in reviewing the figures?" He started.

For the first time since he had entered the office, Vikrant's face turned grim. "Of course, sir," he replied, his voice shrouded in hesitation.

The Chief pushed the file towards him on the desk. His voice continued to be mellow. "Okay, just explain the entries that have been highlighted by me."

While Vikrant's gaze was fixed on the file, the Chief gauged the anxiety lines spreading on his face.

Vikrant's voice faltered. "Sir... I am unable to explain at this moment. Appears, Bhiku, the contractor, has submitted wrong bills."

"But it's been approved by both you and the materials manager, Ranjan." Anger was now apparent in the Chief's voice.

"Sorry, sir. I think I overlooked it."

Ranjan was the next one to be called in. The materials manager shifted the entire blame on Vikrant and the contractor.

After Ranjan left, the Chief pursed his lips. Things were not yet fully clear but there were hints of a nexus building up between the contractor and the company officers. He had to break that. But he should not take any drastic step at this stage; otherwise the entire construction work would get disturbed, delaying the whole project. Also, there could a bigger game being played here. To dig that out and to get the evidence, he needed to go with baby steps. To start with, the checking procedure for bills had to be changed.

***

Manik was prompt in reporting to Rohit about the summoning of officers the day before and the Chief's annoyance with them.

"All of them walked red faced when they exited the office. The boss has now asked me to prepare an office order, according to which from now onwards, the bills are to be jointly checked by Vikrant and you, before they are put up to the materials manager for further verification and finally to the Chief for approval. Meanwhile, all the payments to the contractors are to be kept on hold," Manik whispered to Rohit as they sat in a secluded corner in the canteen.

"Thank you for the letting me know. Now, they must be planning their future action. We need to know about that."

"You're right. I have already gathered some information through one of my friends in the stock room. They met in the stockyard immediately after meeting with the Chief, but Rajiv assured them that he will handle the situation his own way as he knows some senior officers of the company in Calcutta. His advice was that they should lie low for the present."

Manik looked around toward other tables from the corner of his eyes and then added in a low voice, "But more worrying are the words of Vikrant as overheard by my friend...he angrily blurted out that, 'Rohit is behind all this... but he doesn't know how dangerous I can be...he'll have to pay for all this.'"Then, he swiveled his head anxiously and added, "Rohit, I am concerned about you."

Rohit's heart overflowed with turmoil, but outwardly he remained calm. "Don't worry, I will be watchful."

After Manik left, Rohit sat with his elbows on the table, his head cupped in his hands. That was the first step in exposing the growing mafia in the factory. But he had to watch the steps of his opponents. It was becoming a serious game of chess. Only the pawns had started moving yet. The king, queen and other pieces were to follow.

However, there were other things also that needed to be done beyond this. The school had to be started as the first part of plan for villagers' relief.

**

All was set. The Chief had arranged the furniture, furnishings, books and stationery as the company's contribution and had promised more help. Jhilmil had got a couple of self-help books from Bilaspur to get trained in teaching.

A brief ceremony was held for the inauguration of "Udyog Nagar Open School." The Chief cut the ribbon in the presence of a crowd of villagers at a temporary wooden gate leading to the school, which was set in an area cordoned off with bamboo poles.

Ten children, boys and girls, five to six years of age, sat cross-legged on a grey grass-mat, with slates and pencils in their laps, under the *peepal* tree.

Jhilmil, wearing a red-bordered *saree,* and a matching round, red, *bindi* dot on her forehead, stepped forward, bowed and said, "*Namaste.*"

The Chief smiled as he looked at her and turned to Rohit. "I'm glad you've found a good teacher. Let's start the first lesson as a part of this ceremony."

Jhilmil stepped slowly to the black board erected on a wooden stand and placed in front of the children, and wrote the first alphabet with chalk.

The Chief turned to the crowd. "All the credit for creating this school goes to Rohit. The education these children get can be a stepping stone for achieving the skills necessary for them to move into the mainstream."

Ramesar walked to the Chief with gratitude-filled eyes and bowed. "Thank you, *sahib*. These kids will now spend their time in some useful activity. Otherwise, they would be busy all the day pulling the catapult strings to pick tamarind fruit from trees or playing hide and seek."

There was a resounding clapping and a satisfied smile arose on Rohit's face. The first part of the plan for the welfare of these people had already been accomplished. For the next part, he had to await action by Jaidev.

***

"Watch out!" Rohit called as he yanked Daniel away from the path of a crane hauling the rolling machinery.

The two had reached the hot rolling mill area of the plant from the design department. Daniel was deeply engrossed in looking at the layout blueprints. The brisk activity and the construction sounds around had perhaps masked the approach of the crane, making him unaware of the danger.

Daniel gasped for a moment. As he steadied himself his eyes shone with gratitude. "Thanks, Rohit. Sometimes, I'm a bit too adventurous."

As they walked toward the shed, he went on, "Let's check these documents. Seems, we have received all the Indian deliveries, but some machinery from USA is still in transit. We may have to revise our installation schedule."

Another team of civil and mechanical engineers armed with measuring tapes and other instruments joined them and together, they inspected and measured the foundations and the bolt positions for the furnace.

Soon, the Chief arrived at the shed and he and Daniel took a tour to see the progress. Both watched Rohit talking to an engineer from the civil department pointing out some errors in the location of foundation bolts.

As they stopped at the far corner of the shed, Rohit also joined them. A satisfied smile spread across Daniel's face. "Chief, you have a good team here. I'm particularly impressed with Rohit. He seems to be technically strong as well as hardworking."

The Chief patted Rohit's shoulder. "You're right, Dan. I too have been watching him. You know we have a gradation system for the engineers and Rohit has consistently got nine points out of ten for his performance. He is due for a promotion."

Daniel's face lit up. "Yes, he deserves it. I'd like an engineer like him to assist me in the construction assignments that I handle globally."

"Ah! Great," the Chief said. "He also indicated to me that he intends going to USA after some time."

"That sounds good. I can guide him. He'll have to get a master's degree from a US university before he gets a job in the US. Let's wait for the appropriate time," Daniel said as they left for the adjacent shed.

***

As the Chief returned to his office, Daniel's words about Rohit's performance kept ringing in his ears. Rohit was a decent match for Sunita, but Sreedhar had informed in his recent call that Sunita was still indecisive about the marriage. He phoned his brother again. "I just called regarding Sunita's marriage proposal. What is the status?" He asked.

The voice at the other end was rueful. "Nothing so far; Sunita is taking it too casually. It was so nice of you to suggest Rohit's name and we were all happy about it. But Sunita is elusive and still feels it's too early for marriage. As for me, I'm still keen on Rohit."

"Today, I had a talk with one of our engineers from USA. He's quite happy with Rohit's work and he says there are good prospects for Rohit in USA. Of course, for that he needs to pursue his MS course in one of the good universities there. Meanwhile, I'm expecting the evaluation report of all the engineers today. I'm considering a few promotions. Rohit will surely be one of them."

"That's wonderful. I feel it would be good if Sunita visits Udyog Nagar again. Perhaps, that'll bring them closer." Sreedhar suggested.

"Sounds good. Inform me about her plans."

"Okay, done," Sreedhar agreed and hung up.

***

CHAPTER 5

Autumn was over, winter had set in and it had rained that night in November. When Rohit got up the next morning and went to his window, he was pleasantly surprised to see that the valleys and forests near the factory had turned exotic, with a scattering of clouds hovering over the green tree-tops and serpentine streams flowing wild.

"Hey, get up. Why are you sleeping so late in such beautiful weather? This is the time to go and enjoy nature," Rohit called out as he entered Sachin's room.

Sachin stirred in his bed and shouted, "Don't disturb me! It's just seven o'clock on a Sunday. I'm not in a mood to go anywhere." Rohit, who was playing a song on his Sony Walkman, increased the volume to maximum and stuck it near Sachin's ear.

Sachin shot up and threw off the covers. "Okay, what' is this joke? What do you want now?"

"We have such a scenic place around us but we haven't gone trekking so far," Rohit said. "And the weather is fine..."

Sachin broke in, still rubbing his eyes. "Are you crazy? This is not Simla or Ladakh where you can go trekking."

Rohit pulled a chair. "C'mon, don't be a spoilsport. If not the mountains, we have the hills, valleys and forests here. Let's have an adventurous trip, hiking to the Panda waterfalls; about fifteen kilometers from here. I guess it shouldn't be more than eight km through the forests. I am told it's a great picnic spot with good eating places."

Sachin was silent for some time, looking out the window, his gaze fixed at the movement of clouds.

Finally, he jerked out of the bed. "Okay, but you said eight kilometers. Can we make it in a day, and still return by evening?"

"Oh, yes. I've worked that out. Maximum four hours one way with rests in between and staying there for a couple of hours for sightseeing and lunch. So, we're back in ten hours. If we start by eight o' clock, we'll be back by six or seven pm, during daylight," Rohit coaxed. "It'll be a great fun."

Sachin returned to the bed and stretched lazily. "But do you know the route? We could get lost."

"You lazy bum. I know the general direction from the map that I bought from Allahabad. And I've a compass too. Moreover, there must be several forest habitations on the way. We can ask the directions from people there. Don't forget we participated in several scout camps in school."

"Okay, boots, belts and berets; here we go." Sachin' voice boomed across the room as he jumped out the bed and ran to the bathroom.

***

It was a little after eight in the morning when the two, carrying small sling bags, stepped off the tarmac road and paused momentarily to peer at the narrow mud track disappearing into the thickly wooded, forest.

They merrily romped on the fallen leaves and passed the clusters of teak, *sal* and bamboo trees, sunlight peeping through the branches occasionally. In between, they stopped at the brooks to dip their feet in water; other times, they followed the zigzag paths through the ridges and valleys, occasionally stumbling on boulders and slipping on pebbles.

Sachin spotted a slab and, stretching himself out on it for a while, he scanned the unending greenery. "You were right. All these days we've been missing the bounties of nature."

While Sachin was resting, Rohit paced toward the berry shrubs and picked a few. "These are not the red ones that Jhilmil offered to me when I met her last," Rohit thought, while throwing an over-ripe one away.

As they trekked down a steep slope into a trough area, suddenly the sunlight dimmed and total silence fell. No chattering of birds. No fluttering of the tree branches. Soon, the clouds turned grey and occasional thunder could be heard.

"Oh! Weather seems to be turning bad," Sachin warned. "Good that we brought the umbrellas along."

"You're right. Perhaps, we need to look for some shelter till it clears. I see some huts at the top? Seems to be some village habitation. Let me also check our bearings with the compass."

As Rohit pulled out the instrument from his bag, a high wind swept through the valley. The compass slipped from his hand, landing in a stream flowing below. "This goddamn place," he yelled. "Anyway, let's go up and see if we find some people who may give us directions to Panda."

As soon as they started on the uphill climb, dark clouds emerged menacingly, clustering the forest. A drizzle started, and then the rain poured down furiously. They opened the umbrellas, but the wind soon turned them inside out.

"Oh god! It's become like a rain forest," Rohit shouted. "Never saw this kind of weather before. Now, there doesn't seem to be any other option but to take shelter in the first hut we come across."

The village, a small hamlet, seemed to be nestled away from civilization. As they neared it, muddy pools and swamps obstructed their way. In the dim light due to the heavy dark clouds and sheets of rain falling, it became difficult for them, all drenched, to wade through the mud.

Rohit stumbled near a rocky patch and fell down with a scream of pain.

***

"What the..." Sachin shrieked and sprinted towards Rohit. A cobra, with its hood expanding and flattened, slithered away slowly toward the bushes. The nearly five-foot long, grayish-black reptile, with its spectacled spots and yellow cross-bands, looked deadly even in the faint light.

He stooped over Rohit, who lay on his side. "Get up, Rohit," he said in a scared voice.

But his friend didn't get up, despite repeated shaking. Perhaps, he had lost consciousness, Sachin thought as fright overtook him.

His heart missed a beat as he saw Rohit's dangling right arm. It was turning blue. And then he spotted the bite marks, two red fang spots, on his upper arm, a couple of inches from his elbow.

He panicked. "Oh god, he has been bitten by the cobra....and he is now unconscious. What to do now?"

"Help...help," he shouted at a high pitch. But his voice drowned in the roaring sound of lightning. He lifted Rohit in his arms and trudged further toward the village, stumbling many a time.

When he sighted a hut at the periphery of the village, he laid Rohit's unconscious body on a rock and screamed, "Someone, help! A cobra has bitten my friend..."

The village was quiet. No one moved. No human sounds.

Soon, two shirtless, drenched kids, with apprehensive eyes, appeared at a distance. One of them ventured to come close. "A snake bite! Let me call our *vaid ji*, Shambhu *kaka*... he knows the treatment for snakebites," he shouted, and sprinted toward the hut.

Sachin looked to the sky. The rain had changed to a drizzle and the light was now emerging again. *Thank god there is a local practitioner here. He may be able to help revive Rohit with some herbs.*

The creases on his face abated as he saw the boy coming out from a hut with an elderly, balding man supporting himself on a walking stick.

Sachin ran to him. *"Vaid ji,* please help me, my friend has been bitten by a snake."

Shambhu's mouth gaped wide as he bent down and had a look at the fang marks. "Oh god! He's been bitten by the black cobra. He needs an immediate antidote."

Sachin stood shivering. "Is there a hospital nearby?"

"Young man, there is no hospital for miles here." Shambhu's voice was sarcastic. "But don't worry, god willing, he may yet be saved. I've the recipe of an antidote ointment. Hurry up and carry him to my place."

Sachin and the boy lifted Rohit, took him to the hut, and laid him on a bed.

"Jhilmil, come here immediately," Shambhu called out in a frantic tone.

Sachin's ears alerted. "Jhilmil! Another Jhilmil here?"

As a woman appeared at the door, Shambhu gave hurried instructions. "Here is a man with a snake bite. Bring some water and a piece of cloth. Quick! We have to wash the bite area and tie it up with a turmeric poultice so that the intensity of venom gets reduced. And you'll have to prepare the ointment—you know the recipe. My eyes are failing me and I can't locate the herbs."

The woman went back swiftly, without looking at others in the room. Sachin scrunched up his eyes as she left. She was definitely the same Jhilmil—Ramesar's daughter. How come she was there? But this was not the time to check on that. Let them do their work, he decided.

***

Jhilmil returned in a few minutes and hurried to the bed. Her legs buckled as she saw the patient. "He is Engineer *sahib!*" She exclaimed and her eyes misted. "Get up, please." Her voice cracked as she shook his body.

Droplets had gathered in her eyes but she wiped them as soon as she glanced at Sachin. "Ah! I didn't see you earlier. How come you two are here in the interior of forest?"

"We were hiking in the forest and we lost our ..."

Shambhu broke in, "Please, stop talking and attend to the patient. We'll talk about other things later."

He and Jhilmil washed the red spots on Rohit's arm. Then, he applied a layer of turmeric paste with a spatula and tied the wound area with a leaf. A little later Jhilmil applied another layer of a brown ointment.

"That should do," said Shambhu gravely. "But we have to be watchful."

After a while, he lifted the patient's eyelids and checked his pulse. "He is in bad shape. His body has turned purple and he is now becoming convulsive," Shambhu murmured ruefully. "We must take him to the snake goddess temple and make suitable offerings to her to appease her. There is a *tantric* there, who can revive him with his occult rituals."

Jhilmil wiped her hands. "Don't worry; I'll take care of him. I know of herb-mud treatment, which is more effective for the black cobra venom. I learnt about it when my sister was attacked by a snake in Bilaspur. So, no need to take him to the *tantric* for the present. All that is superstition."

She got up, gathered her hair into a bun, tied the corner of her *saree* around her waist and rushed inside. "I'll come back in a minute with all the materials."

***

Sachin watched Jhilmil applying a grey mudpack, removing it every thirty minutes and then refreshing it. "She does have some special feelings for Rohit," he thought as his eyes filled with amazement at her deftness and caring.

As the dusk changed to night, a kerosene lamp was lit. Sachin came out and paced the compound outside the hut, uneasiness swirling inside him. Two hours had passed, but there were no signs of Rohit's revival. He became doubtful whether Jhilmil's and *Vaidji's* treatment would succeed. Should he walk back to the factory and arrange a jeep for taking Rohit to a hospital—even though it might take several hours to do so?

But when he went in, his eyes sparkled. Rohit was moving his fingers. He turned to Jhilmil, who was sitting by his side on a stool, her face weary and her hands smeared with the brown paste. "Thank god! Your treatment seems to have begun working."

"It appears so, but it will take at least till tomorrow morning before he recovers," she replied. "In the meantime, these mud packs and ointment will have to be applied alternately every hour."

Shambhu joined them and checked the pulse. "Sounds good. Body colour is also returning to normal. He's going to be okay now," he said with a satisfied smile. He turned to Sachin and added, "You're lucky that my grand-daughter was on a visit here."

97

"Yes, we are thankful to her," Sachin said.

The dialogue continued as Sachin told him in detail about their identities as engineers from the factory, how they knew Jhilmil and how they started on an adventurous journey that had turned sour. "We did not inform our seniors about this trip. They will be disturbed by our sudden disappearance. When do you think we'd be able to get back?"

Jhilmil broke in. "I think it will take at least three days, because besides getting cured he should gain enough strength to walk. You see there is no transport available. I think you should write out a letter to your boss, informing him about the situation here. I will get that letter sent to my father, who will in turn deliver it to your boss."

"That's a wonderful idea," he said with a satisfied sigh.

***

Jhilmil remained busy with a warm, matronly smile, nursing Rohit's injured arm, till he and Sachin prepared to leave for the factory on the fourth day. Rohit was still weak but he felt confident that with some rests in between he'd be able to make it.

"It's now my turn to thank you, Jhilmil, for saving my life," Rohit said warmly. "And, of course, your grandfather too."

Jhilmil smiled modestly. "No need to do that. Anyway, keep applying the ointment from the container that I've given you for seven more days. I'll also be back after about ten days, and I can check it again when I am there."

During the journey back, the memories of Jhilmil's treatment and loving care kept flickering in Rohit's mind. Ripples of ecstasy flowed in his body as he thought about the gentle touch of her hands, warmth of her breath, her loving gaze and the intense poems about life recited to him when she nursed him. But at the same time, he kept wondering about the direction in which their relationship was headed to.

***

A week later, when Sachin returned from the factory, he went straight to Rohit's room to share the news about developments in the factory with him as Rohit had been absent from work during that period.

Rohit didn't seem to be around. "Must be in the bathroom," Sachin concluded and he cozied up on a sofa and took out a film magazine from the adjoining cabinet.

As he flipped the pages, a paper fell out. He picked it up and glanced casually at the lines written on it. He read them again and mumbled, "Ah! It appears to be a poem. Has Rohit developed a new hobby?" A curious smile crossed his face as he read it aloud:

In the forest paths, near the brooks, I sense you,
Your shadow always chases me
Your scent always pervades me
I always conjure your image and yearn for you

As he was busy with the recitation, he saw Rohit advancing toward him clad in a bath towel. "That's bad manners, Sachin... reading someone's secret papers. C'mon, hand it back to me."

Sachin had a sheepish grin as he heard the admonishing voice, but he held the paper tightly in his hand. "What is so secret about a poem? If you have started writing poetry, you should rather publicise it."

Rohit put up his hand to snatch the paper, but Sachin resisted, laughing hilariously, "And, I see you've grown a stubble. Good signs of being a great poet."

"You idiot. Give it back or I'll punch you in the jaw," Rohit said in an agitated but entreating voice.

Sachin relented, though reluctantly. "Okay, have it back..." he started but paused for a moment and looked at the paper again.

"Ah! I didn't notice it earlier. This is female hand writing," he said with a detective touch. "The plot thickens, Dr Watson."

He handed back the paper and added solemnly, "I'll not insist, if you don't want to tell me who is the poetess."

"Okay, I'll tell you all about it. But first, let's have coffee."

Sachin had a hearty laugh."That's great. In fact, that was the reason I came here today–just to inaugurate your new coffee-machine. But we got dragged into the mystery of this poem."

After Rohit placed cups on the table, his face turned thoughtful for a while and then he leaned back on his chair. "I'll clear the mystery. This poem was written by Jhilmil. She often sits under a banyan tree in the forest near her home, scribbling poems. She says she got the knack of writing poems from her school teacher."

Sachin was wide-eyed. "It seems you have been meeting her secretly and more so after the snake-bite incident. Ah! That explains the mystery of your transformation to an empathetic person as I pointed to you some months back."

Jumbled thoughts had also been rising in Rohit's mind that meetings with Jhilmil had had led to some changes in his attitude to life. But he remained evasive. "It's nothing like that. You keep on imagining things."

"Anyway, it's unimaginable that a tribal girl, who has studied only up to high school, could write such a lovely, heart-touching poem."

"What's so strange about it? Tagore, the renowned poet, didn't have any formal education and he wrote his first poem at the age of eight," Rohit retorted lightly.

Sachin extended his hand. "Okay. Let me have a look at the poem again."

When Sachin got back the paper, a sly smile loomed large on his face. "I think these lines are addressed to you. Hey, friend, she appears to have feelings for you."

"Rubbish! How can you say that?" Rohit retorted, punching Sachin lightly on his arm.

"Of course, she has. Otherwise, what is the meaning of '*Your shadows always chase me*' in the poem that I believe she gave to you to read. And you know how much care she took of you after the snake bite and how warmly she nursed you throughout those nights."

Rohit remained tight-lipped but Sachin was undaunted. He put a pointed question. "Rohit, tell me frankly, do you like her? Have both of you developed a soft spot for each other?"

"Well, that depends on how you define the world 'like.' If you mean whether I like her as a poetess or a teacher or whether I like her caring nature, the answer to all is yes."

He paused for moment and then went on, "If you mean whether we have friendly feelings for each other, yes. But if there is some other thing beyond that in your mind, it's a big no."

Sachin shook his head. "I don't believe you. Sometimes, such feelings are cryptic. They remain hidden, rather suspended in our minds. Then, suddenly, one day…boom…the persons realize that it is love that had been growing in their minds all the time."

"You seem to be a great expert on love. Anyway, I'll approach you some other time for a counseling session," Rohit said sarcastically.

"Okay, whenever you feel like," Sachin extended his arm with his palm down in the blessing pose of a spiritual guru. "I'm leaving now. Have to go to the salon to have my hair cut, otherwise people will nick-name me as a love guru."

***

After Sachin left, Rohit stared blankly out the window with tempestuous thoughts pervading his mind. "Is Sachin right? What answers do I have to his questions? In fact, I'm not too sure myself."

He conjured up the image of Jhilmil sitting against the trunk of banyan tree, cross-legged with her eyes closed. Were her poems meditative, reflecting her solitude? Were her poems in the category of monologues relatable to romanticism or mysticism? Did they relate to her feelings of distress and loneliness about the loss of her mother at a young age? Were they addressed to nature or to some person in particular? Did she feel deeply intimate with nature? Were they confessional, expressing feelings for him?

He recollected her words, sometimes soft and sometimes emotional, spoken at various occasions. In one of the meetings under the tree, she had said, "Engineer *sahib*, you're like this tree, providing me the shade of compassion and warmth, and you wiped away the grief that had accumulated in my heart all these years."

As the images blurred, he walked back from the window and sat pondering. Had he developed some special feelings for her, the ones different from what he would have for a friend? They had not touched each other physically, though they had been meeting for several months, but perhaps their hearts had touched, their feelings had permeated to their souls. Could it be platonic love?

Suddenly, he got up. "No, no, I'm not sure. It's just that I'm friendly with her and she also has the same feelings. I don't think she is in love with me. She has never hinted about that."

Picking up the paper, he folded it and put it back in the magazine.

***

The Chief had laid the matter about Sunita's marriage aside after his earlier talk with his brother, though he still thought that Rohit was a good match for her.

Thus, he was surprised when his brother, Sreedhar, called. "After my earlier talk with you, Anita and I have been able to find a way so that Sunita and Rohit have a chance to meet again during her next vacation. We told her that Anita wants to visit your family, and she'll need company. Sunita needed some persuasion but that was it. Of course, she doesn't know the real purpose."

The Chief twirled his moustache. "That's great. But won't you be joining them?"

"No, I have other commitments during that period. In any case, if the mother and daughter agree to the proposal, I'll put my stamp on it."

There was a heavy laughter on both sides before they hung up.

***

On New Year's Day of 1984, the Chief hosted a party for all the employees. "I'm glad to inform you that our construction work has been progressing satisfactorily in conformity with the targeted dates," he announced amidst jubilant cheers.

He returned to his office with a smug smile spread on his face. As soon as he moved to his seat, his eyes roved to a manila envelope at the centre of his table. It was not there when he had left the office, he thought casually.

He opened it hurriedly with a paper knife and half a dozen photographs slid out. His brows furrowed deeply as he flipped through them.

"What's this nonsense?" He mumbled and after thrusting the photos back into the envelope, he shoved it into his drawer.

He took a glass of water. Rubbing his temples with his fingers he thought of calling Rohit immediately, but shunned the thought. "It is unimaginable. But I should compose myself before I speak to him."

But who could have come here in my absence to put these photographs secretly on my table? He took out the envelope again from the drawer and viewed the photographs one by one.

"It's unbelievable; of all the people, Rohit!" He thought as he looked wide-eyed and puzzled at the photographs—Rohit sitting beside a female, seemingly a tribal, on a rock and then another one of the two of them in a passionate embrace.

Who could be the woman? Someone living in the colony of the construction workers?

There was a sudden realization as he had another look at the photo. "Ah! She is the teacher in the new school that Rohit has started. Perhaps, the name is...Jhilmil."

His mind churned. "So, the romance between the two has already begun? And here, my brother and I are planning his marriage to Sunita. I'll have to find out more. In any case, I'll not allow this romance to continue." His fingers shook as he grabbed the scissors from the drawer. He wanted to shred the photos, but restrained himself.

He picked up the intercom receiver with shaking hands. "Ask Rohit to meet me urgently…right now."

***

Rohit entered the office in his usual cheerful mood. But the contours of his face slackened sharply as the boss didn't ask him to take a seat but instead flipped one of the photographs—Rohit sitting beside Jhilmil—across the table. "What is this?" He growled.

Goosebumps crept down sharply on Rohit's neck as he looked at the photograph. How did the Chief get it? Who could have taken this photograph? Someone must be making mischief. He was pensive for a while and said finally, "Perhaps, someone has taken the photograph when we were discussing the school. You know she is the daughter of our excavation contractor, Ramesar, and a teacher in the school. There have been some meetings between us."

"Ah! Seems you're quite close to her?" The Chief's tone had now a blend of sarcasm.

Rohit looked with twisted eyebrows, wondering about the reason for Chief to ask that question. "Sir, may I ask why you're putting these questions to me?"

"This is why!" The Chief glowered, his voice suddenly rising to a high pitch as he passed across another photograph—this time the one with the amorous embrace.

The Chief held the pack of photographs in his quivering hand. "And there are some more here."

Rohit froze down to the toes as he peered at the photographs.

"Sir, this is somebody's mischief …" he faltered, anger now flashing in his body.

He sat down, took a deep breath and went on. "Of course, as I said, I have met this woman Jhilmil on a few occasions. But this one…this photo…sir, I assure you, somebody is trying to defame us."

Chief's tightened jaws loosened a bit. "You know I've reposed a lot of faith in you. Perhaps, what you're saying is correct. But you must realize that it is a sensitive matter, involving a construction contractor's daughter. It could lead to a flare-up amongst the workers. You know they are quite conservative in these matters. There could be a serious labour problem impacting the factory construction."

Rohit listened intently, but his mind was elsewhere. Who could have done it, Vikrant or someone else?

He gritted his teeth for a few moments but soon his composure changed. He was now in a pleading mode. "Sir, there is nothing secret about it. The workers already know about it. Many of them were present and they applauded when the school started and Jhilmil became the first teacher."

The Chief kept tapping his fingers on the table thoughtfully, and said finally, "I appreciate what you're saying. But the concern is that there are some photographs showing you in objectionable postures. So, you need to submit an explanation for that...and do it fast.

The turbulence in Rohit's heart increased. "Okay sir."

"You may go now. I'll also make some checks on my own."

"Sir, if you don't mind, can I have one of the photographs?."

The Chief hesitated for a moment, but finally passed a photograph to Rohit.

***

Rohit and Manik met the same evening. This time, they were more careful and had arranged a meeting after sunset at the tea stall in the backyards of the colony, though cold winter had already set in.

"Things are getting murky," Manik said, rubbing and warming his hands as they pulled a bench near the coal-fired hearth and settled on it.

Deep lines had formed on Rohit's forehead that was also glistening with the glow from the fire. "It's really serious. Perhaps, you know all about it by now. I mean the photographs, for which I was summoned by the boss."

"Yes, after you left, he called me and questioned me, though tactfully, if there were any rumours floating around about your relationship with Jhilmil. Of course, I stated the factual position that everyone in the factory — staff and the workers — had a great regard for you and that there were no such rumours."

Rohit looked silently at the vapours rising from the hot cup of tea, while Manik continued, "The boss also called Jhilmil's father to his office, perhaps to extract some information from him too. I overheard a part of the dialogue… I think he gave you a clean chit."

The knots in Rohit's mind loosened but he was still skeptical. "Thank you, Manik, for sharing the information and for the good words spoken about me. But what about the photographs? How to prove they are fake?"

He looked around to be sure that there was no one there within a hearing distance. The stall owner was a little away collecting firewood. He then pulled a photograph from his jacket. "Here it is. The bone of contention. Now, the problem is to find some photography expert for his opinion."

Manik had a quick look at the photo. He gasped for a moment and then put it in his pocket. "Don't worry. A friend of mine in Varanasi is a photographer."

"Ah! Tomorrow is a Sunday," he added quickly. "Both of us can go, have his expert opinion and return in the evening."

***

Rohit was calm as he entered the boss's office carrying a folder with him.

"Sir, I have some information that I'd like to share with you," he said as he entered.

The boss, who was making some notes on the file, raised his head."Okay, carry on."

"I went to Varanasi and got the photograph that I had taken from you checked by a prominent photographer there. He's sure it is morphed and he has put it in writing. In fact, he has even given the names of a few photographers who do this kind of work," Rohit said as he flipped a note across. "One of them is in Varanasi and the other in Robertspura."

While the Chief studied the note, Rohit speculated about his boss's reaction. *This should clinch the issue, particularly after Ramesar and Manik have given me a clean chit already.*

Rohit watched a warm smile rising from the corner of Chief's lips. That signified that his speculation was right.

"Rohit, I think you're correct. I'm sorry for my remarks the other day. But all that was on the spur of the moment," the Chief said, his eyes intensely apologetic.

"That's no problem, sir. But now we have to see who did and to what purpose." Rohit frowned in puzzlement.

The Chief moved his pen, doodling a few shapes on paper, and then raised his head. "Yes, it's important, particularly as this also involves the reputation of this girl. It's for sure that someone here hates you. Do you have any one in mind?"

"I have a strong feeling that it has got something to do with the people like Vikrant who were involved in manipulating the bills. But I need to investigate further before pinpointing anybody."

"Can you find out discreetly?"

Rohit grimaced. "Of course, there is no other alternative."

"After you've identified him, we'll jointly work out a strategy. In any case, for the time being his plan has failed because he'll understand that I have not given any weight to the matter."

***

The same evening, Rohit and Sachin were closeted in Manik's house.

Rohit related to them the dialogue he had with the Chief earlier in the day. "What do you suggest," he said, turning to Sachin.

"I'm no detective, but I've a hunch it's Vikrant's doing. He has the double motive. First, he has always nurtured a revengeful attitude toward us. Second, he feels you were responsible for bringing out the truth about the discrepant construction bills," Sachin speculated.

"Looks quite logical. Let's proceed by this theory, and try to follow the trails of these four people... the places being visited by them...the people they meet. And also, we need to check the angle of Robertsura photographer having morphed this picture. We know for sure that many of our senior employees visit Robertspura regularly for shopping or just for a change as it is the nearest town from here."

Manik squirmed in his seat. "Robertspura you said! A thought has struck me. Rajiv and Ranjan, who are a part of this foursome, have been to Robertspura a few times in the last three months. I have seen their travel bills."

"Good information," Rohit said, tapping Manik's shoulder. "What we need to do now is to keep a track on the movements of these four. That might give us some lead."

"You are right. It may take a few weeks, but we sure can lay our hands on the culprit, before he can do any further damage."

Rohit thumped the table. "I'm sure if we play our cards well they'd be trapped firmly."

As they left, Rohit felt a weight being released from shoulders. Soon, the culprits would be found. It was just a question of time.

***

CHAPTER 6

Ratan Kaul

It was the middle of spring when Sunita, her mother, Anita, and her younger brother, Jai, came to Udyog Nagar to visit her uncle's family.

Jai, an ebullient young boy of fifteen, paced impatiently the lawn of his uncle's bungalow, after they had finished their lunch. "Uncle, I hope we aren't going to spend the entire vacation indoors. Are there any sightseeing places here? Please let's go somewhere, maybe just a drive."

The Chief laughed heartily. "Of course, there're many places to see here. But I won't be able to accompany you, as I have important meetings today. I'll have to make arrangements for someone to escort you."

Anita looked with a twisted smile at her son. "Don't bother your uncle. Let him take his own time planning the outing."

The Chief gazed blankly at his coffee mug for a moment and then turned to her, "That's no bother. Actually, I had planned it for tomorrow and had deputed one of our engineers to escort you all. But for today, I was just thinking who'll be the right..."

He paused abruptly as he saw Rohit entering the bungalow. A bright smile flashed on his face. "Ah! There he is... Rohit. He's a godsend. Sunita met him the last time when she was here."

Sunita moved in her seat and arranged her scarf as her eyes met Rohit's.

A strange piqued feeling spread in the pit of Rohit's stomach on seeing Sunita but outwardly he put up a faint smile. "Hello," he addressed all in general and then faced the Chief. "Sir, I came to inform you that I've got a message from the engineer-in-charge of the power station that the water level in the dam reservoir is getting low and they are considering a planned shutdown of the power plant for some time. That may lead to a power outage at our factory for a few hours. If you like, I can go personally and coordinate with him."

The Chief straightened in his seat with a momentary concern in his eyes. "Ah! It will mean temporary stoppage of our

110

construction activity. Anyway, try to ensure that there is a minimum stoppage."

There was a pause after which he went on, "By the way, I have some guests here. They are keen to visit the places in the vicinity here. Since you are going to the dam site, you may show them around. They can also take a walk on the dam top, visit the observatory and also go down the elevators and have a look at the power station. If you have time, you can also go to the forest park and the boat launch, where you can see the water in the reservoir closely. Take my jeep."

Rohit's face was taut with anxiety as they boarded the jeep. *Sunita is quite obstinate and short-tempered, as I remember from the last time on the badminton court. I hope nothing unpleasant happens today. It's better to be aloof from her.* He took a deep breath and tried to sweep away the distressing thoughts as they drove on.

At the power station, he asked the three to wait for some time till he finished his work with the engineer there.

When he returned, he explained to them the layout of the dam and they had a view of the penstocks and the spillways. He noticed that occasionally Sunita looked at him from the corners of her eyes. At one spot where Anita and Jai were at a distance, Sunita came closer to Rohit. "Today, you seem to be quite reserved, unlike last time when you were so lively."

"Oh, it's nothing. I was just thinking of the factory problems."

There was a spontaneous laughter from both, when Sunita quipped, "You should forget your problems for the time being. Let my uncle take care of them."

Ah! This time there appears to be a change in Sunita's manner. She seems to be friendly now. Does she have a dual personality? Rohit tried to put on a friendly gesture, not wanting to offend the boss's guest. "Okay. I'll try."

***

Everyone regrouped on the observation deck. Jai pulled out an Agfa camera from his bag and turned to others in the group.

"Hey, a lovely breeze is blowing here. And what a panoramic view of the reservoir, it's an endless water body. Let's have some photos."

"Let me," Rohit suggested, "so that you too can be snapped with the group."

Guiding them for a proper pose and light effect, Rohit noticed Sunita's rosy pink scarf fluttering in the air and her long, straight black hair flowing down, partly on her back and partly on the front.

His cheerful spirit had now returned. "Please smile," he said and clicked the shutter.

As the group neared the elevator area for going down to the power plant level, Karan, the engineer on duty, who was to show them around, came up and there were introductions. "You'll have to wait for some time as the lifts are slow here," Karan said.

Rohit and Sunita were ahead near the elevator door waiting for the lift to come up while Jai and his mother followed them at a distance, where Karan was explaining to them the functions of the power station, like a guide.

The elevator arrived on the floor and as its grey steel doors started parting slowly, Rohit and Sunita prepared to step in. "Karan, Jai, the lift has come. Hurry up," Rohit shouted, turning his head back.

However, Karan and others were still a few feet away when the elevator doors started to close. Anita with her bulk couldn't pace up with the others though she seemed to be trying.

Rohit fumbled frantically with the buttons to stop it, while Sunita looked on with creased eyebrows.

"Oh god, you people are left behind," Rohit shouted hurriedly through the narrowing openings in the sliding doors. "Anyway, Karan, come in the next trip. We'll wait for you on the Zero floor. Also inform the control room."

"Don't worry, I'll take care of them," Rohit heard Karan's faint voice.

As the lift car started sliding down, Rohit stood fazed. "Sorry, there has been a mix-up here. Now, they've to wait for some time till the lift returns to the top again. But don't worry; Karan is there to take care of them."

Sunita regained her composure. "No problem. It's no one's fault. Your friend being with them, there should be no issue. Anyway, it's just a matter of few minutes."

"Yeah…" he said in a lowered voice, but his mind was elsewhere. *Oh god, this is a very unique situation. I'm now forced to be with her for several minutes.*

Sunita looked at the floor indicator panel inquisitively. "I believe you've visited this place regularly? How many floors down has the elevator to go?"

Rohit's eyes were lowered. "No, not regularly, but I've been here a few times. It'll now stop ten levels down at the turbine floor."

Silence fell for a few seconds. Gradually, Rohit caught Sunita's eyes. He had a whiff of the perfume Sunita was wearing and his heart beat fast as a warm sensation permeated into the pores of his body. A feeling he had never experienced before.

The silence between the two continued. There was no sound except for the whirring of ceiling fan.

Sunita's voice broke the stillness. "Perhaps, you've been annoyed with me since the incident at the badminton court. You see, sometimes I just act impulsively."

She has made up for that day to some extent, but still she didn't say she's sorry, Rohit thought, but there was no sense in arguing about that further. He wore a half-hearted smile, "Ah! That's no problem. Such small things happen all the time."

Suddenly, there was a thud…and then another rocking thud more intense than before. The elevator car swung momentarily like a pendulum and then stopped with a heavy jerk. As the two stumbled towards each other the light went off and it was totally dark. They shrieked in panic.

Rohit's heart pounded. "Are you okay? Don't worry. I think power will be restored soon. They have a back-up power system here," he stuttered and moved towards the panel. Groping in the dark, he tried to locate the emergency call button, but couldn't find any.

"Hey, listen, we're stuck up here," he shouted at the top of his lungs, expecting the phone system to work. But when no response came, he screamed and pounded the door frantically with his fists and shoes.

His whole body was now sweating. On an impulse, he pushed forward and tried to force open the doors with his hands. Nothing moved. "What the hell," he yelled.

Then, he felt Sunita's hand and suddenly, she clasped his elbow. He heard her cry, "I'm so scared."

Cold fear gripped his body in the ghostly silence. He had tried everything. There was nothing more he could do except wait for the power supply to start. Why did it take much time to start the backup power?

Her shrieks turned hysterical and then he felt her arms tightly around his neck. "We're trapped. When will it end?"

Had she swooned? He was not sure. With her closeness, a spirit of chivalry rose in him. He would not allow anything to happen to her. "Don't worry. It's going to be over soon," he hissed, and placed one hand caressing her back and the other on her head, stroking her hair.

They stood in that position for several minutes, until the elevator jerked feebly. Simultaneously, the car was lit up and the fan blades started rotating. Finally, the elevator started moving down.

Rohit promptly composed himself, retracting his arms. Sunita too released her clasp, and her face had a spontaneous streak of crimson.

His heart still throbbed but he wiped his face and turned cheerful. "It was a very dreadful experience. Thank god we're safe."

Sunita looked at her watch. "Yes. Didn't realize we were stuck here for fifteen minutes."

***

Rohit watched two people near the elevator and half a dozen rushing around in frenzy as the elevator doors opened on the zero floor.

"Are you both okay?" Someone asked with a concerned voice. "We have been anxious for you all this time."

Rohit wiped the sweat from his brow and said in a complaining tone, "We're fine, thanks. But it was a bad experience. It's so strange that there was such a prolonged breakdown. I thought you had a backup power here?"

"Rohit, it was not just a power breakdown. There was an earthquake of high intensity that lasted for over thirty seconds. The dam and the power station are being examined for any damage. Thank god you're safe."

Rohit shivered and he saw Sunita's face going pale. "Earthquake?" They repeated in a raised voice.

Sunita's voice was now impatient. "Let's go up. *Maa* and Jai would be waiting for us. We need to cancel the visit to the power station."

***

Next day, Rohit and Sachin were glued to the radio. The details of the earthquake were coming in. It had an intensity of seven on the Richter scale, lasted about thirty seconds and hit the entire Udyog Nagar belt. There was no major damage to the dam, though minor cracks in the masonry and water leakage in the penstocks had been detected. Lots of temporary hutments had collapsed, but there was no loss of life. A team of experts had been dispatched to carry out the repairs to the dam and to strengthen it against future eventualities.

As the news ended, Rohit recalled the fear he had experienced when he was trapped in the lift. He turned to Sachin. "It could have been catastrophic if the intensity had been greater. At eight on the seismic scale, this dam would have suffered a severe breach, leading to flooding of all the downstream villages and towns. That could have killed thousands of people and caused incalculable damage to property. The example of earthquake damage to Koyna dam in the sixties is before us."

Sachin replied excitedly, "You're right. Do you recollect the meeting when the MP Jaidev was here? Kavita had raised the question about the possibility of damage to the dam by earthquakes that could be calamitous. In fact, in the hurry for power projects and industrialization, the planners often forget about the ecological impact."

Rohit nodded. "Oh, yes. I remember that. Seems, she had a premonition about this. I think we should send telegrams to her and Jaidev informing them about this calamity. Also, we need to remind them about the announcement of relief package for the villagers."

***

When Rohit met Daniel that day, the earthquake was the hot topic.

Daniel's face was grave. "I'm so glad you were not harmed when you were in the lift. Such earthquakes can sometimes be catastrophic. I remember that in 1971 the San Fernando Dam in California was hit by an earthquake. The magnitude there was only 6.7, but it got damaged beyond repair."

"That was really tragic. It shows if we continue to tamper with the ecology, nature will surely turn its fury on us," Rohit replied philosophically.

***

In view of the disturbed atmosphere after the earthquake, Sunita, her mother and brother cut short their visit and left for Varanasi two days earlier than planned.

As their car left the peripheral boundary of Udyog Nagar, Sunita glanced back for a while and turned reflective. After the last visit also, she had passed through this place but something was amiss this time.

Jai was as usual playful. "*Didi*, why have you suddenly become serious? Are you not happy we're returning home?"

"Will you keep quiet for a while, silly? I'm thinking about the syllabus for the next semester of my college," she snapped.

Her mother glared repressively at the siblings to stop the argument.

Sunita fell silent again. She had lied to her brother that she was engrossed in thoughts about her studies. In fact, her stomach churned though she didn't know what exactly was bothering her.

Questions swirled in her mind. Was her uneasiness because of the recollection of tremors in the lift? What if there was a more powerful tremor?

Or was she missing Rohit? With half-closed eyes, she relived the scene in the elevator. The sinking feeling she had when there were heavy jolts in the elevator car and then...the physical nearness, the smell of his body and the soothing sensation that seeped even to her bone marrow when he stroked her hair. All these aroused tenderness and warmth in her heart. *He is so chivalrous and caring. I almost swooned, with a sense of weightlessness but he kept on consoling me, holding me and caressing me like a baby. Is it true that a woman in such a precarious situation gets attracted romantically to her male companion? I wanted him to grip me tightly in his arms and...kiss me. But he didn't make any such move. He's a perfect gentleman.*

She was lulled into sleep, till the car entered their bungalow in Varanasi.

***

A week later, Rohit got a phone call from Delhi. The good news that he shared later with all was that the government had announced a rehabilitation package for the tribal villagers displaced by dam construction. Houses in a resettlement township, allotment of land at alternate locations and cash compensation was to be provided to each family—partly within one month and the rest within a year.

Next night, there was a celebration when Rohit, Daniel, Ramesar and others watched the *Chhau* tribal dance in an open field. Torches and fire poles lit the dance arena. Dancers wearing blue, violet and green masks danced vigorously to drums and flute.

Ramesar pulled Rohit to the dance area, putting the mask of a tiger on his face, while Jhilmil and other villagers clapped.

When Rohit resumed his seat, Daniel turned to him jubilantly, tapping his feet. "I'm reminded of clogging, the folk dance we used to have back in the Appalachia Mountains."

***

Rohit and Sachin returned late that evening from the celebration in the worker's colony and were passing through the factory when they saw some movement in the yard behind the stockroom. As no construction work was taking place at that hour, the lights had been switched off except on the arterial roads inside the factory. As Rohit neared the store, he could recognize Vikrant and Ranjan as they passed the lamppost.

Rohit's heart missed a beat. As both tip-toed to the adjacent building and hid behind a column, he nudged his friend and whispered. "Seems, something unusual is brewing up there?"

"Oh, yes. What are these guys up to at this hour?" Sachin's voice was now getting nervous.

Rohit's eyes peered at Vikrant opening a file and handing over some papers to Ranjan. They continued to talk for sometime in hushed tones and then left abruptly.

He leaned toward Sachin. "Perhaps, they've been waiting for some other person, who hasn't turned up. So, they've left."

"Could it be they had planned to smuggle out some expensive

material from the stock yard?" Rohit said. "Anyway, there is no sense in staying on now. Let's also leave."

As they came out of hiding, they saw a paper lying on the road near the place where Vikrant had been standing earlier.

"Ah, Vikrant seems to have dropped some document," Rohit said excitedly, bending down to pick up the paper.

He took out a pencil torch from his pocket and glanced quickly at the paper. "It looks like an invoice from Express Transporters, Robertspura."

Sachin too looked at it and frowned. "Here is another link to the chain. The focal point seems to be Robertspura. We need to go there at the earliest...perhaps, tomorrow."

"Just to remind you to take your camera along; we may need it there," Rohit said with the tone of a detective.

***

The next day, Rohit and Sachin were on their way to Robertspura.

As their taxi reached the town outskirts amid a cloud of dust on the unmetalled bumpy road, Rohit turned to Sachin, "I see a fork in the road. So, we need to ask for directions. Our first stop should be the Express Transporters. Perhaps, we can get some lead from there."

Sachin seemed to have a different idea. "I think we should stop at the first soft drink and betel-leaf shop. Let's have some cold drinks. These small shop owners are great gossip mongers and we can get a lot of information by listening to their commentary on hot things happening here."

The taxi stopped before a kiosk, beneath a *peepal* tree, announcing its name, "Bansi Paan House," on a small painted nameplate. Its counter was lined with soft drinks, a round brass vessel and several small bottles with condiments, while the owner was busy applying lime paste to a betel leaf, his lips moving to the blaring tune of songs from the radio.

The kiosk-owner smiled warmly with a slight bow. "Never saw you before."

"Yes, we're here first time. And, Bansi, that's your name I believe?" Rohit said casually looking at the nameplate. He wanted to continue the conversation to be able to elicit more information about the goings-on there. "You seem to have a nice, well stocked kiosk. We'll have a cola and lemonade and two betel-leaf wraps."

"Please take the chairs and feel comfortable. If you like, I will arrange some snacks for you too."

Rohit thumbed down the marble of the green bottle that Bansi had pulled out from under the slab of ice in a case and took a gulp of cold lemonade. He turned to Sachin, "*Yaar*, I know you'll have the regular cola, but I like…" He broke off as his eyes strayed to the cars parked outside a building at some distance across the road. There was a nameplate, Sonepur Building Material Suppliers.

"Hey, look there…quick…" he whispered leaning toward Sachin.

Sachin was taking his wallet out of his pocket to make the payment, but he withdrew his hand and turned around. "What's that?"

"See that white Fiat car there? That's our company car. It's usually used by Ranjan for official work."

The next minute, their jaws dropped as they saw Ranjan, Vikrant and Bhiku contractor exiting the building and walking towards the car, laughing. Vikrant was holding a yellow bag and another person followed them.

On an impulse, Rohit moved behind the tree and turned to his friend. "That's Mahipal, driver of that car."

Sachin also took position obscured behind a hanging branch of the tree. "Something doesn't seem to fit in here. Why should they be here meeting the building material supplier…both of them together? And you remember, the Chief had issued a memo informing everyone that Ranjan and Vikrant were to attend a seminar today in the factory. But they are here! And what could be in that bag?"

"Yes..." Rohit began when Bansi butted in, "Do you know them? They come here very often. Now, they'll go and see the dance of a nautch girl, in a bar about a kilometer from here. That's their usual practice."

Rohit gave a gasp of surprise. "How do you know these people?"

"Once they were drunk and fought with me over a minor issue. They also hit me. Since that day, I hate them. I'm sure all three are into some shady deals."

The words 'shady deals' impacted Rohit's mind sharply. He recalled the two occasions when he had seen Vikrant with two others in the store yards. Did their meetings have anything to do with the over-invoicing for civil work that he had detected earlier? Were they into smuggling some precious materials out of the factory? Could it be that the two staff members, the contractor and material supplier were in league?

But just finding them together in Robertspura didn't prove anything. Some more missing links needed to be unearthed. Perhaps, Bansi could be helpful.

He took Sachin aside. "Something fishy is going on as this guy has also pointed out. I've a hunch all these three are in collusion."

"You are forgetting that we have also to investigate the other one...the transporter whose invoice we found in the factory."

"Let's ask Bansi about that. He might tell us something important which we don't know so far and that could give us a break," whispered Rohit. Edging toward the kiosk, he asked, "Do you know something about Express Transporters?"

Bansi finished wrapping the betel-leaves and lifted his head, "Yes, I know. It is located in the next street from here. I think the owner's name is ... Rajiv Verma."

"Ah! Does it mean that our admin manager, Rajiv, is also involved? Maybe, he is the kingpin?" Rohit thought.

His gaze darted to the threesome who were still there, laughing. Soon, Vikrant advanced to the car and pulled a camera from the glove compartment. Slinging the camera case, he walked to a nearby "Novelty Photographers" shop. After a few minutes, he returned, a faint smile on his face.

Rohit watched the car leave and he nudged Sachin.

Vikrant's brief visit to the photographer brought back memories of the altered photographs that he had seen earlier in the Chief's office. He was curious to know if Bansi had something to say on that.

"Well, I don't know much beyond what I've already told you," the man said. "But one thing is for sure. The material supplier is a goon, a criminal character in this area. There was a recent instance when he used photography for blackmailing a rich landlady here. I heard the case got compromised on a settlement a week back. Did you notice the yellow bag one of them was holding? I'm sure there is a lot of cash in it."

Rohit's fists tightened. Blackmail. Women's photographs. The words impinged on his brain. Could it be that Vikrant was behind his and Jhilmil's photographs? That blackmail attempt had not succeeded because the Chief had found it to be a hoax and had not given any importance to it.

Now, he had a lead that could pin down the culprits.

During the return journey, Rohit's mind was engulfed with the thoughts of misappropriation, misdemeanor and blackmailing. It was so unexpected; never in his life had he faced such a situation. But now that it was there, he'd do anything to encounter it.

***

Rohit was cheerful, his head raised confidently, when he met the Chief next day. "Sir, I feel I have clues to the issues in the construction bills and the altered photographs. Seems, there is a connection between these two. Our own officers seem to be in collusion with the material suppliers and transporters."

"Don't be so excited. Relax and tell me details," the Chief said pointing to a chair.

Rohit narrated in detail about his and Sachin's observations during their visit to Robertspura.

"You saw them in the afternoon. But at that time, Ranjan was supposed to be attending a seminar here. Maybe, you were mistaken in identifying the people."

"No, sir. Sachin was also there. Perhaps, you can confirm it from driver, Mahipal. A person I am acquainted with corroborated all this... even confirming the blackmailing of women by this gang, who threatened to circulate altered photographs of them."

The Chief spoke over the intercom. "Get me the car log sheets of driver Mahipal for the last month."

His face turned grave as he scanned the log sheets. "Yes, you're right. The log sheet readings are a telltale. They do show a long journey of about four hours by Ranjan yesterday afternoon, though he was supposed to be here. And it seems he has visited the same place at last five times in the last month, without informing me."

Rohit was silent as the Chief's eyes fired with rage. "Oh, my god. I can't imagine Rajiv and Ranjan are also involved. I should have got a hint about the maneuvers of these officers when you pointed out the defective bills last year and when I had found that the photos were not genuine. Anyway, now I'll hand over the matter to a private investigation agency and try to collect all the necessary evidence. If they're found guilty I'll dismiss them and hand them over to the police."

Rohit grinned. That should fix Vikrant and the other officials who had made the factory atmosphere so vicious.

***

Jhilmil looked with widened eyes at Barli approaching the swing with a playful gait, her plaits whirling in air and exclaimed,

"You seem to be very happy! Anything special?" Jhilmil asked her younger sister.

Barli slipped alongside her sister on a swing that Jhilmil had set up for the *Teej* monsoon festival, hanging by ropes from the *sal* tree, and nudged her. "I saw Engineer *sahib* today in the market. He asked about you."

A rush of delight ran through Jhilmil's veins, but she soon regained her composure. "What else did he say?"

Barli smelled the pink banana flowers that decorated the strings of the swing. "He praised you for the good work you are doing for the school and…" She halted for a while, pushing with her feet to increase the speed of upward swing.

Jhilmil was anxious to know more about what Rohit had said. But seeing her sister in a playful mood, she waited for the swing to slow down.

Barli didn't seem to want to stop, so Jhilmil grabbed the ropes. "You wanted to say something more?"

"I think he likes you. Do you like--"

Jhilmil interrupted her mid-sentence. "You're stupid!" She got up from the wooden swing seat, plucked a flower from the nearby banana plant and flung it at her sister.

Barli turned aside, evading the blossom. Then, she pulled her sister back to the seat and held her hand. "All right, I'll not ask you that. You've been meeting him for the last several months. So, what's your opinion about him?"

"What kind of a question is this? I met him a few times and he picked me to help in the school. That's all."

"What about the poems you have been writing under that tree? Earlier, you wrote an occasional poem, but after meeting him, there is a spate of poems."

"Yes. That's because he encouraged me to write them."

Barli's face was now solemn and she shrugged. "I'm just being frank with you; I am younger than you, but I'm old enough to understand ways of the world. The fact is that I'm worried about you. If you develop feelings for him, it's going to be a very difficult situation. You know he is an engineer from a high status family, and…" She stopped, and added finally, "Do you think such a mismatched relationship would work?"

Jhilmil was silent for a while, staring blankly into the faraway bushes. "I don't have any such feelings for him. I just respect him; adore him, because he is so gentle, so caring, and he doesn't consider me of a lower status even though he knows I'm a tribal girl from a poor family."

Barli took a breath and satisfaction spread on her face. But soon her lips curved with a teasing smile. "Thank god, you don't have feelings of love for him. Now, the doors are open for me to begin a romance with him. After all, he is young and handsome–any girl will fall for him."

Jhilmil got up and tweaked her sister's ear, "You are so…"

After Barli left, fuzzy thoughts hovered in Jhilmil's mind. She was still not clear whether she had told the truth to her sister. Did she just admire Rohit? Or was it something more than that? Was she in love with him? But she was not sure what his feelings were for her? Was there a possibility of a high-status man like Rohit getting into a relationship with her?

***

Unknown to Rohit and Jhilmil, the curious hands of destiny were working in another direction.

The Chief had just returned from a round of the factory. "Ah, it's only April and the temperatures have already shot up like in June," he thought.

As he wiped the sweat on his face, he received a call from his brother. "I just called to give you good news. Sunita has expressed her inclination to marry Rohit."

Ratan Kaul

The Chief's voice resonated with cheer. "I'm so glad to hear about that."

"You had mentioned to me earlier about the possibility of Rohit going to the USA for his masters degree and later taking up a job there. Sunita also is keen to do her MD course in the USA. She plans to take the qualifying examination—ECFMG—as they call it, this year," his brother said.

"That would be wonderful. They will make a good couple. Let's try for an engagement soon."

But when the Chief reached home and sat relaxing in his study, questions surfaced in his mind. He walked out and paced across the lawn.

The first issue was how to break the ice with Rohit, who was totally ignorant of the behind-the-scene talks that he had been having with his brother about Sunita's marriage. Second was Rohit's increasing closeness to Jhilmil. Though the mystery of the altered photograph had been resolved and Rohit had been found innocent, the fact remained that they were spending time together. That could lead to some kind of relationship brewing between them in future.

"The second one is the most problematic. I'll have to find a solution to break this relationship. Let me give it a serious thought," he pondered.

After a few days' struggle in his mind, he took a decision and called Ramesar into his office. The contractor appeared nervous when he entered the room, but the Chief tried to put him at ease. He put on a broad smile. "Come, Ramesar. It has been quite some time since we met," he said. "Have a seat."

"So, what's the progress of your work?" He asked, after Ramesar had lowered himself on to the chair.

"*Sahib*, excavation is now complete except for the store and the new administrative building."

A sense of relief crossed the Chief's mind. Ramesar's work was nearing completion, after which he would be moving on, and that would serve his objective. But he had to be sure about it. "How much time do you think it will take to complete your work here?"

Ramesar's manner was now relaxed. "The excavation work for the present contract will finish in 2-3 months, but the civil contractor has promised more contracts to me till he completes the entire work. That may take a year."

The Chief flinched. *Ah! Ramesar is planning to stay here forever. I have to put a stop to that.*

He called his secretary on the intercom. "Put in a call to Himanshu at the New Industrial Township in an hour."

Reclining back on the chair, he put on a warm demeanor. "Good planning, Ramesar. But I have another proposal for you. A township is coming up in a new industrial area about two hundred kilometers from here. My friend, Himanshu, is the man in charge there. He called me yesterday as he wants a reliable labour contractor. I have recommended your name to him — he's the one I'm going to talk to in an hour."

"Thank you. But I want to stay here for some more time. You know my daughter

has just started teaching in the open school here, started by one of your engineers. She is quite happy with this work. She says she wants to be here for a few years, so that she can expand the school to all the children in the neighboring villages too."

The Chief tapped his pencil on the table for some time, his mind meanwhile preparing for the next move. "Ah! That's good work your daughter is doing. But people have to progress and for that they have to move on. You don't want to remain an excavation contractor all your life. You have to become a big contractor and for that it is necessary that you take up new jobs, create a larger workforce and make some investments. I'm only saying it because I like you and your work and I want you to do something bigger."

As Ramesar remained silent, cupping his face, he went on, "And the new job I am referring to will lead you to that new future. It's a once-in-a-lifetime opportunity, building the entire township."

He paused deliberately and then glancing at the phone added, "But you don't have much time, as they may appoint another contractor soon. If you agree, I'll confirm to him on your behalf, when I talk to him in a little while from now."

Ramesar's face had a flicker of glow on his face, though it otherwise remained contemplative. He waited for some time but nodded finally. "I'll do as you advise. I'll finish my work here shortly and leave for the new place soon after that. Please inform your friend accordingly."

The Chief's satisfied countenance belied his shrewd planning. He picked up a file, signaling the end of conversation. "Okay. I'll tell him."

As Ramesar got up and left, a smile erupted on the Chief's face.

***

"Engineer *sahib*..." Rohit heard a high pitched voice as he was nearing the temple, which he visited in the morning once a week.

Rohit turned sideways, and saw Barli getting down from her bicycle. She hurriedly put it on the stand. "Ah! I knew you would be here today. I wanted to give you a message from Jhilmil."

Rohit cocked his eyebrow. "Oh! You had to cycle all the way here to give me the message?"

Barli straightened her dress and set right the strands of flying hair with her hand. "Yes. It's urgent. She wants to meet you today...either in the school or near the banyan tree."

"Okay. But you look worried. Any problem?"

Barli lowered down her eyes. "I don't know. She will explain to you when you meet her."

"Okay, tell her I'll come to the school today during lunch hour."

Barli put her foot swiftly on the cycle pedal. "Thanks. I'll rush back and inform her."

What could be the urgency in meeting, Rohit wondered, as the sounds of chanting, bells and conch shell emanated from the temple?

***

Rohit glanced at a score of children sitting cross-legged, as usual, under the sprawling branches of the *peepal* tree while Jhilmil stood near a blackboard, chalk stick in her hand.

He stopped at some distance, in a dilemma whether to disturb Jhilmil at that time, but after a moment, he walked towards her, while the chant of arithmetic tables from the children continued.

He was expecting Jhilmil to smile, but she just greeted him with her eyes downcast.

Without speaking to him, she turned to the children. "Now, you can go home. You'll get information about future classes later."

Rohit sensed that Jhilmil's eyes were welling up. "What's the matter? You don't seem to be your usual self today. And why did you send the children home–I suppose they are here normally till 4 pm. And what about the future classes? You told them they will get information about that later. What's happening?"

"You have to take those decisions now," Jhilmil replied, wiping her moist eyes. "And perhaps, you have to appoint a new teacher."

Rohit winced. "But why? Has someone objected to the running of this school? Did your father say something?"

"My father is moving away from here for a new contract that the chief *sahib* has arranged for him."

Rohit's brows furrowed. "Ah! It's so sudden. There is so much excavation still left--"

He stopped midway, as Jhilmil rushed away without saying a word.

He sat under the tree, his arms crossed on his chest while disturbing questions clouded his mind. Jhilmil's behavior was surprising. Why was she sobbing and why had she rushed away, though she herself had sent a message to him asking him to meet her? Why was Ramesar shifting to another place when his contract was still in force and there was still lot of excavation work to be done for the new administrative block and other buildings? Why had the Chief arranged a new contract for him? He didn't have any answers to any of them.

He realized he was standing alone in the workers' colony and he felt embarrassed. He'd talk to Ramesar to get some answers.

He slowly walked back to the security gate of the factory. He'd meet her father in the factory. Later, perhaps, he'd try to meet her near the brook or the banyan tree where she used to spend time in the mornings, writing her poems. No, he couldn't let her go away.

***

Ramesar was not to be seen throughout the whole day. But next day, Rohit saw him in discussion with another contractor and a dozen workers near an excavation site.

He walked up to Rohit, but his face was sullen. "Perhaps, you've heard I'm shifting from here to another place, far from here."

Rohit's mind was still engulfed by the questions that were bouncing on his mind since his earlier meeting with Jhilmil. "When are you leaving?" He asked. "Will Jhilmil and Barli also go with you or will they join you later?"

"I'm transferring my present contract to one of my friends. All of us will leave the day after tomorrow. You will have to look after the school now and also arrange for another teacher."

Rohit tightened on the inside. He wanted to ask some more questions. Why was he leaving in such a hurry? Where was he going? But a worker came rushing up to him. "Jayant *sahib* wants to meet you in the rolling mill shed, urgently," he said.

"I have to leave now." Rohit's voice was dampened. "I'll try to meet you later."

***

Stinging pain invaded Rohit's heart. He tossed on his bed all night. As his restlessness increased, he got up and stood on the balcony. Why was he so tense? Was it because Jhilmil was leaving the place permanently? Was it because Jhilmil didn't talk to him properly when he went to meet her? But why should he be bothered about it?

At dawn, he decided he'd go and meet her near the brook where she spent her early mornings, scribbling lines for her poems. He dressed up quickly and rushed to the spot. But he didn't find anyone near the brook or the banyan tree, or in their vicinity.

Then, he noticed a folded paper lying in a hollow of the tree trunk. He plucked it out nervously.

His heart hammered loudly in his chest as he read the lines that seemed to have been scribbled in a hurry:

'The world is large, but a full circle,
and it's also so small they say.
In our journeys, perhaps we'll meet,
Surely, on the way, someday.'

Was it a goodbye message? Had she left already? But Ramesar had said they would leave in two days.

He walked back to the brook briskly. Gazing at transparent stream, he imagined Jhilmil's image reflected faintly in the water. A rush of despair overtook his whole body and mind. His legs buckled under him and he slumped on the ground. As he sat there cupping his throbbing temples in his hands, the events of the last few months rolled in his mind, starting with the first time he saw Jhilmil while he was adjusting his lens on the theodolite.

The sound of the factory siren awoke him from the reverie.

***

In the factory, Rohit was looking for Ramesar, when his eyes caught overseer Balu entering the factory in a rush. "Sorry, I came a bit late for work today. Actually, I'd gone to the bus stop to see Ramesar and his family off. But it seems they took an earlier bus. I couldn't meet them."

"Where did they go?" Rohit asked hurriedly.

"When I talked to him yesterday about it, I got the impression that he hadn't yet made up his mind about his destination."

Rohit froze for a moment and then a sense of hollowness pervaded him. Why did they have to leave all of a sudden?

As he stood there, the painful realization that he'd no longer be able to meet Jhilmil cut through him like the jabs of several knives together.

But soon, he hid the moisture in his eyes and composed himself. "Okay, let's get down to our jobs."

***

CHAPTER 7

A day later, Sachin went to Rohit's room to pick him up to go to the factory, as he did every day. But he found Rohit still in bed.

As he dragged a chair near the bed, Rohit rubbed his eyes. "Don't you have to go to the factory today?" Sachin asked.

Rohit sat up. But instead of getting out of bed, he reclined on a pillow. "No."

"You seem to be tense. Anything particular bothering you?"

Rohit pursed his lips, and his eyes were lowered.

"I never saw you like this before. You need to get over whatever is bothering you," Sachin went on.

Rohit's eyes glazed. For some time, he stared blankly out his window, and then he picked up a magazine, leafing through it.

Sachin touched Rohit's arm. "You don't have to tell me. But we've been friends since childhood, and I can tell surely that you are missing Jhilmil."

"Don't be childish, why should I miss her? After all, what relationship did I have with her? It's just that she was trying to helping me fulfill my dream of running a school."

"Okay, if that's the case, I'll help you find another person to run the school."

Rohit's face was grim. He got out of the bed and put on his slippers. "I want to take rest today. Please go ahead and put in my leave application."

Without looking back, he sauntered to the bath room. He needed a quick shower to get over the shock of Jhilmil having left without informing him.

***

Jhilmil found it hard to adjust in the new township of Shaktinagar, though her father had got a bigger contract and found a larger house.

Nostalgic memories of Rohit kept on chasing her and she thought of writing a letter, so that at least they could remain in contact through letters. But it was not so simple—she attempted to write a few lines and crossed them out. She didn't know how she could express her feelings.

After a lot of mental jigsaw, she managed a few lines and also put her address there to enable Rohit to write back.

After pasting the flip of envelope, she asked Barli to take the letter to the mailbox. Barli looked at the address keenly. "Ah! A letter to Engineer *sahib*. But it looks strange. Remember the day I delivered your message asking him to meet you? When he came over, you didn't even speak to him properly. And, now you're writing a letter to him."

Jhilmil frowned. "You needn't put your brain into all that. Just go and post it."

"Okay. I've to go to get some groceries from the market in an hour. I'll drop it at that time."

***

Barli left for the weekly bazaar, with the envelope in her hand. As she crossed the park near her house, she saw her father coming in from the opposite side.

"Where are you headed to?" Ramesar asked.

Barli stalled. "I'm going to get some vegetables and rice. And *Baba*, you look quite happy."

Ramesar tapped Barli's shoulders. "There is a reason to be happy. I'll tell you when I get home. And what is that packet in your hand?"

Barli hesitated for a moment and said finally, "That's a letter *didi* wrote to *sahib* regarding the school."

Ramesar's smile disappeared. "Let me see it."

He remained ruminative for a while, gazing at the Udyog Nagar address on the envelope. Then, his eyes turned red. "Keep this with you for the time being and don't post it."

He held his daughter's hand and led her to a bench on the park. "Come, I want to tell you something."

Barli sensed there was something her father didn't like about that letter. Her heartbeat increased as she waited nervously for her father to speak up.

Ramesar started cheerfully, "The happy news is there is a proposal for Jhilmil's marriage. The groom's family belongs to the next town from here. They want an early marriage. And, after that I've to arrange your marriage too. You know these are two important responsibilities that I need to fulfill soon."

There was a pause and Barli waited eagerly to hear what her father had to say next.

Ramesar's face was now glum. "So, now I do not want her to continue any kind of relationship with Rohit. I know that they were friendly with each other. I did not interfere because I felt that since their meetings, Jhilmil had shed her gloom and she was feeling jovial with a renewed spirit. But now the time has come when she should forget him completely. Or for that matter even the school in Udyog Nagar...all memories of that place have to be wiped out. And..."

Barli sensed her father had to say something more about the happenings in Udyog Nagar, but he suddenly stopped as some people passed by.

"You wanted to say something more?" Barli asked.

"I have a strong feeling that the factory chief wanted us to leave that place urgently because he didn't want Rohit and Jhilmil to become close."

Barli could hear her temple throbbing. The whole affair was so unimaginable.

"Forget about that," her father continued. "Now, what I'm going to tell you is important and you've to help me in that."

"Okay. What do you want me to do?"

"Don't post this letter," he said sternly. "And if there is any letter from Rohit–the possibility is remote as he doesn't have our address–but whatever, you have to take care that letters from both sides get destroyed. That way, they will forget about each other quickly."

She remained inert for some time. *Sahib* was so nice. So caring. He gave her elder sister a fresh lease of life. And she had always been a confidante of Jhilmil but with this betrayal, how was she going to face her? But what her father said also made sense.

She slowly, hesitantly, handed over the letter to her father and walked away, guilt following her like a shadow.

***

Some days later, the Chief relaxed in his reclining chair, recalling the events of the last few days. The factory construction was going ahead on schedule and he had received a letter two days ago from the head office commending him for that. The four unscrupulous staff members had been dismissed and booked for misappropriation and theft by the police.

And his plan for Rohit and Sunita's marriage had proceeded well. Ramesar and his family had left much before the deadline of one month. And Rohit had been promoted.

A pleased smile rose on his lips. "I have played my cards well."

But what next? He pondered. Should he talk to Rohit and get his views about marriage to his niece? Or should he leave it to his brother, Sreedhar, to approach Rohit's father in Delhi?

Let his brother take it from here, he decided and asked his secretary to connect him to Sreedhar at Varanasi.

***

"Papa! How come you're here?" Rohit exclaimed as he looked out the window of his house. His father, Vineet, and mother, Kamla, stood beside a cab, enquiring from a passer-by the location of their son's house.

Rohit rushed down the stairs and hugged his parents. "I am glad to see you here? But you could have wired or phoned me."

Vineet laughed. "First, let's get our baggage out of the cab. I'll explain everything to you."

As they entered the house, Rohit called out to his domestic help. "Bhure! Papa and mummy have come. Get some water and then, tea."

Vineet beamed as he sat on the sofa in the hall. "I'm happy to see the new flat allotted to you. Looks quite decent. Last time I came, you were in the bachelor quarters. Congratulations on your promotion and this flat."

Sparkles of happiness and pride flowed through Rohit's body. "Thanks, papa."

"Come, sit here alongside me," Vineet said affectionately. "We made this plan to visit you as there has been a development that we wanted to share with you. We're here for a day and it would be good if we know your mind about it before we leave."

Bhure placed a tray on the table and Rohit passed the cups around. "I'm sure it would be good news."

"Yes, of course," Vineet said cheerfully. "It's about your marriage."

A jolt passed through Rohit's body momentarily. "My marriage! Why has this come up all of a sudden when I'm thinking of going to the USA for further studies?"

Vineet passed his fingers through his grey hair. "Actually, Sreedhar–you know, the brother of your boss, Divakar, came and met me in Delhi. He had also phoned me a couple of times earlier."

Rohit gasped, taken aback. Things had reached that far and he hadn't even got a hint about it. The boss seemed to have been playing games. He had a half-twisted curious smile. "Very strange! How does he know you and how come he got your phone number?"

Vineet laughed lightly. "It seems your boss gave the details to him, after which he approached me with the proposal of his daughter, Sunita's marriage to you. I suppose you know her… I'm told she came here a few times and you two have met each other."

"Yes, we've met a couple of times, but just as acquaintances or you may say friends," Rohit said with a shrug.

"That's right, but the parents are always anxious to keep finding matches for their grown-up sons or daughters."

Rohit's eyes were quizzical. "But have you seen Sunita? By the way, you didn't tell me whether you have come directly from Delhi or you have been visiting other places."

"No, we didn't come from Delhi. In fact, we had planned to come to Varanasi to visit the holy temples and offer our prayers there. So, Sreedhar suggested that we meet him and his family there. And that's where we met their daughter, Sunita, also. After that we drove here. We have to leave in the evening as I have an important work to attend to in Delhi tomorrow."

Rohit retreated into an irked silence, disturbed about this sudden development, while his father went on, "You already know the girl. You know her family."

"But the important thing to be considered first is whether I'm willing to marry at this stage in my career," Rohit retorted.

Kamla, who had so far not spoken, joined the conversation now. "Son, your papa and I like Sunita. She is beautiful and modest. She's appearing shortly in the finals of MBBS and has a good career ahead of her. And she is from a decent and reputable family."

Rohit wanted to say firmly, "No, I don't want to marry her or anyone else for at least two years till I complete my post-graduate work," and put an end to the discussion. But in view of the respect which he had for his parents, he didn't want to sound discourteous or impetuous, particularly when they were his guests, just for a day. He needed to resolve the issue sensitively.

"Papa, Ma, I don't think what you are saying is logical. Marriage is an important decision and it requires a careful consideration of several vital factors."

Kamla took over in a slow, pleading tone. "Son, there is a very sensitive factor that your papa didn't broach so far. Your younger sister, Nilu, is twenty-two now and she has already finished her studies. Now, we feel she should get married soon. She is younger than you and according to our customs it is appropriate that you get married first. However, if you go abroad for studies, it will take two to three years before you visit India again for your marriage. In the meantime, she may outgrow the best marriageable age."

Rohit rubbed his chin with his fingers. "I don't think any harm would be done if she gets married first."

"But Nilu has insisted you get married first. Also, you know our family believes in traditions and customs."

Rohit raised his hands in resignation. "I understand the importance of traditions and customs, but they need to be somewhat adapted to the times and circumstances. In any case, all this is so sudden. It's difficult for me to take a decision right away. Let me think it over, I'll write to you or we can talk on phone."

***

The discussion had ended there and Rohit's parents had left for Delhi in the evening. They had also stressed that an early decision was important, particularly due to the circumstances about his younger sister's marriage.

Rohit spent the night listlessly, sitting on his chair. He was angry deep down on the inside. How could he be forced to marry someone he didn't love or when he didn't have an inclination to marry at that particular time? He almost banged his fists on the table.

It was only in the early hours of morning that drowsiness began to overtake him. But sound sleep eluded him and he drifted in and out of short naps. The semi-lucid images of Jhilmil in different dresses, sometimes in a turquoise *saree*, other times in a mustard yellow *choli lehenga* or in a purple *salwar-kameez* dress passed across his dreams.

They are sitting under the expansive canopy of banyan tree. He puts his arms around her neck, feels her breath and brings his lips near to hers. "Do you love me?" He asks. Jhilmil is silent, lips quavering but closed. He restrains himself, waiting patiently for that perfect, sensuous moment of bliss, when her lips will part. But she doesn't answer, gets up and walks away, her anklets creating a sweet music.

He opened his eyes for a few moments. "Ah! It was just a dream."

He rubbed his aching eyes to soothe them for a few minutes, turned over and drifted into sleep again.

Jhilmil is still there, this time near the brook. Both look at their images in the crystal clear water and she laughs heartily. "We are eternal lovers. No one can separate us. Not your boss. Not my father. No one. We're meant to be together. "

Then, she moves near him and puts her head on his chest, her arms circling his neck. As he caresses her long hair, she pulls him close. He feels the heaving of her chest and sparks fly in his body. Spontaneously, he lowers his lips to hers which are now parted, questing and seeking. He cups her cheeks and says aloud, "You can't go away. I'll keep chasing you wherever you go."

***

Next morning, the sunrays had spread to Rohit's bedroom through his glazed window when Bhure knocked at the door.

He sat up and stretched when Bhure entered. "*Sahib*, are you all right? It's already nine o'clock. An hour ago, Sachin came here asking for you, but didn't want to wake you up. He's already left for the factory."

Rohit's voice had an irritated tone. "I'm okay. Get me some tea."

But his mind was still occupied by the lingering thoughts of his dream, the embrace with Jhilmil, the touch of her soft shiny black hair, and the kiss.

"No, I can't sit here idly while Jhilmil may be yearning for me. I have to go find her... wherever she is," he mumbled. "But where will I find her? Perhaps, her father has shifted back to Bilaspur. She had mentioned to me that she was brought up and educated there. Ah! Why didn't I think of that before?"

After taking a few sips of the tea, he jumped out of bed. "Bhure, I'm going out for a few days...may be two or three. Go and tell Sachin to inform the office."

"But what should I tell him if he asks where you're going?"

Rohit remained silent as he hurriedly gathered his bag, paced out and kick started his bike.

***

After three days, Sachin found Rohit in the family cabin of Dholakia's *dhaba*. A half-empty bottle of whiskey and a half-filled glass lay on the table in front of him.

Dholakia spoke in whispers from a slight opening in the cabin door. "Sachin, can you come out? I want to speak to you."

Sachin came out hurriedly. "How come he's here? I've been waiting for him for three days."

Dholakia was glum. "I don't know. He came here at dusk in a weary, disheveled state and asked for a drink. Since then he's been drinking one shot after another. He seems to be in some great distress. Never saw him like that before. Any problem in the factory?"

Sachin had guessed the problem. Perhaps, Rohit had gone in search of Jhilmil and returned without finding her. But Dholakia shouldn't know about it. "Don't worry. I'll take care of him."

Rohit had slumped to a side of the chair by the time Sachin re-entered the cabin.

"I think you've had enough for today. Let's go home."

Rohit didn't answer. His face was strained.

Sachin panicked and ran out to Dholakia's counter. "I'll take him home. Can you arrange a vehicle?"

***

Rohit's head was fuzzy. The abundance of liquor he had the night before was having its effect. He didn't want to get up from his bed. But his heart palpitated heavily even lying down.

He got up reluctantly. His eyes burned with anguish and desperation. For three days, he had been on the dusty, pot-holed roads searching for Ramesar and Jhilmil in Bilaspur and the nearby towns and villages. Some people had known the family there, but in the last two years the link had broken. Other had given some clues and directions but those didn't work. He had used all his ingenuity and investigative skills, but had failed. Jhilmil had vanished.

He looked up as Sachin walked in, holding a glass. "Hey, here's some lemon water for you. Gulp it and the after-effect will vanish."

Rohit took a sip. "Thanks."

"So, how was your journey..." Sachin started.

Rohit gestured sharply with an open palm. "Please, I want to be left alone. No sermons."

"All right. Take your time. But take my word, you need to open up. The sooner the better. I'm leaving now and will return in the evening."

As the sound of his friend's footsteps receded, Rohit's mouth dropped and his eyes were downcast. Sachin had always been so helpful and caring, but he had never taken his friend seriously. But now, he needed a shoulder to weep on, a well wisher to open out his heart to, a person to heal his wounds.

As he got up, his legs buckled under him, but in a moment he steadied himself and called out, "Bhure, hurry over to Sachin's house and give him a message that we'll have dinner together tonight at my place."

***

By the time the two friends took their seats at the dining table, the turbulence in Rohit's heart had calmed down.

"I hope you had a good rest during the day," Sachin started on a cheerful note, placing the napkin on his lap.

Rohit wore a dry smile. "Oh yeah, lots of it."

"Daniel asked about you. I told him you'll come in tomorrow. Perhaps, you need to resume your work now."

"Yes," Rohit replied.

Sachin turned to Bhure, "You're really a good cook. The cheese dish is delicious," and then after a few moments to Rohit, "By the way, may I know what adventure you have been up to on your bike? Have you been to some hermitage to seek solace?"

Rohit's mind brainstormed. How much should he tell his friend? In any case, Sachin would have already guessed about some parts of it. Should he now bare it all?

Finally, he opened up. "Don't be silly. I did what any person in my situation would have done. I hadn't got any letter from Jhilmil after she left and I wanted to be sure she is comfortably settled down wherever she is. All these three days I biked like crazy in Bilaspur and adjoining towns and villages, trying to get some lead about Ramesar's whereabouts, but it turned out to be fruitless search."

Sachin patted Rohits arm. "Ah! It must have been quite strenuous."

After a while, he added, "But now, my pointed question is: why do you care so much for her? Are you in love with her? Is she in love with you?"

"I don't know."

Sachin took a few spoonfuls of fried-rice from the bowl on to his plate. "Has she ever displayed any romantic signs implying she wants a relationship with you?"

He didn't wait for an answer and went on humorously, "By the way, there has been a lot of research on the signs that a woman displays if she is romantically attracted to a man, like adjusting strands of hair or running her fingers through her hair, or..."

Rohit conjured up the images of Jhilmil's expressions at various occasions... downward glance, red cheeks...stammered reponses during their conversations.

Outwardly he snapped, "Now, for god's sake, you needn't go into the details of your research. I'm not sure about the answers to your questions."

Sachin took a glass of water. "Okay. Now, on a serious note: how long are you going to remain so despondent? I realize you and Jhilmil were friendly or, let's say more than just friendly; yet it's also a fact that she has gone away and you may never meet her again. Perhaps, her father would presently be looking for a match for her. So, you also need to move on. And remember, you have plans to go to USA for further studies and you wouldn't want anything to get in the way."

"Perhaps, Sachin is right," debated Rohit in his mind. *I did have a soft spot for her, and we cared for each other, but there was no explicit relationship between us beyond sharing some thoughts, discussing the emotions in her poems, and our association in running the school. And if she had any special feelings for me why didn't she express them.*

"You may be right," he said hesitatingly, his eyes cast down.

Sachin took a deep breath. "And take that as a part of your destiny. You can't bend it to your liking. And you can't play the game every time by your own rules. So, be practical and treat that chapter as closed," he counseled and turned to Bhure. "Please get coffee for both of us."

"And after that let's go for a movie. *Sholay* is running in the touring theatre tent that has come up recently in the outskirts of the factory. We haven't seen a movie– particularly the night show–for ages," he added.

Rohit nodded his head in silence. But agitating thoughts still lingered in his mind.

***

Jhilmil became silent and aloof in her new house. For her, life had lost its charm and luster and she kept herself occupied with the routine work at home.

One day, she stood at doorstep, as usual awaiting the postman eagerly. But though the man came at the appointed time, ringing the cycle bell, he just passed by to deliver a letter in the neighborhood.

"No letter today either. Rohit must be busy; he must have gone on a tour," she speculated in anguish.

When Barli joined her, Jhilmil asked in a dim voice, "Are you sure you posted the letters in the right box at the post office?"

Barli held her sister's arm. "Of course, *didi*. Now, why are you spoiling your health for a person who doesn't care for your letters? It's time you forget him."

Jhilmil sensed that Barli was averting her eyes. "Perhaps, she doesn't like to see me in such a distress," she guessed.

She sat silently with her hands in her lap, trying to stop the tears that threatened to flood her eyes.

Barli pulled her chair closer to her. "I think you should resume your studies. Take up the correspondence courses of the distance education programs of the universities. I'll also join some private courses for my high school examinations. It'll be so thrilling, you being my teacher... and you can also start writing poems again–you haven't written a single one since you came here."

There was a sound of familiar footsteps and Ramesar entered the room, holding a packet in his hand. "There is good news and here are the sweets for that. The couple and their son who met us last week regarding Jhilmil's marriage have given their approval. Our priest says the tenth of next month is the auspicious date. So, we've to start preparations for the wedding soon."

When her father and Barli left, two large drops slid down Jhilmil's cheeks and she slouched on the chair, her mind in a swirl. *Why is it that the girls in our society don't have much say in their marriages? Oh god! I'm going to miss Rohit, his smile, his laughter, his touch, his care...I can't imagine life without him.*

***

Rohit sat in his room, pensively looking at a letter he had received from his father:

"I was awaiting your letter and the decision about your marriage. Your mother has already spoken to you about the gravity of this matter, particularly as the marriage of your sister is also linked to your marriage. Think about it and let me know. I'll call you one of these days."

Rohit had read this paragraph of the letter several times. No, he was not sure whether he wanted to marry Sunita. He had found her annoying initially though she seemed to have calmed down and was more likeable now. But still he was not yet sure what she really wanted from life, whether she really liked him or wanted to climb a social ladder by marrying him and going to USA. At the same time he didn't want to displease his parents and the most logical step forward seemed to be to marry her. But what about Jhilmil? How could he forget her? The emotional connect he had with her could not be matched by Sunita.

Rohit was unsure of which direction to take.

***

CHAPTER 8

SAN JOSE, USA
2005

Rohit saw a mail from his partner, Tony, on his Blackberry as he entered the lift on way to his office. "Rohit, I'm forwarding the presentation sent by a start-up company 'Usher'. The concept looks good for investment. Can you send me your feedback ASAP?"

"Okay, got it. I'll check it when I get back to my ..." he began replying, but left it unfinished when he heard an alert tone.

His jaw dropped as he read the message. It was from the headmaster of Sam's school. "Please meet me urgently, preferably today noon. There is a serious case of misconduct against your son, Sam."

He stiffened sharply. "Something urgent has come up. Will catch up with you later," he texted to Tony hurriedly.

Returning to the lobby, he stilled for a moment, prickly feelings sweeping through his body. He had met Mr. Steve, the headmaster, a few times before but there had been no complaints about his son. Even Sunita didn't seem to have an inkling of this. But how serious was it?

He looked at his watch. It was time to leave as it would take at least 45 minutes to reach the school through the heavy traffic.

Rushing through the school gate, he ignored the impressively designed grey facade and the building's four-storey tower that rose over the entrance that he always admired.

When Steve rose to shake hands, Rohit looked at the furrowed forehead of the headmaster. He broke the momentary silence. "I'm sorry for my son's misconduct. What has he been up to?"

"If it had just been the conduct, I wouldn't perhaps have bothered you," the headmaster's voice was solemn. "Your son is into...drugs."

Rohit's heart sank, while he faintly heard the man across the table speaking falteringly. "He has been taking drugs...small quantities of cannabis have been found in his possession... in his locker."

"Drugs! Oh, my god." His heart pounded. "Sam is just twelve!"

He cupped his face in his hands and took a deep breath. "Mr. Steve, it's just not possible. His behavior has been normal at home. His report card is good, too. May be there is some misunderstanding."

Steve's face wore an indignant expression. "I wish it were like that. In fact, we suspected three boys of his class, and our school committee on drug abuse kept a watch on them. The committee reported their confirmation ten days back. But we didn't inform you as we wanted to be doubly sure. Only after an external agency confirmed it and the boy was tested positive, did I send this message to you."

Rohit's phone dropped from his hands as his body shook. Sam was such a precocious child, and what had he landed into?

"Where's he now?"

"You should know. He's absent from the school today," the headmaster shrugged.

Rohit picked up the phone and tried to compose himself. "Do you mind if I make a call? Perhaps, my wife would know about his whereabouts."

His fingers tingled as he heard the voice from the other end. "Dr. Sunita is checking a patient. I'll ask her to talk to you when she is free."

"Mr. Steve, she is not available at the moment. If it's okay with you, let me go back and talk to my wife and my son and ascertain the facts. I'll then come back...let's say tomorrow this time," he said as the nervousness still gripped him.

"That's okay. But meantime, I've to put him under suspension till the matter is cleared by the Discipline Hearing Authority."

Rohit froze. "I'm sure there will be a milder alternative?"

"I'm sorry, but we have a zero tolerance policy against

drug usage," Steve said in an imperative tone. "I cannot imagine that Sam, with such good upbringing, should have done it."

Rohit bit his lower lip and sat speechless in his seat, as Steve went on with an exasperated look on his face. "The sad and ironic part is that these are good, promising boys brought up in decent homes. They are fully aware of the consequences of what they're doing. They know they could even be rusticated from the school and also jailed if they indulge in drugs. But they still do it."

He paused and then rose in his seat, stone-faced. "And, now if you don't mind, I have to go out for a meeting."

Rohit's legs shook beneath him as he exited Steve's office. He walked unsteadily to a nearby park and sat fidgeting on a bench, lamenting the mess caused by this unexpected development. "I always thought Sunita was keeping a good watch on the children. But the situation has turned otherwise. It was unimaginable that Sam has turned to drugs. Who is to blame?" He reflected as multiple twinges of pain exploded in his chest.

***

Late evening that day, Rohit walked into his home, a disturbed, agitated person, and slumped on the sofa. As Sunita joined him, he narrated the conversation he had with the headmaster. "Can you ring up Sam and find his whereabouts?" He asked in a feeble, distressed voice.

Sunita tried but Sam's phone was switched off.

An hour later, a young boy with short, black, heavily gelled tapered hair entered the hall with a Walkman and stepped toward his room, seemingly unmindful of his parents sitting there, when Sunita accosted him with a shout, "Sam, it's already nine o'clock. We were worried."

Sam took off the earplugs. "Ah, we had some after-school programs," he replied casually.

Sunita looked at Rohit who was sitting on the adjacent seat on the sofa. "I told you that…" and then turned to Sam. "Ah! I am so happy you're focused on your studies. We just got worried as your headmaster made a complaint to your dad today."

As she told Sam the happenings of that morning, Rohit saw his son's face going pale for a moment, but soon getting into a combative rhetoric. "No, no, it's all rubbish. I'm not doing any drugs."

"Okay, come with me to the headmaster tomorrow and prove your innocence," Rohit shouted.

***

Next day, Mr. Steve, two other teachers and Sam's football coach were present when Rohit and Sam met them. Sam broke down when the headmaster presented the evidence, and finally he admitted his guilt.

Lawyers were engaged, but ultimately when the children's department presented the case before the juvenile court, Sam was committed to three years of rehabilitation.

That night, Rohit cried the whole night, for the first time in his li fe.   ***

Rohit sat on his chair, still brooding about the altercation with Sunita earlier in the evening, while returning gloomily after meeting Sam at the Rehab Center.

"It's no fault of mine," she had said in a high-pitched tone. "Go and blame the school."

"Anyway, now we have to take care of Annie. At fourteen, she's at such a vulnerable age."

But Sunita had shouted adamantly, "Don't bother about her. She's going to be okay."

Presently, the tumultuous thoughts wobbled inside him to a crescendo and drained him totally in body and mind. He dropped unsteadily in his chair. *Oh! God, this is becoming too much to bear. I need to run away from all this.*

"Where did I go wrong? Was Sunita a wrong choice for me?" He moaned.

***

His thoughts travelled back to India... twenty years back... when he was in a dilemma whether to marry Sunita or not.

***

CHAPTER 9

UDYOG NAGAR, INDIA
1985

Rohit was in a great anguish as conlifting thoughts had been invading him about his marriage for the last several days.

On one side was Jhilmil, whom he loved and on the other hand, Sunita, for whom he didn't have a liking but was under pressure from his parents to marry her. At the same time, the procedures for immigrating to USA for post graduation loomed large in his mind.

Soon, Sachin joined him. "You seem to be in a deep thought. Is it about your admission to colleges in USA?"

His gaze fell on the letter in Rohit's pocket. "And by the way, what's that letter? Is it from some college?"

Rohit shook his head, but remained silent.

"Something seems to be bothering you. If you like, you may tell me about it."

Rohit pulled out the letter from his pocket. "I don't hold any secrets from you. Here see it for yourself. Dad wants me to marry Sunita before I leave for the US."

Sachin's eyes narrowed for a while, but soon relaxed. "Rohit, I know your feelings, but I think what he says also makes sense. Sunita looks to be the best match for you in the present circumstances. And there are good career prospects for both of you in USA."

Rohit stood up and flailed his arms furiously. "This is absurd. I don't love her. You know how arrogant and snobbish she was when we met her first time." He pursed his lips for some time and then went on, "Of course, she regretted that later, but don't forget that in a marriage there has to be a deep involvement and commitment. A relationship built by pressure or desperation can only be termed as a compromise, which doesn't last for long."

"Cool down, my friend," Sachin said pulling him back on the sofa. "You're right to some extent. But you know that in India there are mostly arranged marriages. The love starts after the two start living together. Over time, the relationship grows and evolves gradually and the two get adjusted to the partner's shortcomings and differences in nature. Moreover, we have our social systems and obligations and we have to live within their parameters."

Rohit sat in silence and took a sip of water. He pondered his dilemma, leaning against back of the chair and holding his head in his hands. *I don't agree fully with Sachin. But the fact remains that I've not been able to find Jhilmil, for whom I had intense feelings, despite my best efforts. She has also remained silent. Perhaps, I too need to move on. My marriage can pave way for my sister's marriage, which is very important for our family. And during her last visit, Sunita seemed to be a changed woman, more cordial and friendly. As a professional couple, we can have a bright future in USA"*

The lines on his face smoothened gradually. "All right, I'll think over and talk to dad."

"All the best." Sachin closed his fist and raised his thumb.

***

It was monsoon time. Sunita was looking out the window gazing at a conglomeration of white, grey and dark clouds chasing each other, when she saw the postman in his khaki uniform, pedaling towards the house.

She went down the stairs, jumping the steps, holding the hem of her gold embroidered *saree* that she'd got as a gift for her wedding a fortnight back. "Ah! It could be a letter for me."

She was almost breathless when she came up. "Rohit, things are moving fast after our marriage. Yesterday, you received your admission letter from Columbia University and it's my turn today. There are two letters: one from Weill Cornell confirming my admission to the post-graduate course and the other from New York Hospital accepting me for their residency program. How exciting!"

Rohit sprang up from his chair and extended his hand for the letters. "Congratulations," he said throwing up his hands for a high-five.

"Thanks. And gear up now. There are only two months left before the fall semester starts in the US universities. Lots of work has to be done before that."

A fired excitement ran through Rohit's body. "Oh yes, we've got to get the visas, write to the colleges for lodging arrangements, apply for loans and get in touch with our relatives and friends there. Perhaps, we have to look for an apartment if the on-campus residence is not possible. That's really tremendous work."

"And I forgot two important tasks," he added quickly. "First, I have to meet the boss and submit my resignation. And, second, I have to say good-bye to my friend, Sachin, as well as my mentor, Daniel, who has been a great inspiration for me. He'll also be leaving for the US in the next six months, when his assignment finishes here. We've decided to stay in touch."

***

CHAPTER 10

WASHINGTON, USA
1985

The Washington-bound Pan-Am flight from Delhi had left Amsterdam after a stop-over of three hours when Rohit, who was getting lulled to sleep, felt Sunita's head resting on his shoulders.

He opened his eyes for a while and gently smoothed back a few strands of her hair from her face. Warmth surged in his body. "Let me not disturb her. It has been such a hectic day before we boarded this flight; lots of shopping and then meeting all the relatives."

"This journey is also an extended honeymoon for us. And we are going into another world, another environment among another set of people, to build our career, set up a home and raise a family."

***

After they collected their baggage at the Washington-Dulles International airport and advanced toward the exit, Rohit's eyes spotted Prof. Kartik Menon, his father's friend and erstwhile colleague in India, now a professor of Physics at the University of Baltimore.

The bespectacled man with a receding hairline, in his late fifties, extended his hand. "Welcome to America. I hope you had a comfortable flight."

Rohit shook the professor's hand excitedly. "Thanks. The journey was perfect. Please meet Sunita. Sorry, you couldn't attend our marriage."

Sunita was still a bit drowsy but she managed to fold her hands. "*Namaste,* uncle."

"All this is so different from India," Rohit said when the car had proceeded a few miles from the airport.

Kartik was silent for a while as he negotiated the cloverleaf, turning his head to find a gap in the traffic and then merging into the traffic on the highway.

"This is the Washington-Baltimore Parkway," he explained. "We live in Baltimore, just about 35 miles from here. That comes to about 55 km," he clarified.

"That's far, like say, Delhi to Sonepat."

Kartik laughed. "Yes, for India. But here the traffic is fast and we'll be home in just about 45 minutes."

During the drive from airport to Kartik's home, Rohit looked wide-eyed at the wide multi-laned highway, the expanse of blue sky, gas stations and motels, when he heard Sunita's voice after a long silence. "Everything is so big and beautiful here."

"Ah! We're just there!" Exclaimed the professor, as Rohit noticed the Charles St.road sign and a few minutes later, the car entered the Silver Oaks Apartments.

Rohit tilted his head upwards and looked cheerfully at the tall, multi-storied complex with a red-bricked façade and a huge lawn with a fountain in the front, while he and Sunita waited for Kartik to return from the parking lot.

"Such a wonderful place," Sunita commented with a smile. "I am reminded of the new high-rise apartments coming up now in Delhi, but they're not so tall."

As the three entered the house, Rohit's eyes went to the kitchen where a woman in an orange polka dot dress stood near the granite counter, her back to them. The familiar smell of fermented rice and lentil batter pervaded the room as she wiped the iron *dosa* griddle with a soft cloth.

"Krishna, our guests are already here," Kartik announced.

She turned off the stove and came into the hall. "Ah, Rohit and Sunita, I'm so happy to see you." A big smile loomed on her round, high-cheekboned face. "I haven't seen Rohit in over three years—that was in Delhi when he was still in college."

After Rohit and Sunita greeted her, Krishna held Sunita's arm and then turned to Rohit. "And you have such a charming wife. But Kartik and I are annoyed because your dad didn't inform us in advance about your wedding. We missed the chance to participate in the celebrations."

"Oh, aunty, it happened so suddenly, we didn't have a chance to invite anyone except for a few relatives in Delhi."

"So, Sunita, how do you feel here?" Krishna continued.

"It's great. Though I'm in a foreign land, I feel quite at home because of you. Thanks for your hospitality."

Kartik looked at the bags lying to the side and turned to Krishna with a sly smile. "Dear, we have to treat them like a honeymoon couple and make arrangements for their stay accordingly."

"Don't worry, all that's arranged. They'll stay in the same bedroom on the first floor that we prepared for Lakshmi and Tony last year. Please escort them there. Meantime, I'll get some *dosas* ready," she said warmly and hurried back to the kitchen.

Rohit exchanged glances with Sunita. "Thanks, aunty," he called over Krishna's shoulders.

He picked up the two pieces of luggage and looked forward to savoring his favorite *dosa* and *sambhar* dishes after the bland food that had been served to them during the flight.

***

"Let me make the introductions," Kartik said, a radiating smile on his face.

Rohit knew that the smile was special. A kind of reunion was taking place that evening. Kartik's daughter, Lakshmi, and son-in-law, Tony, who lived in the neighbouring Hill Apartments, had just come over to meet him and Sunita and everyone had assembled in the hall.

While the cheerful handshakes went on, he admired Tony's six foot frame, broad shoulders and short curly brown hair. Then, he looked at Lakshmi, wearing a short purple dress, her black hair neatly pulled into a ponytail. His eyes promptly switched to Sunita in a bright blue *saree*. *How different the women's dresses are! And how would Sunita look in the kind of dress Lakshmi is wearing?*

Steaming dishes of pilaf and curries were being passed on at the dinner table, when Kartik turned to Tony with his usual professorial tone. "Rohit and Sunita would be with us for a few days, before they leave for New York—Rohit will join Columbia University for his MS in engineering and Sunita will take up her post-graduation at Weill Cornell Medical College as well as her residency in the affiliated New York Hospital. I'm wondering if in the meantime you can drive them to some scenic spots around here this weekend. You all happen to be in the same age group, so you'll enjoy it a lot."

"Oh, yes, of course," Tony replied briskly and then said to Rohit, "Washington is one place we may visit. We can plan a trip to places overlooking the ocean and the bay. And if you're interested we may also drive toward the Appalachian Mountains, where the landscape is superb. That'll also give you a glimpse of the rural areas."

"That'd be thrilling," Rohit was about to say when Sunita broke in feebly, "Oh no. Not the villages, please. I'd like to go to some lively places. I'm sure there'd be many of them around here."

That led to hearty laughter but Rohit smiled faintly on the inside. "That's the reason she didn't like the tribal area of Udyog Nagar. She'll get attuned to American life much sooner than I will."

***

After a visit to the Six Flags amusement park in D.C., it was time for the beach. Sunita and Lakshmi strolled and at times ran on the sandy beach alongside the Chesapeake Bay, frolicking like kids on the water-front, collecting seashells. Rohit's eyebrows rose and his lips curled slightly as he watched their sandals sinking into the sand.

"We want to go to the edge of the water. Why don't you two join us?" Lakshmi shouted over her shoulder.

"Thanks, but we'll join you later," Rohit called out as he and Tony sat back and relaxed under the shade of a canopy. During the few hours spent with Tony, Rohit had developed camaraderie with the man who seemed to have some common interests with him.

After watching the rolling surf intently for some time, he turned to Tony. "I was told by Uncle Kartik that you work in a software company. What's your role there?"

"Ah! I'm in a team which is collaborating on the development of a new computer operating system."

"That's great. Computers are future of the world," Rohit laughed. "By the way, you talked about Appalachian Mountains. Are you acquainted with that area?"

"Oh, yes. One of my close friends, Al, grew up in Allegheny County, not far from here. His family is still there. I used to spend time with him there during our vacations and many a time we went on long walks in the terrace fields at the foot of mountains."

"Ah! It'd be quite scenic."

"Yes. But the area is underdeveloped as compared to other regions. Al told me the stories of his childhood. His family owned some agricultural land but his father had to work in a mill, as there was not much income from farming. But even with that he had financial problems. Of course, a lot of development has taken place since then."

Rohit stared blankly at the distant horizon line dividing the grey of the water body from the blue of the sky, recalling his days at Udyog Nagar, the remote tribal area. For a few moments, the memories of his meetings with Jhilmil and the events leading to the opening of a school there came to the fore, tormenting him. But he shook his head and managed to put them out of his mind.

Tony broke the silence. "You seem to have some interest in these places. Any particular reason?"

"Oh yes. There are some coincidences. One is that back home in India, I worked in a place, which has some similarity with this Allegheny that you just mentioned. Second, Daniel, the American engineer who came to supervise the erection of a plant in our factory, also belonged to some remote village in Appalachia."

Sunita came running towards them, followed by Lakshmi. She dusted the sand off her sandals and laughed. "Wow, what a great place. I had never been to a coastal city in India and I didn't know what a seashore is like. I'm having such a wonderful time with Lakshmi."

Rohit was buoyed at her child-like exuberance and he gave her a cheerful smile. "I'm so happy to see both of you enjoying the place. My father lived in Bombay for a few years and I spent my childhood on the sands of Chowpatty. But this place looks more beautiful. Anyway, you may carry on for some more time. And when you return, we'll ask Tony to guide us to some good beach restaurant. "

As Sunita and Lakshmi disappeared again in the crowd of visitors, Rohit's glance fell on the two women, one in a two-piece white bikini and the other a blue polka dotted one, and both wearing black sunglasses, relaxing on deck chairs at some distance. "The days are not far when Sunita will ask me to take her photograph in this pose," he chuckled in his mind.

Moments later, his cheer dissipated as he doodled some geometrical figures in the sand. "Tony, I was just wondering, what kinds of lives we, Sunita and I, would have here, in a foreign country. I mean starting from scratch, getting our degrees, then a job and on top of that adjusting to a foreign culture and lifestyle."

"To some extent your concerns may be realistic. You need to put in hard work for your studies and then for landing a suitable job...there is a lot of competition. And, yes, there have to be lots of adjustments, too."

Rohit grabbed some sand, squeezed it firmly in his hand and then let it drop. "Ah! Hard work and competition, that happens in India, too. The only difference being that in India, the rewards are smaller and they take a lot of struggle and time to be realized."

"That's okay, pal. Don't lose heart from day one. Remember, there have been hundreds and thousands of foreign students here who have not only survived here but done wonderfully well," Tony said, getting up. "Let's now walk to the water's edge and join the ladies."

They stilled momentarily and then stepped back for a while as a white, thick spray of water was thrown into the air by the high-crested waves lashing the shore.

After the waves abated, they were wiping the moisture from their faces when Tony's pager flashed. "Excuse me," he said and stepped aside. "Ah! There is a message for me. I'll have to go to a pay phone booth to make a call."

"That was a message about a conference I have to attend in Manhattan, Monday evening," Tony said when he returned. "And Rohit that gives me an idea. You two have to be in New York that day. I can drive you and Sunita to your college and hospital there in the morning."

"That'd be wonderful. But hope that's not too much of a bother."

"No, not at all," Tony said and added with a laugh, "Moreover, there is a commandment from the professor that I do my best to make you comfortable here."

***

"We're now driving to the northeast," Tony announced, as the car exited the I-895 ramp and merged with the traffic on I-95. "It'll take over four hours to reach New York."

Rohit sat in the front, his chin dropped to his chest. "Nice drive," he said tepidly. In spite of the bright fall sky and colorful autumn leaves, his nerves were on edge with apprehensions about adjusting to the environment in his new college. He could also clearly see Sunita's lowered, tense profile, when he occasionally tilted his head back to the rear seat.

Tony's cheerful voice soothed Rohit's mind. "Relax, both of you. You'll enjoy your stay here."

Soon, they were at the Garden State Parkway when Tony made a suggestion. "I feel we'll proceed first to the New York Hospital, that is Upper East Side of Manhattan and get Sunita's admission process completed. As she said, she has been in touch with some seniors she knows and other students joining her program. They'd be able to help her in completing the paperwork and also getting settled in the dormitory allotted to her. That should do it."

"Yeah, that's fine, I have informed them in advance about my arrival today," Sunita replied.

Rohit looked at the speedometer. The needle was crossing seventy-five. "Tony, I hope you are driving within the limits."

"Don't worry, that's the usual on this highway," he laughed. "Anyway, after dropping Sunita, we'll drive to Columbia, near Broadway Avenue and put you in touch with the admission guys. Your new friends there will take care of the rest."

"Thanks. You're a big help."

"Oh. It's my pleasure," he said. "One more thing that will interest you a lot. One of my friends has a furnished apartment in Manhattan and that's presently vacant as he's gone for a long overseas assignment. You see, an apartment in Manhattan is a prized possession and only a few have the opportunity to enjoy this luxury. So, you'll be the lucky ones to stay there, though only temporarily. I'll get you the keys so you can spend good time together during the weekends. You can even do your cooking there."

Rohit turned to Sunita and winked. "Tony, you're a gem," both said in unison.

***

Rohit and Sunita stood hand in hand walking toward the glazed balcony of their apartment, next Saturday evening.

"Ah! What a spacious apartment. You could get lost in it. And have a look at the floor- to-ceiling windows and the elegant interiors," Rohit exclaimed. "Tony was right; we're greatly privileged to be able to use it."

As he gazed with admiration at the vast expanse of the river, he added cheerfully, "This apartment has a great location too. You can see the skyline and the Hudson clearly from here."

Sunita squeezed his hand lightly. "And what a superb view of the Statue of Liberty, particularly against the setting sun."

Rohit pecked her on the cheek. "Wonderful place for another honeymoon, isn't it?"

She circled his arms around him and edged her head upwards with her lips quivering. "Then, what are you waiting for?"

***

On Sunday, they went out to the neighbouring store to buy groceries. Rohit gazed wide-eyed at the never-ending lineup of juices, breads, eggs, salami... "Such big stores are not common in India yet," he said, nudging Sunita. "But they are sure to be there soon."

Returning to the apartment, they got ready to fix up a quick breakfast together, wearing blue aprons.

"I don't know whether the omellete will get the correct texture. Never entered the kitchen in my house in India." Rohit threw his partner a smile, beating the eggs with a spoon.

"Don't worry, it will be fine," Sunita said warmly as she collected the popped up toast and put them in a holder. "I, too, am not expert…see my toast is also overdone. But together, we'll manage."

***

As they sat cozily having coffee late that evening, Rohit asked, "Tell me, how it's working for you in the college."

"Ah! Nothing much for the time being. But it's a bit tough waking up daily with the alarm, working through the hectic morning chores and then reaching the hospital before eight. You can imagine the hurry. The real problem is that I have to attend classes too for my MD, besides my residency."

"And how about the lectures?"

"They're okay, except that sometimes they get too boring. I like genetics, but hate microbiology. And I feel sleepy if there are two consecutive periods of any subject."

As Rohit poured another cup, Sunita continued, a smile now crossing her face, "But there is a fun time after the classes are over. We meet and spend time with new people. I have now a few friends–Ashwin, Stephanie, Christine, and Ganesh. I've also become the member of an outdoor club that arranges trips for skiing, cycling, rock-climbing, and surfing. And how about you?"

Rohit didn't speak for some time. There were not many Indian students in his class. And he had yet to get accustomed to the quirky American slang, because of which he remained somewhat aloof in the class. The only solace was provided by Graham, the bearded professor, who had earlier been a visiting faculty at one of the IITs in India. The two used to chat after class, building a good rapport between them. But he need not display his feelings to Sunita, he decided.

"Ah! It's going fine. I think it'll not be so tough for me, at least to start with, as I've already covered part of the syllabus of some of the majors in my degree course," Rohit said with a tight-lipped smile.

"Seems things will work out by themselves gradually." Sunita said, placing her hand on his arm. "By the way, we may not be able to meet here next weekend and even the weekend after that as the outdoor club has organized cycling trips outside New York City. All my friends are joining. Sorry for that."

Rohit's lips twisted ruefully with tumultuous thoughts for a few moments. "Ah! Sunita won't be free for two weekends. She has already built up her network of friends. Gradually, she will be too busy to spend time with me." But soon he steadied himself. "Sunita, that's no problem. Prof. Graham has an open invitation for me to visit his home on weekends. So, I'll plan to complete my assignments on Saturday and spend Sunday with him."

As Rohit joined her in the bed, Sunita giggled, "Let's not be naughty today, we have to get up early in the morning and rush to our colleges." Soon, she curled up on one side of the bed and her eyes closed.

Rohit switched off the light but sleep eluded him. He got out of the bed restlessly and padded to the balcony. As he watched the night sky, pangs of sadness hit his chest.

He'd be getting only occasional opportunities to meet Sunita, though they had been married only a few months back. She would gradually have a different set of friends, different likings, and a different lifestyle. Would it lead to their drifting apart even before they had begun their married life? Fleeting thoughts of a troubled relationship with Sunita in future invaded his mind.

***

"Catch up soon with you," Sunita said as she waved with a flying kiss, boarding the first M-66 for her college, at 6 o'clock the next morning.

When she left, his eyebrows slanted in a frown as sadness overtook him again. He didn't return to the apartment, but sat laggardly on a bench in the bus shelter that was secluded at that time. Gazing at the light trickling through the slanted, transparent roof of the shelter, he reflected on the initial hiccups that had started in his marital life.

As another bus stopped near the shelter, he was reminded of his college days when commuting by buses used to be a great fun.

Then, suddenly, the image of his college friend, Shalini, standing in a bus shelter near their college in Delhi, flickered in his mind.

***

After the first brief meeting with her in the college corridor, when he was a first year student, Rohit longed to meet her, speak to her and spend time with her. But he didn't have the courage to approach her except to say an occasional hello.

But there came an opportunity that Rohit grabbed. His father had presented him with a Yezdi Roadking bike and he was fond of flaunting it before his friends. One day, when he was returning home late after the extra classes, he whizzed past the bus stop and found Shalini standing there. It was dusk and there were only a few commuters there.

A tingling sensation arose in his heart. This could be a good opportunity to meet her. But would she mind if he offered her a lift?

Finally, he gathered courage, put on his brakes and turned back. "Can I drop you somewhere?" He asked hesitatingly.

Shalini didn't speak for a while, looking beyond. "Hello, Rohit. Thanks for asking," she said finally. "But I see my bus No.10 coming in. I'll take that."

Rohit's face was downcast. "Okay," he said, as he pulled the bike reluctantly to one side making way for the bus.

But the bus skipped the stop and sped away, leaving a trail of black fumes from its exhaust. He turned and looked at her keenly. "That bus was full. I think the next bus will come only after half an hour."

Shalini's forehead furrowed. "Yes, you're right. Perhaps, I should take a lift from you, if it is not too much of a diversion for you. I live in the Gole Market area."

"It's no problem at all. In fact, that place is on the way to my home in Karol Bagh."

When she had settled on the saddle, he kicked off with a nervous, clumsy kick start. Soon, waves of pleasure shot through his body as she came closer to him and placed her hand on his shoulder.

***

His reverie was broken by the increasing movement of commuters at the bus stand as the rush hour approached.

He got up and lazily walked toward the apartment. Pleasant memories of days spent with Shalini during his college days pervaded him till he entered his room. "Ah, those times will never return," he lamented and dashed to the bathroom to get ready for his meeting with Professor Graham.

***

For two weekends, Rohit and Sunita couldn't meet. But the next Friday afternoon, Rohit called her. "Hey Sunita, there's good news, and I can't wait to share it with you. Let's meet this evening."

"Rohit, I'm happy to get your call. What's the good news?" She asked from other end, amid chatting and bouts of laughter from her room.

171

Rohit's voice was exuberant. "I'll tell you only after we meet and..."

"No spicy talk on the phone," Sunita chirped. "Anyway, I have some other plans for this weekend too. We are also going to the movie *American Fliers* on Sunday. I've become a crazy fan of Kevin Costner, who is playing the lead. Why don't you too join us?"

Rohit's jaw dropped slightly. But he modulated his voice to say softly, "Good that you're enjoying. I can't join you for the movie on Sunday, as I have to complete an assignment. But if you meet me for a few hours on Saturday, I could share the news I was talking about."

He heard Sunita's whispers. "Look, guys, Rohit wants me to meet him Saturday. Don't worry, I'll return in time for the Sunday movie," and then, "Okay, Rohit, I'll be there Saturday morning."

***

"Good that you could make it," Rohit said cheerfully, hugging Sunita, after they met in the apartment.

He looked curiously at her short, black, embroidered dress in which she looked very much an American. "You look gorgeous in that dress," he said aloud.

"Thanks. I bought it at Macy's last week," Sunita said bubbling with excitement.

Rohit wanted to spend more time sitting cozily with her on the sofa, and telling her the good news. But he felt she was tired by the bus journey, perhaps also hungry. "Let's have breakfast first. It's ready," he offered.

"Oh! You're a darling. Actually, I'm famished," Sunita said, circling her arms around his neck.

After they finished the breakfast and lounged on the sofa, having coffee, Sunita straightened in her seat. "Ah! I forgot. What is the good news?"

Waves of cheer surged through him. She would be excited to hear the news, especially because it would ease the problem of meeting the expenses for tuition fees and other bills. That would reduce the burden on his father, who was making remittances from India. He grinned merrily. "I got the job of teaching assistant...Professor Graham recommended me. It carries a good compensation."

"That's wonderful, congratulations." She moved closer to him and let her head tilt towards his shoulders. He circled his arms around her, caressed her hair and whispered, "Thanks."

"I love you," she said giving him a quick peck on the cheeks. "Now, you can give me a car on my birthday in December. I'll tell all my friends."

Hearing Sunita's unexpected demand, Rohit winced internally, abating his effusiveness. Buying a car was not a priority, as they didn't have to go long distances yet. Public transportation was easily available in NYC and few residents there used cars. Even a used car would cost a lot. Meeting other expenses was more important, particularly as her bills on dresses and other items were shooting up.

But he didn't want to hurt her feelings though she was very demanding and her behaviour was irresponsible. "Of course, buying you a gift on your birthday is at the top of my mind. But I was just thinking whether we can postpone buying a car for at least a year, till we have enough savings. I'll get some other gift for you," he said putting up a smile.

"Rohit, other expenses would be taken care of somehow. But the car is important for me. Maybe, a Honda Concerto, a couple of years old, will do. I have always to depend on my friends whenever we go for long trips," Sunita pleaded.

He himself could manage without a car, for some more time. But Sunita would be exuberant getting a car. So, he should manage the expense somehow. Perhaps, he'd take a few hours' part time job at McDonald's or Burger King.

He shrugged. "Okay, if you think so, we will look for a car after I've settled down with my new job."

"Thank you, Rohit," Sunita beamed.

"By the way, have you considered taking up some part-time jobs in the hospital?"

Sunita turned somber. "I've thought about that, but I remain busy for at least eighteen hours a day. The residency duties, documentation of patient histories, lectures and preparing for tests, take up not only the entire day but also a part of the night. Not much time is left for other jobs. Besides, it's so chaotic and tiring. These medical courses and jobs are so strenuous, you know."

These were testing times. But in less than two years, he would complete his post grad and possibly join Steelco, where Daniel had promised to help him find a job. By that time, Sunita would also complete her MD as well as her residency in the hospital. Then, there would be smooth sailing. With these comforting thoughts, he drew her closer and caressed her cheeks. "Okay, let's not spoil the day worrying about these things. After all, you're here only for a few hours. So, let's make the best of it."

***

CHAPTER 11

Two years passed by, after which Rohit finished his Master's and got his dream job in Steelco in Pittsburgh. His results had yet to be announced, but with a strong reference from Daniel, he had been interviewed and offered a job in the company.

"Good morning, Rohit." Daniel rose and greeted him on his first day in the company. "Welcome to Steelco headquarters."

Rohit's mind had ripples of anxiety and excitement, blending with each other, when he had earlier entered the plaza of the sixty-four-storey triangular skyscraper, clad in pastel gray tile work.

But on meeting Daniel, his chin rose with a surge of self-confidence. "Thanks a lot, Dan," he said fervently.

He now looked keenly at the company logo--three stars within a circle--hanging on the side wall. "I had seen only the miniature logo in the engineering documents that we studied in Udyog Nagar but this is the real three-dimensional one in a steel frame."

"Yes, this logo is very important for us." Daniel smiled and got up. "Now, as for your role in the company, you'll work in the design section. Let me show you around the office and brief you about your first design assignment. After that we'll return here and have our morning coffee together."

Daniel led him toward the far end of the hall and stopped near a cubicle. "This is Harry's seat. He's another design engineer, on leave for two weeks. You can use it temporarily," he said. Rohit looked keenly at the workstation with a computer screen displaying an electronic drafting system and some drawing sheets, a couple of them rolled, protractors and pins scattered on the desk.

Walking back, Rohit heard the murmur of people gathered near the copying machine. "A new kid on the block, they would be thinking," Rohit chuckled internally.

After they returned from the coffee machine, Daniel asked, "So, how's Sunita? As you say, she is still in New York. What are her plans now?"

"She's not sure yet. She's just completed her MD and also put in two years of her residency in the New York Hospital. They want her to continue with residency for another year, after which they could offer her a job as an ob-gyn doctor. Of course, she has an option to approach other hospitals for the continuation of her residency. She is undecided yet whether she would like to continue there or move to a hospital here."

"I think it will be good if she relocates here. I know some doctors here in UPMC hospital. They may be able to guide her in transferring from her earlier hospital."

Rohit's eyes sparkled. "That'll be great. I'll talk to her about it and let you know."

***

After he exited the office in the evening, he was exuberant. His first day at Steelco had been enjoyable. Sunita would possibly move to Pittsburgh soon, they'd have a new apartment, new cars. For the first time, they would have a chance to live together and that would put an end to the conflicts in their relationship so far. They'd now raise a family with perhaps two or three kids. And they would get all they had been aspiring for.

His heart bumped with joy as he looked at the red, crescent-shaped, setting sun and visualized the glorious life ahead.

First thing was to phone Sunita. "Hi, good news; I joined Steelco today. The first day was wonderful. Daniel has been so nice I'm already feeling at home."

"That's great, Rohit." Sunita' voice was cheery. "Why don't you come over to New York for the weekend? We'll have a grand party...I'll call all my friends."

"Of course, a party is due. But I was thinking of having the celebration here in Pittsburgh. You, me and a candle-lit dinner," Rohit said excitedly. "Moreover, you can use the opportunity to explore the possibility of a job in one of the hospitals here. Daniel said he knows some people in UPMC. It'd be so nice if you relocate to this place at the earliest so that we can be together. You know how much I miss you."

"But Rohit, I'm rostered for on-call duty next weekend." Sunita's voice was subdued. "And presently, I can't get long leave from here to enable me to scout for a job in Pittsburg."

Rohit's voice dropped as the euphoria over expectation of meeting Sunita soon dissipated. "All right, let me know when you can come...maybe even for a couple of days," he said feebly.

***

As Rohit's car left the highway and approached the car parking at Greater Pittsburgh Airport, he whistled. How would Sunita greet him when they met at the airport exit? Just a brief hug or a long kiss? Whether Sunita stayed in New York or Pittsburgh, their lives were now on the threshold of a booming career for both of them and it was a great moment. Where would they celebrate? Would it be the Black Porch Restaurant on the bank of the Mon River, which was known as one of the most romantic places in Pittsburgh? Or would it be in Hyeholde, housed in a castle in the Woodland Gardens? He'd book a table for two after knowing her preference.

He waited at the arrival gate. The flickering green on the flight board showed that the flight had landed. Perhaps it would take some time before she got her baggage.

His pulse raced as he spotted her among a mass of passengers, in her orange dress, her hair trimmed, carrying a small handbag. He waved his hand and their eyes met. Soon, he saw a young man, around her age, join her. After they exited the gate, she moved with a cheerful smile toward Rohit and gave him a quick hug. "Ah! After a long time," she said joyously. "...And meet my friend, Ganesh."

Rohit frowned internally by the unexpected intrusion but extended his hand, half-heartedly. "How do you do?"

Sunita broke in. "Rohit, as I told you earlier, we have been together in the New York hospital andbecause of him and some other friends I am having a good time there. Actually, we were thinking of

continuing there for some more time. But after your phone call, we thought we may as well try for jobs for both of us here.

***

As Rohit, accompanied by Sunita and Ganesh, entered the four-storey, fawn-colored building of Grey's Inn, where he had been staying, he asked hesitantly, "Ganesh, would you like to stay in this hotel or do you have some other arrangements?"

Sunita broke in hastily. "Of course, he'll stay here. It will be convenient as we'll go together to visit the hospitals and check about the availability of jobs."

Rohit shrugged, as he signed Sunita into the guest register at the reception desk. "Yeah, okay."

While Ganesh moved a little away, looking at the glass chandelier in the lobby, waiting his turn to register, Sunita whispered, "Rohit, perhaps you'd like to invite him to the dinner that you're planning to celebrate your new job."

Rohit's hand shook and his excitement for celebrations dampened. The candle-lit dinner at a romantic restaurant, which he had planned after spending a few hours scanning the Yellow Pages, was now out of question due to Ganesh's presence. Maybe, he'd now arrange a small get-together at the hotel restaurant and invite Daniel also there.

"Yes, of course," he said with a dry smile and then turned to Ganesh. "Let's meet for dinner in the restaurant here at seven this evening."

Then, he picked up the room keys, held Sunita's hand and started for the carpeted stairs to level one, following the red-liveried bellhop. But internally, he felt uneasy by Ganesh's presence when he wanted to have some private moments with his wife.

***

Two days later, when Rohit entered the hotel lobby after a grueling day at the office, his mind was still engaged in the design parameters of steel converter. What refractory material would be suitable for the vessel, had been the subject of a hot debate with his colleagues.

However, when he stepped into his room, his attention diverted as he found Sunita seated pensively on the sofa.

Ratan Kaul

"How was the day, dear?" He asked softly.

"Rohit, in a way it was good. I can get a transfer to the hospital here to complete my residency," Sunita said plainly.

Rohit's voice resonated with exhilaration, "That's excellent. Let's have another celebration." But he could sense that Sunita's face remained sulky. "But I'll be in a totally new system here, with a different kind of routine and no friends."

"Don't worry about this place being new. In a few weeks, you will get adjusted to it," Rohit said warmly. "Look at the plus points. We can now live together...after such a long period of celibacy. Tomorrow, I'll call a property agent to look for a good apartment for us."

Rohit moved slowly toward Sunita. He had an intense urge to lift her off the sofa and embrace her in a loving hug. But he stilled as he looked at her stony face. "She is perhaps not comfortable with the relocation. Let her take her own time to get over it," he surmised.

"Hey, let's order our dinner. I'm starving and so must you be," he said, stepping toward the house phone.

As Sunita went to change her dress for the night, Rohit conjured up the images of moving into the new apartment, painting his bedroom pastel blue–his favorite colour. They would make several big trips to buy furniture and appliances. They would dust and mop till they were dog tired and then they would rush to the bed together.

There was a break in his reverie as he saw Sunita in her night gown, slipping under the covers.

"We need a baby soon," Rohit whispered, caressing Sunita's cheeks before they fell into a deep slumber.

***

CHAPTER 12

A month before Sunita's due date two years later, Rohit's mother, Kamla, landed in Pittsburg on a bright sunny afternoon.

There was an atmosphere of jubilation, though Sunita looked uneasy, dragging her feet while walking.

"Sunita, there is an increasing glow on your face and you look prettier. I am sure you'll have a girl… that's what we believe in India," Kamla said in a cheery and affectionate voice as they sat in the living room.

Sunita smiled faintly. "You're right, mummy *ji*. The ultrasound too says that," she said and abruptly shifted in her seat. "This pelvic pain is awful."

"Ah! Take care," Kamla said tenderly. "Now that I'm here, I'll help you in all the chores."

After they had tea, Kamla opened her suitcase. "Sunita, look, here are some *sarees* for you," she said warmly, handing over a large packet to Sunita. After picking up another smaller packet, she announced with rising exuberance in her voice, "And these are for the small one who will soon join our family soon."

"Thank you, but I don't wear *sarees* here except on some special occasions." Sunita feebly opened the packets. "Now, I'd like to go to my room and rest."

Kamla stilled and her voice dropped. "Ah! Yes. Please carry on. There are some more gifts for both of you and I'll hand them over to you later."

Rohit's chin tilted in a frown as he reflected on Sunita's disappointing behaviour while his mother sat pensively, her shoulders sagged. He went over to her and touched her arm affectionately. "Ma, you also need rest due to jet lag. Let me show you the bedroom we've arranged for you."

***

When Rohit returned to his room, he shifted a chair near the bed, where Sunita was reclining. "How are you feeling now? I was concerned as you left the living room abruptly."

Sunita edged toward him. "I'm having cramps and my feet are swollen. Would it be okay if you and mummy *ji* take care of the kitchen for a few days?"

Rohit's voice took a somber tone. "I know you have problems. Of course, you need more rest. But she's come just today and she is jet-lagged. It may not be good to ask her to cook for today..."

He broke off but added after a moment, managing a weak smile, "But don't worry, I'll take care of the kitchen for some time."

A little bitterness arose in him. His mother had come all the way from India to help them during the birth of their child and she deserved the best treatment while she was here. But how far would he succeed in making sure that she was comfortable and at home and not get a feeling that she was an outsider?

***

In the late hours of a night before the appointed date in July, Rohit woke up hearing faint sounds from the other side of bed. He switched on the light and found Sunita doubled up, pressing her abdomen.

"Are you okay?" He asked as the sounds became more prominent.

She gasped for a moment and then composed herself. "I think it's time to go to the hospital."

Rohit dressed up hastily and drove her to the UPMC hospital, apprehensively pushing the gas through the almost deserted streets.

"It'll take a few hours, perhaps four hours more," announced the obstetrician, Dr. Hailey, who was also Sunita's colleague in the hospital. He turned to Rohit. "You can leave it to us now, and wait in the lounge in the meantime."

It was in the mid-afternoon that Rohit was called in the ward. His heart throbbed out of expectation as he saw the nurse filling in the details in a card and Sunita reclined on an inclined bed with a set of white pillows, her eyes slightly drowsy. The newborn lay slept in the crib beside the bed.

"Rohit, you wanted a daughter...she's here," Sunita said, turning to her side.

Rohit and Kamla beamed at the doll-looking baby girl, clothed from top to toe in a woven wrap, sleeping peacefully. He stepped forward with open arms to pick her up in his lap but looking at her snuggled with bent elbows, and legs folded close to her body, he restrained himself.

"I think you should allow her to sleep for some time," the nurse suggested. "Meanwhile, you can be comfortable in the waiting room."

***

After three days, Sunita was back home. She, Rohit, and Kamla sat relaxed in the hall, having tea, while the newborn rested, blissfully curled up in her baby cot.

"What name should we give to her?" Rohit asked, stirring sugar in his tea cup.

"I have thought about some names. In fact, while in India itself, your papa and I had thought of some boy and girl names. Some names for baby girls were Akriti, Kavita...I have a list in my purse. Let me get it," Kamla said excitedly, opening the zip of her bag.

Rohit got up and standing by the side of the bassinet, he caressed the cheeks of the baby, her eyes closed in peaceful sleep. "Let's see those names. Sunita and I would also have some suggestions. We can discuss and pick up a good name for our cute little daughter."

Sunita winced. "Mummy *ji*, since we are now settled here in America, we need to have a name by which she can identify with the mainstream here. I have already picked a name after consulting my friends," she said in a demurring tone, but laced with a half smile, and then turning to Rohit, "I thought Anita... meaning grace... would be a good name. It's popular both in India and America."

She got up, lifted her daughter from the bassinet and caressed her cheeks. "And it resembles my name too. We'll call her Annie," she continued excitedly.

The child moved slightly, seemingly ignorant of how she was going to be addressed throughout her life.

"But Sunita, let's discuss other..." Rohit broke in.

He saw the colour fading from her mother's face as she put back slowly the paper that she had picked up from her purse. Then, she turned to Rohit resignedly, "If Sunita likes that name, let's all agree to it."

Rohit's eyes were downcast and his teeth clenched. How could Sunita have taken that decision without first consulting him and his mother? And it was a rubbish argument that migrants from foreign countries needed to shed their cultural identities for joining the mainstream.

He sneaked a look at his mother. Even she seemed to be peeved though she didn't express it outwardly. But it won't do good to create a fuss at this time, he argued in his mind.

"Okay," he shrugged with a faint smile.

***

Next evening, when Rohit returned home from the office, he stilled for a moment at the door smelling the aroma of black cardamom, bay leaves and nutmeg spices flavoring the chicken curry, his favorite. "Ah! My mother is cooking the special dish for me," he thought effusively. He should thank her for that.

"Hi, sweetheart," he said to Sunita, sitting with the laptop open in the hall sofa. As she waved back, raising her head slightly, he turned to cuddle his daughter in the crib. "Ah! My little angel."

He had just settled on his favourite reclining chair when his mother entered with a tea tray. He held the tray from her and looked gratefully toward her. "Thank you, Ma. How was the day for you?"

"It was okay," she said flatly and briefly, fiddling with the corners of her *saree*.

A few minutes passed when Rohit sensed that no one had spoken for some time. He looked around at Sunita and his mother and the sleeping child and found that the silence filled the room more eloquently than on other days. Was something the matter?

He broke the stillness. "*Maa*, you seem to be quiet today. Are you feeling well?"

Kamla's voice continued subdued. "Oh, I'm okay. Actually, during the day I got a call from your father. He has not been feeling well."

Rohit shifted in his seat, his eyebrows raised. "But you didn't tell me earlier, how's he now?"

"I didn't want to disturb you. Anyway, now that everything is settled here, I'm thinking of returning to India in the next two weeks."

Sunita turned her head toward her mother-in-law while Rohit spoke in bewilderment. "Ah! So soon? I think you should stay on for a few months more."

"I would have but I also need to look after your father, who must be feeling lonely. And soon, it'll start getting colder here," Kamla said. "But..." Her gaze turned toward the crib and warmth grew on her face. "...there is an important ceremony that I thought needs to be done before I leave."

Sunita pushed a button and closed the lid of the laptop and straightened, while Rohit asked, "And what's that?"

"Formal naming ceremony for the child...the *Namakaran*. We need to consult an Indian priest for fixing the auspicious date and also conducting this important ceremony with a 'hawan' and a get-together. According to our customs, it's important to do so in order to invoke the blessings of the God for protecting the child. ...Let's do it this week itself. By that time, we can also get the horoscope of the child made and place it before the deity. "

Rohit turned contemplative. Mother had taken a sudden decision to leave. Was it that she didn't like to stay on with him? Were the conflicts increasing between her and Anita? In any case, yes, the naming ceremony was important. He knew an Indian priest, Shankar, who conducted ceremonies at Sri Venkateshwara temple. He'd talk to him.

Sunita's slightly edgy voice startled him. "Mummy *ji*, those are old fashioned traditions. We should move with the times. Let's have a brief blessing ceremony at home one of these days. That'll take just a few minutes."

Grimness grew on Rohit's face and he stared blankly out the window, as distressing thoughts stormed his mind. Mother would feel disappointed. She and Sunita had such divergent views. It was a great quandary. Were they Indians or Americans? Even if they became Americans by way of citizenship, did their faiths also change? Did they not have any identity of their own? Should they shun their traditions altogether? Anyway, he had to work out a balance between his own culture and traditions with those in America. This time, he had to put his foot down; He'd not be guided entirely by what Sunita feels.

He took a deep breath. "I think we'll have a small ceremony in the temple tomorrow," he said decisively and got up. "I have to go now. I'll make all the arrangements during the day."

He didn't look back, but he hoped both his mother and wife would be reconciled by this arrangement.

***

A year and a half passed. Sunita and Rohit lived their lives in different worlds. Sunita was busy with her classes and hospital duties and Rohit busy with furthering his career in Steelco.

On an August day, Daniel approached Rohit's workstation where he was giving finishing touches to a process flow drawing. "Hey, Rohit, we've been talking about a trip to the Appalachian Mountains that never came off so far. But now there's an opportunity," he said pulling a chair. "I've got an invitation to attend the Heritage Celebrations of Appalachia. Every year in August, the residents there have a weeklong celebration to commemorate the days of old coal mines and railroad. There'll be races, parades, amusement rides and of course the food courts."

Rohit straightened with a puzzled look. "Good to know that, Dan. But I thought we were planning the trip to get acquainted with the social and economic conditions; not to attend any musical concerts."

Daniel leaned forward putting his elbows on the desk. "Ah! You get me wrong. Of course, we'll do that, too. A glimpse of the abandoned coal mines and the railroad remnants of the past will be included in the itinerary. And through these celebrations we'll also have a glimpse of the culture there. And to top it all, we'll have a chance to celebrate my Uncle Joe's birthday that comes around the same time. He lives in a nearby village, so we can explore more interior regions."

Rohit's eyes glowed. "Okay, got it. Let's plan it out."

***

Rohit and Daniel spent a few hours excitedly in Appalachia, partaking in the annual celebrations, and then decided to drive over to Uncle Joe's village thirty miles away.

As the car turned from the paved to dirt road, it traversed an almost barren area, sparsely interspersed with trees and bushes. Rohit's eyes roved to a scattering of small houses at a distance with smoke emanating from the chimneys.

All seemed quiet till there was a bark from a dog and from the nearby tinkles of bells round the necks of a herd of white and brown goats and billies grazing on thorny bushes. "Ah! I'm seeing goats in the USA after a long time. Of course, it's a common sight in India," exclaimed Rohit.

Daniel smiled but drove on silently till they reached a place where a bearded man in his seventies was sawing a wooden piece. The man got up and exclaimed joyously, "Daniel! Good to see you here after such a long time."

After the introduction with Joe was over, Rohit sighted a rusted car-trailer, seemingly a primitive model, parked nearby. While his eyes were set there, a sharp wind blew and the door of the trailer was flung open. His eyes widened as he saw a boy sitting on a chair inside it, amid a stack of small wood logs, cutlery, stove, a chimney, a table, unwashed utensils and other articles which could at best be termed as a clutter.

"Johnny, come here, we have guests," Joe called out and then turned to Rohit, pointing at the trailer. "That's where I live and that's how most of the people, including some of my relatives, live here in this village."

As Joe stored his saw and tools behind the trailer, Rohit whispered to Daniel, "We need to celebrate your uncle's birthday in some good restaurant…maybe we'll find one some distance away. On our return, we can have a look at the old coal camps. But the most important part would be to return here and listen to his story about the living conditions in this region."

While driving over dust-laden dirt roads, Rohit noticed more such trailer houses, shops in wooden shacks, an old-style barber shop and a cycle repair shop. *Seems, they are at least 50 years behind from the mainstream US.*

***

By the time they returned to the village, it was late afternoon and they sat on chairs outside the trailer, sipping coffee.

"Joe, how has life been here? I think the government is doing a lot to improve the conditions," Daniel started, while Rohit listened keenly.

Joe stoked his bearded chin. "Ah! I'd say life is better than before but still tough. There aren't enough jobs anymore, because nobody's buying coal or lumber like they used to. There are only about five hundred of us left, and we're all hurting. Of course, there's aid from the government." The wrinkles on his face had deepened.

After a while, his lips curved into a smile. "But I feel one thing is good here. We may not have money but we still care about each other…you can't find that elsewhere."

"True. Let's hope other facilities will also improve soon," Daniel said and got up. "Anyway, it was good seeing you. I'll come again soon."

Ratan Kaul

As Daniel drove on their six-hour journey back to Pittsburg, turning from the countryside onto highways, Rohit was mostly silent, gazing blankly out the window. The living conditions in Jose's village kept reminding him of the scene in the workers' colony in Udyog Nagar.

Daniel's voice broke his thoughts. "I can guess what you're thinking about. Your social activism spirit is perhaps getting revived."

"You're right. I was just wondering whether some corporation will adopt this village for community assistance. We can also put in our efforts."

"Good idea. But given the pride of people in this region, it has to be done sensitively. Anyway, I'll talk to our CEO, Jonathan, and plan something."

***

Rohit returned on a Sunday evening after the weekend trip to Appalachia, but he felt something amiss in his home. "Sunita! Annie!" He called out and then repeated.

But there was no answer. He walked up the steps and then to his bedroom, where he found Sunita lying in bed, pillow at the back and a book in her hands.

"Ah, you're here! I thought you'd be downstairs," he thrust himself in the easy chair. "And where is Annie?"

Sunita didn't stir, but hurled a jibe, gesturing with her hands. "You always expect me to be waiting for you eagerly at the door, like the traditional Indian wife, while you're having a good time with Daniel in the godforsaken tribal hills."

Her words stung his heart sharply. She always had an unreasonable attitude. But she was in her second pregnancy and he should not upset her. His lips pursed momentarily and then his tone grew mellow. "Sorry, dear. But you knew about it when I left. If you'd mentioned that you had reservations about my trip, I wouldn't have gone."

190

Sunita's eyelids tightened and her voice was raspy. "You should have realized it yourself. I'm now in the fourth month and need some care. But I have to take care of myself as well as Annie. Thanks for asking where she is. I sent her to spend the day with Liz in the neighborhood, as I needed some rest."

Rohit was in no mood for any cantankerous arguments. He needed coffee urgently to soothe the throbbing pain in his temples. "Sorry, again," he mumbled and left for the kitchen.

***

Sunita gave birth to a baby boy, who was named Samrat, shortened to Sam. From his naming to his and his elder sister's upbringing, learning of mother tongue, following of religious prayers, admission to schools and parenting issues, conflicts continued to rise between Rohit and Sunita.

One day, the arguments turned unusually sour. It was a Sunday morning and Rohit had opened out an alphabet picture book before the-four-year-old Sam to initiate him into learning his mother tongue, Hindi, when Sunita came over and gestured with her hands irately. "Rohit, what're you doing? He's just a small child and already overloaded with learning English. Now, you want him to learn Hindi, too."

While the child was still looking at the glossy pictures of colourful fruits and animals, Rohit had a prickly feeling surging in his stomach. "Sunita, it's important that he learns his mother tongue, at least the basics. We may have become Americans now but our roots are still in India. He needs to be acquainted with our language, culture and traditions. Besides, this is the best time to learn another language," he scoffed.

Sunita's voice turned vituperative and she got up. "No, I don't think so."

"You must understand that we need to keep a balance between the assimilation of foreign culture and retention of our own values" Rohit retorted. "Otherwise we would regret it later."

"All right, do whatever you want," she said and left in a huff.

Rohit's heart palpitated, resonating with the retreating beat of her high-heeled shoes.

He didn't want the conflicts to escalate but at the same time, he was of the firm opinion that the children, whom he loved a lot, should not be totally alienated from the Indian culture. So, he decided to spend time with them, relating stories about Indian mythology and scriptures. But Sunita kept on interfering, with the result that the children themselves got confused by the clash of cultures.

***

Gradually, there was an inevitable alienation between Rohit and Sunita, while both progressed in their professions. After an eight year stint at Pittsburgh, he had relocated to New York, now as Vice-President of Steelco and Sunita had taken over as a perinatology specialist in the New York Hospital. Annie, now seven, and Sam, two years younger also grew up in their own world of schools and friends. In order to avoid any conflicts with Sunita, Rohit tried to spend time with them mostly for their outdoor activities while she took care at home. But he started getting a feeling that children felt aloof.

Meantime, a local community assistance project had come into being in Joe's village and Rohit and Daniel continued their trips there to overlook the programs. These regular trips however caused a further rift between Rohit and Sunita as she did not like his philanthropic programs, terming them as a waste of time and money. He had a hunch that the real reason for her dislike for his Appalachian visits was because she linked these visits to his old friendship with Jhilmil.

***

"Ah! It has been a long time, Tony," Rohit said as he answered the phone on a July morning. "When did you come to New York?"

Laughter echoed on the other side. "I came to meet a client and thought that I should look you up too."

"That's great. Let's meet up. How are you placed this evening?"

"I, too, am keen to meet you," said Tony with excitement. "I expect my meeting to be over by five in the afternoon and I can perhaps take the six o'clock ferry to Staten Island. Of course, this is rush hour, but I think I can make it in an hour. I hope that works for you."

"Oh yes. I'll pick you up at the jetty."

***

Rohit and Tony passed through the well manicured lawn and stopped at the concrete porch of the red brick building in Strawberry Lane.

Tony's eyes widened as he admired Rohit's house. "A quiet place near the sea, and such an elegant house. The sun was quite harsh in Manhattan, but here on Staten Island it's pretty cool."

Rohit had been feeling a bit lonely, with Sunita away to Pittsburg for a conference and Annie and Sam, as usual, gone with their friends. Quiet. Too quiet, he wanted to say. Instead, his lips extended slightly into a weak smile. "Thanks."

They drew the chairs onto the balcony and Rohit brought the drinks. After Rohit filled the glasses and handed over one to Tony, he stared blankly across the sea.

"You seem to be quiet today. Any problems?" Tony asked, looking at the small, light, sparkling bubbles inside his beer glass.

Rohit was saddled with stormy thoughts about his job and then his family relationships...his wife and both children slowly drifting away from him. But he should not bother Tony about his family problems, he reasoned.

He straightened in his chair and leaned forward. "Tony, for some time, I've been thinking that I'm not doing what I should be doing at this time of my life."

Tony looked keenly into Rohit's eyes. "Hmm. But I thought you were doing well— vice president in one of the major steel producers in the country. In next few years, you could be the president. What else would you want?"

"You're right in a way. But I've lost my interest in the steel industry. I'm impatient to try something else."

"Anything specific you have in your mind?" Tony bent forward.

Rohit wiped off the foam sticking to his chin. "Yes, I do have. Something related to computers, software or telecommunication…these are the sunrise areas. I'd like to make some investments there…" After a brief pause, he continued, "You've been in this field for many years. I thought I'll bounce some ideas off you."

Tony stretched back on his chair. "Sure, Rohit. As for internet, it is, of course, on its way to a tremendous growth. Same for information technology. But with so many players around, I don't know which investment will click."

Rohit got up to draw the drapes, as the crescent of setting sun splashed its colours. As he returned to his seat, his face wore a smile. "Do you remember what Dale Carnegie said? 'The person who gets the farthest is generally the one who is willing to do and dare.'"

"You're right," Tony laughed. "Well, another area which come to my mind is mobile technology. You see the plain, weird-looking black and white phones at present with long antennae? I'm sure all this is going to change with the advancements in the wireless technology. I'm sure that in the next five years, which is by the beginning of the twenty-first century, this technology will revolutionize our world. Why not explore this?"

"Eureka!" Rohit thumped the table in excitement. "That's a superb idea."

Tony too appeared thrilled. He gulped the remaining beer in his glass and poured a refill. "Of course, there are already several companies in this sector. Nokia for one. But they would be looking for some new features, new technologies and new vendors. This is a field in which someone can make a killing."

"The more you talk about it, the more I am getting fascinated with this idea, Tony," Rohit said excitedly, but he soon turned contemplative, rubbing his chin. "But there is one problem. I'm not sure whether I can do it alone."

Both were silent for some time, looking at their glasses.

"Ah! That should be no problem. You can hire some good people," Tony suggested. "But you need to decide whether you will take the risk of leaving this cushy job and start from a scratch."

Rohit was quick in his answer. "To your second question first. Yes, I tend to think that I'll take the risk. And to your other question about hiring, I was just wondering if you can work with me on part-time basis, while you continue with your other job?"

Tony extended his hand, "Sure, I'm game for that."

"But one last question, Rohit," Tony went on. "Did you have a chance to discuss it with Sunita? This is a major decision that can affect her as well as your kids."

Rohit had already thought about it. Sunita, Annie and Sam could stay on in New York while he might relocate to another city... may be San Jose. That's what Sunita would want, too. Away from him.

"Yeah, that's important. I'll speak to her, too," he said and jubilantly raised his freshly filled glass for a toast. "Now, let's say cheers for the new venture."

***

Rohit moved to San Jose the same year and things worked well for his projects and investments as he progressed to be a major venture capitalist in the Silicon Valley. He was now keen to focus on his family relationship, particularly as he loved his children immensely and didn't want them to remain away from him during their growing-up years. Sunita and the kids finally joined him after Rohit's repeated pleadings. However, he had to continue with the unwritten arrangement that he would not interfere in the way Sunita wanted to bring them up. She thought that even after so many years in the US, he was still idiosyncratic about his notions of Indian culture and traditions.

***

Five years later, Rohit was waiting at the arrivals terminal of San Jose International Airport and he shaded his eyes, looking over the incoming passengers.

"Great to see you after a long time, Sachin," Rohit said buoyantly as he hugged his friend.

Sachin's face glowed. "Yes, it has been more than seven years since we met in New York. After that somehow, I couldn't make it, though you have been inviting me every year. How are Sunita, Annie and Sam?"

A dry smile loomed on Rohit's face. "Happy in their own worlds," he wanted to say. But he just said, "They're okay. Sunita is busy in her hospital and the youngsters are busy in their teenage pursuits...both of them."

"Ah great. So, we are in the Silicon Valley," Sachin said joyously as they passed a long avenue line with palm trees.

"Hope you like the autumn here. In any case, the weather on the West Coast is always moderate," Rohit said after they drove home.

He pulled up two chairs. "Make yourself comfortable. I'll change and join you in a jiffy."

"You have not changed much. In USA also you dress as an Indian!" Sachin exclaimed as Rohit returned wearing an Indian style white dress ensemble, *kurta with trousers.*

As both laughed heartily, Sachin's eyes grazed the vast expanse of the bungalow.

"This is the advantage of living in the US, large lawns, big houses… it must be at least half an acre, I believe,"

"Yes," Rohit said, offering a cup of coffee that the liveried house-help had brought from the kitchen.

After a short silence, he asked, "How's Kavita?"

"Ah! She's doing fine. You know a lot of activity is taking place in the media in India and so many new TV channels have come up. She's now a senior executive with *TVNOW*. That keeps her quite busy."

"And what exactly have you been doing of late? You wrote to me sometime back that you left the job in your earlier company."

Sachin's eyes diverted to a flock of colourful parrots flying overhead and squawking noisily. "Never seen so many parrots together," he said with a faint smile and then continued, "One of my relatives, Vikas, came up with the idea of setting up a software company. So, I left my job and both of us made investments in a small way."

"That's wonderful, I'm sure you'll do well." Rohit beamed and looked at his watch. "Now, let's go have some food. I have reserved a table at Rangoli Indian restaurant."

***

As the orders were placed, Rohit stared blankly into the menu-card for some time, his lips pursed.

Sachin's voice broke the stillness. "Rohit, something is bothering me. When we were at your house and I spoke to you about Sunita and your children, you seemed to be quite evasive. There seems to be something missing... I mean you're not the spirited, cheerful kind that you used to be. I think you have all what you dreamt of, a beautiful wife, two sweet children, a large bungalow, latest model cars and your flourishing software business."

Rohit laughed dryly. "That's what people from India say about the immigrant Americans, or Indian American as they call us."

Sachin straightened in his seat as Rohit went on, "But the picture is not as rosy as it appears to an outsider. First of all, this business, and this status was not achieved in a day. There have been lots of compromises, sacrifices and tremendous hard work."

"Ah! That's the story in India too..."

Rohit's lips twisted into grim smile. "But think about it. How much you have to adjust to foreign culture. It is particularly hard with the kids who are born here. Take for example, Annie who is now fourteen and Sam who is twelve. They're still uncertain about their cultural identities and that makes them feel caught between the two worlds. As a result, they are more vulnerable than the normal teenager. Frankly speaking, I'm quite worried about them."

There was a short break as the waitress began serving the dishes.

"By the way, have you been meeting some of our old class mates?" Rohit asked as the table was laid out.

Sachin dug into a piece of duck with his fork. "Ah! That reminds me. I forgot to tell you something important...of a very special interest to you..."

He broke off for a moment and then went on, "Do you remember Shalini?"

Rohit's face was blank for a moment.

"That's surprising, Rohit!" Sachin exclaimed. "I am talking of Shalini, the girl from the Arts department of our college. Strange that you have forgotten her as you had a crush on her from day one in the college."

Rohit missed a beat. Soon, a faint smile emerged on his lips and he tapped Sachin's arms animatedly. "Ah! You mean Shalini Mehra. How can I forget her? She too seemed to like me, but I didn't have the courage to take the relationship further. Anyway, what about her?"

"I recently met our classmate Arjun in Delhi in one of our reunion parties. He seems to be in touch with her and he told me she has become a renowned artist."

Rohit listened keenly as Sachin went on. "Seems, she has been organizing exhibitions of her paintings in India and perhaps in the US too. Perhaps, you will have a chance to meet her, if she happens to come here. I'll give you Arjun's email ID and if you like you may contact him to get more details."

"What's the use? She might have forgotten all about me during these twenty years." Rohit pursed his lips. "Anyway, SMS Arjun's email ID to me. At least, we can share some news about other college friends. We need to remain in touch. "

After Sachin left, Rohit was still in his nostalgic reverie, reliving the moments shared with Shalini during his college days.

***

Rohit had a hectic week. A ring on his phone interrupted his thoughts. He straightened and looked at the caller's name. The screen read 'Tony calling.' Normally, he would have picked up Tony's call promptly in view of urgent business matters between them, but that day was different. He was feeling stressed. He pushed the phone away and closed his eyes.

The phone rang again. This may be something important, he thought tensely.

"Hello, Tony," he spoke wearily.

"How're you doing?"

Rohit's tone continued to be indifferent. "I'm okay. Anything important?"

"Yeah, but nothing related to business. Just thought of letting you know that there'll be an exhibition of an Indian painter at one of the galleries in LA next weekend, both days. Perhaps, you might be interested."

It was an inappropriate time to discuss art and paintings but Rohit impulsively straightened in his chair as he recalled Sachin mentioning during his last visit that Shalini had become a painter. "What's the name of the painter?" He asked, for a moment his distressed feelings subsiding.

"Let me check. It is on one of the community websites," he said. "Okay, it's here. Her name is Shalini Mehra and she is from New Delhi, your hometown."

Rohit gasped with excitement. The image of his first meeting with Shalini near the staircase in the college conjured up in his mind... the accidental dropping of her drawing board and his quick reflex action to jump and retrieve it....their rides on the bike.

"Are you still on?" Tony's voice jolted him back.

"Ah, yes. I'd like to have a look at her paintings."

"The place is Galleryvista in the downtown. I'll SMS the address to you."

As he hung up, Rohit leaned his head on the chair and closed his eyes. The iconic heritage building of his college, the green lawns swarming with students. The corner where the girls in bright *kurtis and tight chudidar* dresses, wearing puffed hairstyles chatted animatedly during lunch hour... passed in a slideshow before his eyes.

***

He flew to LA next Saturday morning. As he drove to the art gallery from the airport, a corner of his mind was still saddled with grouchy thoughts–the shouting matches with Sunita had taken their toll. But that day, he wanted to shut his mind to all that. The clear crisp blue sky helped him dissipate those thoughts and by the time he took the exit from Santa Monica on way to the downtown, it almost looked like a spring festival anointed with the warmth of expectation of meeting an old, dear, friend.

A flash of smile crossed his face as he noticed a board, set up in a bed of pink and white flowers at the entrance, announcing the 'Exhibition of Nature paintings by Shalini Mehra.'

As he stepped into the gallery on the upper level, a well-illuminated, long hall with gilded roof, a thrill shot through him. The expectation of meeting Shalini, his old-time crush, turned him into a spirited, youthful college student, and blood rushed through his body.

Passing through the rows of framed paintings hung on wall panels and some on free-standing panels, he wondered how he would face her, what he'd say and how she would react. "Let me go directly to the artist's desk at the far corner so that I have an opportunity to meet her before others come in," he thought as his eyes were riveted towards the small desk and a chair near far end of the hall.

But the corner was empty. He was now undecided whether he should start a tour of the gallery and view the exhibits or wait for her near the desk. By that time, visitors had already started sprinkling in, some viewing the paintings silently and others commenting on it.

Soon, his eyes roved to a painting depicting a rural or a tribal scene with people dancing to the tune of drums. He inched toward the black frame and viewed closely the noting beneath the painting:

"Tribal dance and drums"

By Shalini Mehra

Acrylic on Canvas

His gaze remained focused on the painting for a few minutes, as he recalled the tribal dance in which Jhilmil, wearing a pink *choli* and *lehnga* had participated along with her friends in the workers' colony in Udyog Nagar years back.

He was still in front of the frame, busy in his reverie, when he heard the rustling of dresses near him. He turned around to see a couple looking at him curiously. "Hello, too engrossed in the painting? It seems to have evoked some memories of the past," he heard the man saying.

"Yes," Rohit said sheepishly, as he paced to another section of the gallery where he keenly viewed an oil painting of a yogi in meditation with the backdrop of forests of Himalayas. He didn't know much about art but he was fascinated by the various shades of blues and green—deep, light and pastel—used for portraying various facets of the nature.

He moved on to next painting but soon his attention diverted as he heard some voices. Turning around, he saw some activity around the artist's corner.

He stood still. A woman in her early forties, draped in a turquoise *saree*, locks of black hair immaculately flowing on both sides of her face, was arranging a pile of booklets, perhaps table top brochures. He went into a trance momentarily, recalling the face of Shalini in the college. *Yes, she is Shalini. These twenty-five-odd years have not brought much change to her, except that she has put on some weight.*

Rohit's heart pounded with excitement and he inched toward her. As he neared the desk, her gaze slowly turned toward him.

His lips quivered briefly but he managed to say, "Hello."

A welcome smile broke on her face. "Hello. Did you have a look at some of the paintings?" She asked with a slight dip of her head in curtsey.

Rohit fumbled for appropriate words but said finally, "Ah! Yes. Excellent paintings on nature."

He soon noticed a faint sign of recognition on her face. "Have we met earlier, Mr...?"

"Yes. If you try some more, you may be able to recognize me, Miss Shalini," he said with a hearty laugh. "Okay, just a hint. I am from Delhi."

"Oh, my god! Are you Rohit from the engineering college?" She said with an intense gaze and her cheeks flashing with a smile.

"Yes," Rohit said, his heart thumping.

Shalini extended her hand. "It's great meeting you again. Imagine, after more than twenty years!"

With the touch of the soft skin of her palm, sparks of warmth ran through his body for a moment. "Same here. Now that we had a reunion, let's remain in touch," he said.

His eyes diverted to visitors streaming into the gallery. "I think you should attend to the visitors. We'll meet some other time," he went on. "Meanwhile, I'll also have a look at the exhibits. Luckily, it is not modern art which is totally incomprehensible to a layman like me. I can understand these nature paintings very well," he laughed.

"Okay, please carry on. If you have any queries about the paintings, please let me know,' she said. "And I will be free after five. If you like we can have coffee together. There is a restaurant in this block."

"Sure, I'll come and pick you up at five."

***

At the café table, nothing was said for few moments. Without being too conspicuous, Rohit was trying to sneak a glance at her facial expressions and getting aware of her perfume.

His mind went back to the college days and to her innocent face and her shy smile when he had met her for the first time…the growing relationship between them that had not survived for long.

She broke the ice. "When did you come to the US?" Rohit narrated to her the sequence of events from his first job, marriage to Sunita and the journey after that.

"Lucky guy. You seem to have done pretty well," she said cheerfully.

She is looking at only one face of the coin. I have not told her the facets of my personal life. But why should I bother her with that? "Yeah, in a way," he replied aloud, faking a smile. "Anyway, you have become a renowned painter. How has your life been?"

Shalini's face turned somber. Her hands were on the table while she stared blankly into her cup of coffee. "Well… it has been good and bad. Let's talk about that some other time. But I can say that I focused on the nature paintings thinking it would wash away the disquiet in my life."

Rohit winced. So, she had also been through some rough times. He tapped her hand slightly. "I'm sorry…"

Shalini didn't move her hands and in an impulse the two were holding each other's hands. Sparking tingles shot through

Rohit's body and gradually ecstasy engulfed his entire body down to his toes.

But within seconds, both withdrew their clasp. Rohit straightened. "Where are you staying and for how many days you plan to stay here? Can I help you arrange your accommodation or in any other way?"

"Thanks a lot, but I am staying comfortably with my longtime friend, Suzie," she said. "And it's a question of just three days more as I'll be flying back to Bombay this coming Monday."

"You're leaving so soon! Can I show you around some good sightseeing places here, if you are free one of these days?"

Shalini's lips moved without words for a while but finally parted with a warm, pleasant smile. "Okay...let's plan for morning on the day after tomorrow. We'll speak on phone and fix up the time and place before that."

Rohit was nearly breathless with happiness at the prospect of getting an opportunity to spend more time with her. He nodded, "Okay, great."

"I think it's time to go now; Suzie will be waiting for me," she said softly.

That night, Rohit tried to dispel the thoughts of his tangled relationship with Sunita as memories of the touch of Shalini's hand kindled warmth in his body. In a corner of his heart, conflicts still pricked him. Could his disturbed mind find solace in Shalini's company? What would be the outcome of this short liaison with a woman, who was almost a stranger meeting him after over twenty long years?

***

Two days later, after a hectic tour of the Little Tokyo District and Natural History Museum in the city, they drove past a park in the evening. Shalini looked out the window and her eyes brightened. "Hey, Rohit. Let's rest here for a while, I'm feeling a bit tired."

As they entered the gate and looked at the sprawling landscape, their shoulders brushed against each other and then Shalini slipped her hand onto his arm. A flash surged in his body and he suddenly turned into a college boy on a date with his girlfriend.

They now held hands and walked silently through the spacious lawns overlooking a fountain with colorful lights. "It's so beautiful, looks like it's dancing to the tune of a piano," Shalini said, stopping for a moment.

These were the first words spoken since their entry to the park and her voice sounded musical to Rohit, like the glissando on a musical instrument. "Yes," he said joyously. Then, looking a distance away, he went on, "Ah! There is an amphitheater near the fountain. Not many people there now. Let's go and sit on the steps. That'd be quite relaxing."

They walked close together, their arms touching. When they settled on a corner of one of the semi-circular steps, Rohit started, "Ah! It feels so wonderful sitting here with you. Our college days come to my mind. By the way, you may not know, but sometimes I used to bunk lectures to be with you on the same bus...sitting on your adjacent seat."

A shy smile rose on Sunita's face. "Ah! That was so clever of you. But even you would never have guessed that I too used to wait for you at the bus-stop and missed some buses till you came."

The two laughed till the corners of their eyes wrinkled.

Soon, Rohit's voice turned sober. "Unfortunately, we can't get back those carefree and romantic days. Anyway, the other day, you said you'll tell me something about your life."

She stared blankly at the lake in the far corner of the park. "Well...it's been like a sine curve as they call it...lots of ups and downs. You know I had to leave my studies unfinished in the arts college at Delhi after my father's transfer to Bombay. I didn't want to go as a relationship was building up slowly and silently between you and me. That was giving a lot of solace to me from the daily bickering between my parents. I had quite a troubled childhood. But I had to go as there wasn't any alternative."

Rohit patted her arm. "I too was shattered, but in any case, we were too young and it couldn't be helped."

Shalini bent her other arm and placed her hand on Rohit's, intertwining the fingers. "Anyway, I graduated from an arts college in Bombay. My parents arranged my match with a businessman, but that never worked. We separated in five years..."

"Ah! Sorry to learn that. Divorce, just in five years! Did both of you give the relationship enough chance before separating?"

"Yes, we tried compromises several times, but finally felt it was not working out. Better to separate and lead lives peacefully than to remain in artificial bondage."

Rohit listened silently while thoughts about his own troubled relationship with Sunita swirled in his mind. But he shut them out as Shalini leaned toward him and placed her head against his chest, her hair draping over his arms. Soon, a gush of cool breeze with a flowery fragrance blew through the amphitheater and impulsively they clasped each other in a passionate embrace. "Oh, I loved you so much," she mumbled, while he felt her warmth and her scent permeated into his lungs.

Slowly, his mouth lowered to her parted, trembling lips and intense passion flooded his body traversing to his bones and marrow. For a few moments, the world came to an end for him—the only sounds were the chirps of the birds and the music from the fountain.

Gradually, they loosened their grip and moved apart. "It seems we were destined to meet like this and make up for the lost time," Rohit said.

"You're right. But it's time to leave now, Rohit," Shalini said, her eyes downcast, seemingly hiding her feelings.

Rohit clasped her hand tightly. "When shall we meet again?"

"I don't know. Perhaps, when you come to India. I am leaving for Bombay by the morning flight tomorrow."

Rohit could not fathom whether the solemn expression of her face reflected her sadness about those tender moments being so short-lived. Bleak thoughts of parting from her filled his mind. "Okay," he said gloomily. "May I drop you at your friend's apartment building?"

On his return home, he grappled with conflicting thoughts. On one side, was the latent guilt in a corner of his heart about having spent those stolen moments of intimacy with her and on the other side, was the tenderness and spontaneous pleasure of that fervent kiss.

It was so comfortable to be around her, he thought fondly. She was the kind of woman he should have married, the kind of woman who would make him realize how much he missed home.

*****

"You seem to be a changed person since you returned from your recent tour of LA," Sunita remarked casually as they had dinner together after a gap of few days. "You look very cheerful and relaxed."

Rohit stiffened. Was his face giving away indications of the joyous time he had spent with Shalini, he speculated tensely. But he soon regained his cool. "Oh! Nothing. It's that some of my investments have done well in the last few days."

"I hope it's that and nothing else," Sunita snapped.

He was grateful that it had passed of peacefully...without the usual vitriolic ranting.

*****

He returned to the present, pondering the roller-coaster journey of his life from Udyog Nagar to San Jose in the last twenty years after he had married Sunita. But Sam's drug addiction was the one that had inflicted the deepest scar on his heart.

Anyway, life had to go on, he surmised. He would now try to reason out with Sunita for building an amicable atmosphere in the family, if only pretentious; as that was important for ensuring that daughter Annie too didn't fall into bad ways.

***

CHAPTER 13

On a December evening, Rohit returned late from office. White flakes had started falling suddenly as he had exited the garage of his office building. Was it snow? But that would be a rare happening as San Jose didn't usually get a snowfall, only hailstorms sometimes that gave the illusion of snow. "If it's snow, it'll stay for some time as San Jose isn't really geared to remove the snow," he chuckled as the thought.

The roads had started getting a bit slippery, but he was able to maneuver the car and soon reached the driveway of his house.

As he entered the hall from the side door of the driveway, his gaze fell on sets of wet footsteps from the front door and going up the stairs that led to bedrooms at the top.

"Don't know who has done it. Maybe, Annie; she is becoming so careless," he muttered with irritation. "I'll ask Sunita when she is back."

He went to the kitchen, made a cup of black coffee and settled with his laptop. It was 11 o'clock at the night when he heard the footsteps. He lifted his head. "Hope you had a nice day," he said as a ritual, as he saw Sunita coming in.

"Yes, lots of cases today," she replied casually and sank in a sofa. "Seems, you'll be reviewing some presentation till late night. That's the story every day."

Rohit was irritated at the jibe but he remained silent.

"I too am not feeling sleepy," she mumbled and switched on the TV serial "Grey's Anatomy."

Rohit had just finished reading an email when his ears perked up to the sound of loud music accompanied by intermittent bouts of laughter from the upper floor.

"Is Annie having a party? It's already past midnight," Rohit asked.

Sunita shrugged without shifting her eyes from the scene on the TV. "Maybe, yes."

"Did she inform you about it?"

"No, but don't bother about it. She has perhaps invited some friends over. Let her enjoy the party."

It was one o'clock in the morning when Rohit's eyelids began to droop. He yawned and then shut the lid of his laptop. The music was still on. "Dear, seems this is a whole night party, can you please go and check?"

Anita tilted her head a bit. "Don't be bothered. Wait till this serial is over," she said loudly.

Soon, Rohit heard footsteps. As he looked up he saw Annie accompanied by a boy, about her age with ruffled blond hair, coming down the steps of the stairway.

His breath stuck in his throat for a moment. *This guy was with my daughter in her bedroom till so late. This was no party. Just the two of them.*

"Mom, dad, you're still awake," Annie babbled. "Anyway, meet my new friend, Kevin. We were finishing some school assignments together."

Rohit's eyes furrowed and fury simmered inside him. But he remained silent as Kevin said a quick hi to him and Sunita and walked away hurriedly through the door.

Annie retraced her steps and ran up the stairs.

"Did you see that? That boy was in our daughter's bedroom for so many hours in the night. All because of the liberties given by you to her," Rohit shouted. "Call her here right now and let her explain."

Sunita's face turned red. "Oh really? Am I responsible for everything?" She yelled back. "In any case, I am not in a mood to discuss anything now. We'll talk about it tomorrow."

He wanted to roar at her but he was so frustrated that he just threw his hands up.

His eyes were ablaze as she scurried away to the bedroom.

***

It was a torturous night for Rohit. His body and mind cracked up as he recalled the recent reports about teenage pregnancies becoming common. In the past, there were social pressures to be secretive about it, but lately the scene had changed. Teen motherhood was no longer a matter of scorn.

Annie, my child! What kind of relationship does she have with this boy, Kevin? Have they been meeting here frequently in our absence? What if they have crossed the limits? He shuddered at the thought.

***

"When do you have the time to discuss family problems? You are only busy with your office, visits to the Appalachian Mountains, conferences, presentations," Sunita replied coldly when Rohit broached the subject the next evening.

The situation needed to be handled tactfully, Rohit thought. "Okay, let's discuss it now," he said softly. "Let's call Annie too."

"She said she will be late today."

Rohit looked at his watch. It was already past nine. "It is all a result of your encouraging her to go for late night parties and unescorted out-of-town visits. I've been cautioning you for the last two years that she's now in her adolescent age and you need to be watchful about her activities."

"Don't be old-fashioned with the Indian mentality," Sunita said scornfully. "These things are quite common here nowadays."

There were sounds of hurried steps on the front door.

"Where have you been?" Rohit asked his daughter, in a high pitched voice.

She rolled her eyes. "Dad, I'd gone to a party. But what's the matter. You never spoke to me in that tone before."

"Can you please sit here for a few moments?" He toned down his voice and tapped on the sofa, indicating her to sit beside him.

He patted her head lightly and lovingly. "You know how much I love you. There are some things that I need to discuss with you."

Annie was silent when Rohit continued, "What is your relationship with Kevin?"

"He is my boyfriend and we have been steady for some time. So, what about it?"

"Okay, I don't have any objection to that." Rohit started and then went on with a persuasive tone, "But I'd like that from now onwards you don't take him to your bedroom, and also don't go to late-night parties."

Annie jerked herself away from her father in annoyance. "That's ridiculous. You can't stop me from doing that."

Hearing her words, Rohit's heart was torn into two and his eyes turned watery. The girl he had pampered and showered with affection since her infancy had turned a rebel.

Sunita, who had not spoken for some time, broke in with a bitter scowl on her face. "Rohit, she is correct. It's her life; let her enjoy it."

"But Sunita..."

She raised her voice and gesticulated with her hands vociferously. "You're totally ignorant and in spite of long years in America, you still have those backward and orthodox notions."

"But we're Indians by our roots...we have our own culture." Rohit's voice had now turned aggressive.

Annie glowered. "Dad, you must understand that I'm an American. I don't have anything to do with your archaic, orthodox Indian culture. I'll live my own life and no one will interfere in that."

Her words struck like a bolt hammering his head. Helplessness in the presence of defiant mother and daughter crept through his mind, when Sunita's shouts choked off abruptly into a scream, "You have been interfering in my life too–my job, my postings, my friends and my lifestyle–and I'm not going to take it any longer."

His flesh crawled with disgust. "Perhaps, both of you want me out from here."

"No one said that. But if you..." Sunita stopped abruptly mid-sentence.

Her every word came crashing on him. He shifted his gaze to Annie, expecting a conciliatory stance. But she had a dark, blazing look and her lips moved querulously. "Mom is right. And I'm going away to a friend's house ... and will be out for the night. Don't phone me."

Within seconds, Rohit heard her stomping out. Sunita left in a huff too. "I've to go to the hospital and will return only in the morning."

As her car roared out of the garage, he banged his fist on the table and dropped his head in his hands. The events of that evening had sucked out his soul, leaving an unfathomable vacuum in his chest.

***

Next morning, Rohit was calm after a deep churning in his mind the whole night.

"Sunita, I want to have a frank talk with you," he said mildly when he met her at breakfast. "I'm sorry I have been interfering in your and Annie's life. But that's because of my Indian roots. I admit I'm conservative or old fashioned as you may call it, but you know how difficult it is to change these ideas."

Sunita moved the strands of her hair hastily and shook her head. "I've also thought about it at length. I feel there is a big gulf between us, and it's now too late to bridge it. It would not be possible for me to live under one roof with you. I'm ready to move out."

His jaw dropped. He hadn't thought that the situation had become so grave. What he wanted was to plead for a give-and-take situation. But now it was clear that Sunita was defiant.

"I didn't mean that..."

Sunita's eyes were fiery. "But I surely mean that. You don't like me; you don't like Annie. You don't like Sam. So, we'll move out. You can lead a life wedded to your work, that's all you want. Or you can go live in the backward places, where you have been donating hundreds of thousands of dollars..." she broke off. After a couple of heavy breaths, she added sarcastically, "in the memory of your old love Jhilmil in Udyog Nagar...whom you don't seem to have forgotten even after so many years."

Sunita's venomous words stung him sharply. Such insinuations, bringing in the name of Jhilmil, who had gone out of his life more than twenty years back, were just rubbish. On the other hand, she should have been in the dock for her closeness, rather intimacy, with her colleague, Ganesh, to which he had been turning a blind eye. No, no...this had gone too far now. "Well, let it be so if you want it that way. It's time for us to part and go our separate ways. Let's file for divorce. I'll schedule an appointment with my attorney," he said in a decisive tone.

Sunita got up and barged out of the room.

***

Rohit scrambled to his feet and moved to the balcony. As he rested his elbows on the balustrade, looking at the vast stretch of greenery in the front, the iciness in the breeze entwined around him, and his body shivered tip to toe. But he did not move, just swiveled his head in one direction and then the other, pondering the breakdown of his marriage.

Agitating thoughts ricocheted in his mind. His life was now totally dismantled. Could it have been avoided? Who was responsible? Was it because of the children? Was it that with increase in age, people tend to grow in different directions with changes in temperament, likes and dislikes, attitudes and habits? Was it an intractable situation?

His wife had gradually alienated herself in the last few years and because of her, both the children were now like strangers to him. What else was there which could bind them together?

He straightened. Yes, for him, it was over. He would be very civil about it and part in an amicable way. He would not contest custody or any other issues relating to the division of moveable and immovable properties. Let the attorney take care of that.

He needed to go back to his roots...to India.

***

CHAPTER 14

BACK TO INDIA

"How're you feeling today?" The image of a non-descript female passing before his eyes seemed to be saying slyly. "At the age of forty-five, you had to leave behind your family, business and all that you strived for during all these years. But don't worry. Life is a full circle and I'm sure we'll keep on meeting even if destiny ordains to separate us temporarily."

The words reverberated in Rohit's ears in his semi-awake state, but he woke up with a strong jolt as the plane suddenly dipped down with a vibrating sound. "Perhaps, it has struck a turbulent pocket. Don't know how much time it will take to get out of it," he thought tensely. He'd never felt nervous when aircrafts were in turbulence, but now he wiped the sweat from his face and gripped the side rests tightly.

A *saree* rustled by the side of his aisle seat. "Please fasten your seat belt, sir," the air hostess said with a concerned tone. "Perhaps, you didn't hear the announcement."

"Sorry." He made an apologetic gesture. As the hostess moved away, he latched the seat-belt and closed his eyes again.

A spasm rose in his stomach. The thought of having left behind his family and business in the US in his middle age haunted him again.

When the plane had resumed its gliding pace, Rohit's mind wandered to his first trip to the US, when Sunita sat cozily by his side.

"We're entering a new phase of life. We have new careers for both of us ahead. We'll raise a big family…and return to India only after retirement, except for short trips," he'd said, edging toward his wife. But here he was, going back to India when his retirement age was yet too distant.

Agonizing thoughts had been agitating his mind and making him restless since his departure from JFK. He had alternate feelings of gloom, disillusionment, and a desire to renounce all worldly things and go to the Himalayan mountains to seek solace…or to restart his life with new beginnings, coming back to a full circle?

"Unlike me everyone else—the Indian couple in the front and their child looking out the window or the two Americans in the middle row, sleeping hand in hand— seems to be enjoying the flight," he thought with a sigh.

Soon, the food service started, with the hostesses moving along the aisles with trolleys and the passengers opening their tray tables. While the inside of aircraft bristled with such activity, teeming with liveliness, he had a persistent listless feeling swarming over him.

The thought of his wife, Sunita, for whom he'd sacrificed his love; his son, Sam, whom he brought up with so much affection and daughter, Annie, whom he treated as a doll–all had built a fortress around themselves which made him look like a stranger to them. Now, all that he'd cherished and the business which he had groomed for ten years had come to naught. Even his parents had left him for the other world. He felt totally alone.

He closed his eyes, but sleep evaded him. The newspapers and magazines lay untouched in the back pockets of his front seat, and his vision was blurred as his mind incessantly looked back. Did his judgment fail him, leading to turmoil in his family and his life?

An announcement interrupted his thoughts. "Ladies and gentleman, this is your captain speaking. We're now flying over the Atlantic. The weather is perfect and we expect landing on schedule." He checked his watch; only four hours into the flight...fifteen hours more to reach Delhi.

He reclined on his seat, returning to the realm of the present, and wondered what his unplanned visit to India was about to bring up.

***

At Terminal Two of IGI airport, people were waiting to receive the arriving visitors–a mix of Indians and foreigners. But he hadn't informed anyone about his arrival as he didn't want to answer any questions. Not yet. He wanted to give it a few days, perhaps a week, and think about his plans and destination.

He had heard that a lot had changed at the Delhi Airport since he had come here last, with several new terminals coming in. But at that moment, he was oblivious to that. He absent-mindedly cleared a serpentine queue for the pre-paid taxi, and reached the Centaur Hotel.

His mind returned to the present only when the bell boy turned on the TV, and the anchor in a TV channel announced a program of *pandvani* tribal songs, the sound of which he loved.

Suddenly, the voices from the TV faded from his mind, as the sour memories of his unrealized or failed relationships with the two women in his life–Jhilmil and Sunita–pervaded him.

And Shalini? The charming memories of the time spent with her arose again in a corner of his heart momentarily. While parting in LA, she had said they could meet when he was in Delhi. But would he like to indulge in such an affair? No, he should drop the curtain on that too. No more women in his life. Perhaps, he was not destined for such relationships. He clenched his fists and got up hurriedly.

***

After he had a shower and finished his dinner, the nostalgic, acrid memories gradually subsided and Rohit began brooding about what the future had in store for him.

Sleep eluded him. He heard himself asking, "Should I renounce all I have achieved in life and go to a hermitage in the Himalayas to seek solace from some renowned spiritual guru? Should I bequeath all I have and make a trust for some philanthropic cause?"

Restlessly, he sat up, dangling his legs from the bed, and his eyes shifted from one framed painting to another on the walls of his room. Then, he got up and looked out the window at the moon and stars in the sky, his eyes fixed on the lode star.

"I'm in a land that, though my own, is today alien to me. Now, I need a guiding star like this to tide over this mid life crisis, but who would that be?" He mumbled. "Ah! Would Sachin be able to help?"

Soon, his eyes were drowsy. He switched off the light and threw himself into the bed.

***

At 10 am sharp he received a call. "Hi Sachin, wait for me in the lobby. I'll be there in five minutes. We'll have breakfast together," he answered and hung up.

Sachin's well appointed cream-color suit, pointed moustaches and receding hair with streaks of grey set him apart from other guests in the lobby. Rohit stepped toward him, extending his arms. "Hey, seeing you after two years...what a great physique. Have you been gymming a lot?"

Sachin laughed. "Yes."

"Hope this place is fine," Rohit pointed to a corner table in the Triveni Restaurant, near a latticed window overlooking the swimming pool of the hotel. The serenity of the place captured him and by the time the waiter came to take the orders, the remnants of cloudy feelings and jumbling thoughts that he had during the night had abated.

He turned the pages of the elegantly bound menu card lazily. "Sachin, what will you have?"

"The usual...continental."

Rohit moved his fingers on his chin. "*Aloo-poori* for me."

After the man left, Sachin laughed. "Seems, you're going to revert to Indian lifestyle from day one...in a fast forward mode."

Rohit's cheer had started to return. "Yes, sooner the better."

"Let me bounce some ideas off Sachin," he thought as the bearer placed the dishes on the table. For a moment, he looked expectantly at the puffy *pooris*. "Ah! They are so tempting and good."

He then turned to Sachin, "As I said on the phone, I plan to stay on in India this time. But I need rest and some introspection.

Maybe, I'll go to a hermitage in Rishikesh and spend a few months there."

Sachin shook his head. "Oh, you seem to be unduly charmed by the spiritual gurus. But what happens after you turn into a monk? In three or six months or a year you'll be done with the introspection part. After that, what?"

Rohit dipped a slice of the *poori* in the curry as Sachin went on with a philosophical edge to his words, "There isn't any better therapy than work. You know very well about the epic *Bhagvad Gita* that dwells on *Karma Yoga*–the discipline of action. The point is that you must move on with your life."

Rohit took time trying to express his sentiments, as he was unsure of himself. He wanted to just live his life and pursue his passions his own way. "Maybe, you're right. But I'm lacking direction… not sure where to make a start. I'm also not acquainted with the present conditions for business entry in India or which field is the favoured one at present."

Sachin had a sip of the orange juice. "Don't worry. I can help you in that."

Rohit straightened as he recalled that Sachin had started a business sometime back with his relative as a partner. "By the way, how is your company getting along?" He enquired.

Sachin's eyes turned glum. "Unfortunately, it is not working out as my partner is keen to move to the construction sector. He is keen that we start winding up the operations soon." After a pensive pause, he went on, "I am quite distressed as I had done extensive marketing and I was able to bring many clients in the USA and Europe on board for outsourced jobs in the financial sector. Besides that I have many more leads in the pipeline. A business plan is also ready. But all that's a waste now."

Sachin's words clicked in Rohit's mind. He could start a new project with Sachin, his friend of many years. And if Sachin had the expertise and access to the pool of clients as he said, the time to market would be pretty short.

"Ah! That gives me an idea," Rohit said, rubbing his chin. "If your partner ultimately decides to close down the company, we can start another one, the two of us. Don't worry about the funds, I'll manage all that."

Sachin's face brightened. "That'd be great, buddy."

"But there's a caveat. The company will not be located in metros, but in some less developed area. You know my stance on this."

"That's no problem," Sachin was quick to reply.

Rohit was elated. The cobwebs in his mind had cleared away. "Okay, done. Can you email the business plan to me? Also think of a suitable name for the company. Let's meet as soon as you'e ready and have a brainstorming session."

***

Sachin was ready with the presentation two days later. "That's pretty fast," Rohit said when he received Sachin's call. Let's meet in the hotel tomorrow morning. If you can get hold of a projection system, it would be helpful."

In the slides, Sachin displayed business plans for the outsourced banking and insurance services outsourcing fields. "Given the present outsourcing business scenario, let's start with just the banking vertical and add the insurance part later," Rohit said rubbing his stubble that he had grown in the last few days. "Can you just tweak the figures to project the revenue and profitability if we just have the one vertical to start with?"

Sachin returned to his lap top and made some quick calculations.

Rohit had some more questions and finally, he said. "Well, sounds good. I think I should be able to finance it with my own funds...so no loans are necessary. So, let's get going with the nitty gritties... but it should be at a jet speed."

"Great!" Sachin said joyously. Now, we need to finalize the location. You were suggesting some backward area."

Momentarily, Rohit was reflective. "Yes, I've thought about that. My preference is for Raipur, capital of the new state of

Chhatisgarh. It was formerly a tribal area. I'm sure you're well acquainted with that area. It was quite near to Udyog Nagar."

Sachin smiled. "Yes, I remember. And, I could also guess that you'd prefer that area."

"And what about the name of company?" He asked after a pause.

"What do you say to 'XPRO'? Does it give good vibes?"

Sachin raised his thumb. "That sounds perfect to me."

"We need to work out the nitty gritties...the company formation and suitable business premises...and, of course the hiring of professionals. Personally, you'll need to focus more on marketing that will involve lot of overseas trips. Meanwhile, other guys can tie up the things here."

Sachin's face brimmed with enthusiasm. "That should be no problem."

"Alright then; three cheers for the new partnership," Rohit said and then extended his hand.

"That calls for a bottle of champagne," Sachin said as the two shook their hands.

***

Year 2006

Raipur, India

Swinging in the leather swivel chair in his new office, Rohit gazed blankly at the soft rays of the autumn sun percolating through his glass paneled office, a letter clutched in his hand.

Minutes earlier, he had entered his new office building with the glowing sign 'XPRO DIGITAL SERVICES' at the entrance and passed through the reception area with its gleaming brass-potted plants. Lofty feelings of having created a new world for himself had arisen in his heart, but the letter on his table had distracted him.

He re-read the letter from the labour department and unsettling thoughts spiraled in his mind. "Oh, god! Our US clients are going to cancel the outsourcing agreements if we don't start our operations in time...and our entire investment of over half a million dollars will sit idle." Stringent conditions in the government letter regarding job reservation could seriously delay the recruitment of operational staff for his company.

He looked up when Sachin entered and announced, "All is set for the interviews of candidates. We can start whenever you like."

"Good job. Let me email this presentation to the Pacific Agencies, our US client, and we can begin the interviews after that. Meanwhile, have a look at this." He flipped the letter across to Sachin.

Sachin's lips twisted in a frown. "I'm not sure why the government keeps on fixing job quotas for these tribal people."

"Keep in mind that the government has to ensure employment in these areas. The only thing bothering me is that they informed us about this job reservation policy at this late stage, which is delaying our recruitment process."

Sachin shrugged his shoulders. "All right, I get the point. Anyway, I suggest you have a look at the candidates now, and let's see how it goes."

"Okay, buddy, let me check the bios," Rohit said. Scrolling the short-listed résumés of candidates on his laptop screen, he particularly focused on the birthplaces and the categories they belonged to. Most of the candidates did not satisfy the criteria of being from the tribal area. But an entry caught his eye.

'JHARNA, Father's name: Late K. Munda, scheduled tribe, Chhatisgarh.'

He drummed the table excitedly. "Let's call this candidate, Jharna. And I suggest you carry on with the questions. Meanwhile, I'll have a chance to run through some more mails."

On taking her seat, Jharna started with the usual salutation, "Good morning, sir."

His mind tugged sharply as the tone of her voice and the accent sounded quite familiar. He inquisitively lifted his head, his eyes rising to the woman in her early twenties with long, meticulously tied hair, draped in a light blue *saree* with the loose end held smartly by a brooch.

Seeing her kohl-traced eyes, contour of lips and the flexing of her neck, he straightened up and rubbed his head. "Have I met this girl before....where could it be?" But he was unable to recall having seen her and a sense of déjà vu preyed upon him.

He took over from Sachin. "Tell me something about your background, place of birth and academics."

"Sir, I had my schooling and college education in Bilaspur..."

The word 'Bilaspur' sounded a bell in Rohit's mind and goose bumps surged in his body. Jharna's remaining words came across only as faint whispers as Rohit retreated in his thoughts. Something mysterious was going on here. There was no question of ever having met her. Yet the intense feeling of having met her or someone closely resembling her and some kind of bonding with her remained unabated.

He took a deep breath. "Get me a coffee," he said on the intercom and then to Sachin, "Please continue if you need some more information from her."

Sachin went on with more questions, which she answered confidently. He was about to ask more when Rohit looked up again. Thoughts quickly spun in his mind. "There is something compelling about her, though I am not sure what it is. Moreover, she is well qualified to be a human resource executive. Also, being from the tribal area, she fulfils the government criteria."

He took a snap decision. "Okay, you're in."

Her lips curved into a smile. A gradual transition in the facial muscles at the corner of her lips created tiny depressions and dimples appeared on her both cheeks. Suddenly, Rohit relaxed as he appeared to have found the answer to his mental zigzag. Dimples are hereditary, he had read. Did he know anyone in her family? His mind raced. He had to somehow complete the links in the chain.

A beep on his phone distracted him. He got up hastily and called Sachin aside. "I have to rush for a meeting, so I'll catch up with you later. Meanwhile, you may issue an appointment letter to her — give her the position of Senior Human Resource Executive, with a decent start and perks. Also ask her to join immediately."

***

Back in his office, Rohit wanted to be left alone, but the ring on his mobile distracted him. Sunita was calling from New York. *Perhaps, she wants to talk about the divorce proceedings. Let her discuss them with my attorney.* He pressed 'Delete' on his cell.

Sunita's call had to wait; he ruminated, as his mind gradually drifted towards adding up pieces of the jigsaw puzzle. Udyog Nagar 1983 A shy girl with dimples His eyes focused on his monitor with his hands sliding on the mouse and suddenly he felt the fonts of words in Jharna's résumé subtly *dissolving and transitioning to video images from the past.*

Destiny is intervening. The incidents which I had relegated to the past appear to be reviving. Seem, this girl is the bridge between my new and old worlds.

There were clear indications that she was Jhilmil's daughter. But should he ask her about her mother and her father? What all had happened in their lives in the twenty-odd years since they left Udyog Nagar? And her grandfather, Ramesar? How was he doing? The series of questions perplexed his mind.

But soon, he rubbed his eyes and leaned on his chair, cupping his face in his hands. "No, I should not re-dig my past. I've started a new life and that should not be clouded by the past events."

***

Rohit swiped the security card as he and Sachin stopped for a moment to enter the office six months later.

"Seems, the recruitments for the second phase have also been completed?" Rohit asked looking at the line-up of executives in the cubicle-type grey-blue workstations of the operations hall.

Sachin smiled. "Oh yes, but don't give the credit to me. Jharna has worked tirelessly for the last six months."

Rohit hadn't met Jharna for a few days. He had mustered every bit of mental effort to focus on his work and not be distracted by the memories of the past evoked by Jharna's presence. But that appeared to be in vain as the feelings of affection and an urge to meet her surged in his heart.

Sachin turned toward his cabin but Rohit tapped his arm. "I have to discuss some points. Let's go to my office."

As he threw his jacket at the back of his chair, he thought of enquiring from Sachin how Jharna was grooming up but he did not want to appear too inquisitive. "Let that come later," he decided.

He scribbled figures of financial projections and milestones on the white-board and asked for Sachin's opinion.

"So, let's finalize these figures," he said, returning to his seat. "Now, there is another pending issue, Sachin. Have you received any résumés for HR Manager yet?"

"No, I've inserted the ads again. Just awaiting the responses."

"Ah! That'll take time. I recall you mentioning that Jharna was doing a good job. Why don't we promote her as Manager?" Rohit suggested, his eyes fixed to his laptop.

There was silence for some time as Sachin rubbed his forehead. "Could be a good idea. But don't you think she is too young for that? I'll check up her bio again, but as far as I remember, she has only two years experience."

But Rohit's voice was now decisive. "Don't look at her experience. With her consistently good performance here, she deserves that position."

"Okay. I'll issue the promotion letter to her."

A tide of gratification swayed in Rohit's heart. Jharna needed to be groomed for senior positions.

***

Jharna slung her bag on her shoulders and locked her room in the YMCA hostel, where she had taken up residence.

Rashi, her friend and colleague in the company, and hostel-mate too, joined Jharna on their way down the stairs. "Hey, you're looking gorgeous today...and why not? You are the new boss of HR."

Jharna recalled the moments that she had spent before the dressing table that morning. After she finally adjusted the silk ponytail holder, and had a full-body view before the mirror, she had seen something different about her face–a sort of glow that she had never seen before–as she visualized having her independent cubicle in the office after promotion.

Returning to the present, she laughed. "Thank you. But you too are the boss in the operations department."

As they stepped into the office van, there were cries of hi's, hello's and congratulations as young colleagues, men and women, clambered up on their seats to greet the two.

"Ah! The blue-eyed girl of the boss has got a promotion," someone remarked, while others pipped in, "Sure, she is a favorite of the big boss."

"Shut up," Jharna said in a voice laced with slight annoyance.

A period of silence followed as the van traversed the heavy morning traffic areas, amid blaring of horns, speed-reducing bumps and overtaking by the two wheelers.

As they neared the outskirts of the city where the Technology Park was situated, the van was abuzz with excited chatting.

"Hey, Jharna, there seems to be a major recruitment spree. I see a lot of ads on job sites," Shankar said. "What else is new?"

Jharna laughed. "First is the news about your new nickname for the voice desk. It's Ben. That's how you'll be known among our US and European clients."

"Ah! I like the name, I'm reminded of Ben Kingsley, the famous English actor," Shankar laughed hilariously.

As the van took the final turn toward their office, Jharna looked out. How fast had the city changed in the last year...new buildings with glass-paneled walls of blue and green cascading down, new glamorous offices, exotic eating-houses and cell phone towers reaching the sky.

Her phone vibrated with an alert tone. She looked at the SMS: "U r late 2day. I'm already here."

Oh, that's Varun. He goes by bike and zooms to the office before the shift starts. Perhaps, I will get a car after my next promotion as senior manager. Looking around to make sure no one was watching, she punched briskly: "b there in 10 mts."

***

This was a scheduled day for a review meeting. "Let's have a round of the office and check the partitioning of new workstations," Rohit pinged Sachin.

"I'll come in five minutes," Sachin replied instantly.

They stood at a section of the hallway on the ground floor of the building. "We have already twenty clients now. It would be good to segregate the stations for each client," Rohit said effusively, satisfied at the business growth. After a quick scan of the facility, he was about to proceed back to his cabin when he stilled. "Wait a minute; let's also have a look at the upper floor too."

As they exited the lift on the first floor, they passed the employees' lounge, which had been completed recently for the relaxation of executives during their break.

Rohit gasped as his eyes were set on two executives, a male and a female, in the lounge, laughing with soda cans in their hands, their hands touching occasionally.

His eyeballs fired with fury. It was Jharna with someone whose name he couldn't recall. But he restrained himself and turned to Sachin, "Let's continue this discussion tomorrow."

***

"Come to my office in two minutes," Rohit pinged Jharna the next morning as soon he had settled down in his cabin.

Jharna greeted him cheerfully as she entered the room. In the light-grey coloured jacket and black jeans, she looked elegantly smart, Rohit thought. But this was not the time to commend her for her dress sense. He had to discuss some serious things with her.

"Have a seat," he said roughly.

Jharna's lips tightened as she lowered herself slowly in the seat.

I should come direct to the point, Rohit thought. "I should have talked to you yesterday, but normally, I allow my anger to subside before I confront the person who has been a cause of my anger."

"Anger, sir!" Jharna exclaimed, as stress lines grew on her face. "Did I do anything wrong?"

Rohits' eyebrows slanted inwards. "Not one, but two wrongs. First, you were in the employee's lounge yesterday afternoon when it was not the time for your break. And, being a senior executive you need to maintain a certain discipline in the office. I don't think the way you and the other executive with you were behaving was appropriate."

Jharna's eyes lowered and she folded her hands in her lap. "I'm sorry."

"What is the name of the executive?"

Jharna's lips quivered for a moment and then she replied feebly. "Varun Mathur."

"Which department and when did he join?"

"He is the group leader for the voice section of our US client New Citizen Bank. He joined about two months back."

Rohit prodded her on. "Ah! I see. Now, how close are you with him? I know you'd not like me interfering in your personal matters, but I surely would like to keep my eyes open about what goes on within the premises of my office."

Jharna's voice choked. "Sir, it's just that we're colleagues. Nothing more."

"Anyway, whatever," Rohit faltered for the right words. He had been grooming her for a senior position in the company and he wanted her to focus on that–just that–for at least a couple of years. But at the same time a faint streak of possessiveness pervaded in a little corner of his heart.

"Now, listen carefully. First, I want everyone here to focus on his or her work. Second, I want everyone to maintain decorum in the office. Do you understand that? And particularly you have to ensure it as you're the head of the HR."

"Yes, sir," Jharna said, raising her eye brows slightly and wiping the moisture in her eyes.

"All right. You may go now," Rohit said.

When Jharna rose and turned toward the exit, Rohit looked at the long, glossy, black, thick hair hanging up to her waist. He smiled for a while but soon his fingers shakily drummed the hand rests of his chair with deep conflicts in his mind. "No, no, I shouldn't rake up my past," were the thoughts one moment that were overshadowed by his fond memories the next moment.

Ultimately, he couldn't take it anymore and his hand moved to the bottom drawer of his table. He pulled it open and picked up his old diary. After leafing through some pages, he looked at a photograph. There stood Jhilmil, a replica of Jharna, at the time of the inauguration of the school in Udyog Nagar, twenty-three years back.

Should he show that photograph to Jharna? Should he point out the resemblance of the mother and daughter to her? Should he narrate the entire story of his Udyog Nagar stay?

No, let things be as they are, he reaffirmed his earlier decision and put back the diary in the drawer.

What he needed now was to focus his attention on knowing more about this man, Varun Mathur, with whom Jharna seemed to be getting close. He grabbed the phone. "Sachin, can you discreetly get the résumés of all the executives recruited in the last two months?"

***

Jharna was scanning the résumés on her desktop on a Friday evening when she heard a message tone.

"Let it wait," she murmured. "I've to shortlist the candidates and send them to Sachin sir in an hour."

After a few minutes, there was another beep. Could be urgent, she thought and opened the message. The multimedia screen had the image of a cake with the words HAPPY BIRTHDAY TO THE CUTE GIRL.

"Thanks," she replied quickly and dialed Sachin's number on the intercom. "Sir, the candidates have been shortlisted. I'll mail them to you?"

As she put down the receiver, a call flashed on her phone. "Oh God, what's it again? Seems, Varun has no work today," she thought, her irritation peaking up.

"What's it now? It's office time and I'm very busy."

"I want to celebrate your birthday. How about meeting some place tomorrow–you and I," she heard Varun's pleading words on the other end.

But Rohit's words about her career and decorum resonated sharply in her ears and that set her thinking. Yes, she was fond of Varun, and they had been meeting in groups but in any event she wasn't sure whether she should go on a date with him. Stormy thoughts invaded her mind. Should she continue this relationship or quit it as it might hamper her career? She took a snap decision and replied hurriedly, "I'll call you later."

Her hands shook as she switched off the phone. She cleaned up her table and exited the office hurriedly.

***

It was a Sunday evening when a call from the vice president of New Citizen Bank in the USA flashed on Rohit's phone. "Call on a holiday from Tom! Seems, something is urgent. What could it be?" He speculated.

The voice at the other end sent shock waves through his body.

"Tom, listen...it's impossible. We have all the security arrangements in place here," Rohit protested fiercely.

"What I'm saying is correct. There are reports coming in of siphoning of funds from the accounts of one of our customers. She has claimed that there has been an unauthorized debit of twenty thousand dollars from her account," was the agitated voice on the other end. "And that is a very serious matter. Your voice agents could be involved."

Rohit got up frantically. "It can just be your conjecture, isn't it?"

Without waiting for an answer, he went on defiantly, pacing to and fro across the room. "I can't understand the role of our people in this. They are just doing the coordination work, and they don't have any access to your customer accounts or the database."

"That's what you feel. But I consider your attitude to be totally unprofessional. Anyway, I'm getting the matter investigated in detail here. What I would like is that you also conduct an inquiry at your end and send me a report within the next week. Otherwise, I'll have no other alternative but to refer the matter to my legal department and terminate the contract with you."

Rohit's stance was subdued now. "All right, I don't mind making an inquiry."

He dumped the phone on his table and wiped the sweat beads from his forehead.

Picking up the instrument swiftly a few minutes later, he bellowed, "Sachin, can you come to my house right away?"

Sachin was there in half an hour. "Something serious?" He asked, hurriedly pulling up a chair.

Rohit was grim. "Yes, it's bad news. Tom called. He feels something fishy is going on in the voice support we are providing to them. He said some unauthorized transactions have taken place in the bank. I don't know how he can pin it on us."

"But we have secure systems and no one can tamper with them."

Rohit took a deep breath. "He wants a report within a week; we have to do something about it. I feel we should have investigations on two fronts–internal and external."

Sachin was silent with questioning glances as Rohit went on, "I mean we should keep a close watch on our executives dealing with the bank and also check the recording of their conversations. If we find someone with any kind of suspicious conversations, we'll confirm it by an external surveillance. We can hire a detective agency for that. I'm sure you know some good people?"

Sachin nodded. "Good idea. Let me work on this. I have got some jobs done earlier by Alpha Detectives. I'll speak to them too."

"Let's meet again tomorrow morning in the office to review it."

***

Two days later, Rohit deleted a mail from some Bangalore institute offering a week's refresher courses in HR management. "Many mails still sneak into the inbox in spite of the spam filter," he reflected peevishly.

He looked up as he saw Sachin entering. "I've checked the recordings," Sachin said excitedly as he rushed in, "and I think we have a suspect, though at this stage we can't be sure."

"Okay, go ahead."

"Varun Mathur. First, on a couple of occasions, he has asked for the passwords from the bank customers. Second, he seems to have tried to call some customers and bank executives repeatedly on his own. There is a strong possibility of someone from the US bank also involved in this. The detective firm is already on the job, and we should be able to get the initial feedback on this in two days."

Varun Mathur. The name rang a bell in Rohit's ears. Jharna had mentioned his name and said he was a friend--maybe he was something more than that. Could he be involved in all this? Was the friendship a part of his ploy to gain confidence from her and cover up his maneuvering activity? No, he couldn't be sure. Not till he had the confirmation.

"Good job, Sachin," Rohit said aloud. "Keep tabs on the recordings and let me know." He stopped and his forehead furrowed as a thought rumbled into his mind. *While Varun is under surveillance, Jharna should not be seen with him. Otherwise, she may also get involved in the muddle. She needs to be packed off to some place for a few days.*

As Sachin began to rise, Rohit gestured him to stop. "Wait a minute."

He recovered the mail about the Bangalore institute that he had deleted a few minutes back, from the trash to the inbox and resumed, "Here is a mail from an HR institute that I'm forwarding to you. They are offering a one-week refresher course for HR professionals, starting tomorrow in Bangalore. I feel two of our HR executives–Jharna and one more person from the department–should attend. Can you please make arrangements for their travel? The institute will provide facilities for stay in their hostel."

"Okay, I'll get the flight bookings done for Jharna and Renu," Sachin said, as he exited.

***

The first report from the Alpha Detectives came after two days. During the last month, Varun had been spending evenings with an American woman, Lisa, in 'Hot and Juicy', a high end restaurant-bar. The woman had splurged a lot in the last two days, buying gifts for him.

The next one was clinching. Lisa had been arrested in her hotel in a midnight swoop by the police for possession of drugs. Varun was also likely to be questioned as an accomplice by the police.

By next day, Rohit's nerves had calmed. "Sachin, we did a good job by informing the police about Varun's suspicious activities," he said with a smug smile when they met in the office next day.

"Yes, of course. It's for sure that Varun has been a part of this dirty game in connivance with some counterparts in the US bank. But it's still not clear whether there was another person from the bank involved and what the mode of their operation was."

"Police will have the full story after interrogation."

***

Rohit was still in his bed next morning when he got a call from Sachin. He had been tossing and turning throughout the night, still worried about the NC Bank episode.

"I have to give you some bad news," Sachin said on the other end, "but in a way it's also good news."

"Okay, go on," Rohit said, his voice groggy.

"Varun was interrogated at the police station last night," Sachin said. "He has admitted he helped Lisa in laundering off twenty thousand dollars from a customer of NE Bank."

"Oh God!" Rohit yelled out. "Anyway, it'll be better to discuss this in person. Let's meet in the office in an hour."

"Okay, shoot," Rohit said impatiently, as he rushed into Sachin's cabin in the office.

Sachin rubbed his temples. "Well, it seems the twosome, Varun and Lisa Ashworth were in it together. Lisa, a former employee of NE Bank, was the mastermind. Varun got in touch with her on a social site and become friendly with her."

"And, how did they carry out this operation?"

"Varun would keep track of the accounts which had been dormant for long periods. Then, Lisa, being acquainted with the bank's database, managed to hack the database and generate fictitious requests for change of address and issue of debit cards on the new address."

Rohit flinched in his chair. "Hacked the database?"

"Yes–a neat job," Sachin said. "The new address belonged to Lisa. So, she received the debit cards with the PIN. She was the one who would withdraw the money from the customers' accounts. Then, she would split it with Varun. It was for this purpose that she came here about a month back."

"Oh god!" Rohit exclaimed as Sachin went on, "Perhaps, this would have remained a secret, if Lisa hadn't been into drugs, too. In a case of drug trafficking, the police got a lead from an informer about Lisa's involvement in that. They picked her up from her hotel room and got the entire dope about her involvement in drugs as well as her source of funds. That's when Varun's name cropped up."

Rohit leaned his elbow on the table, resting his palm on his chin. "It surely will bring some bad name to our company, though it is clear that NC bank was also involved. Let's give an additional assignment to our PR firm. They must carry out a damage-control exercise, with press releases clarifying our role–after all, we reported this matter to the police ourselves and we are clean on this."

As Rohit left for his cabin, he recalled his talk with Jharna, when he had advised her indirectly to keep away from Varun. Did he have an intuition about Varun's nefarious activities at that time? Would this episode hurt Jharna, as she was friendly with him? Anyway, it was good that she was far away in Bangalore, isolated from all the happenings here, he thought.

Of course, all this will be flashed in next day's newspapers and on the internet and she is bound to know all the details. But let her make own guesses why she was packed off to Bangalore at such short notice.

He rested his head on the back of his chair. "Now, let me speak to Tom. He is also responsible for this fiasco. His former employee, Lisa, was the mastermind."

***

CHAPTER 15

"Jharna, look for some good candidates for the data processing work. We have a new client and we want five dedicated people. Look in all the databases for which we subscribed recently," Rohit said into the intercom.

There was a few seconds silence from the other end. Then, he heard her weak, shaky voice. "Sir, I am in a bit of problem. Can I meet with you just now?"

Rohit straightened. What could be the problem? "Okay, come over," he said.

"Sir, my grandfather is seriously ill. So, I'll have to leave for Bilaspur immediately," she said hurriedly, wiping the moisture in her eyes. "Can you please allow me leave for a week? Meantime, Renu can handle the new recruitments."

Rohit's heart pounded heavily as the name 'Bilaspur' again activated memories of his past. Many years back, he had gone to that city frantically searching for Jhilmil. But who was her grandfather. Ramesar? He needed to make sure.

"That's so sad. Please hand over the charge to Renu and proceed on leave. Don't worry, your grandfather is going to be okay," he consoled her. "By the way, what is his name?"

"We call him *Baba,* but his actual name is Ramesar."

"Ah! I was right." Names and events crawled out like the worms from the earth after a heavy rain in Rohit's mind. Ramesar... Jharna's grandfather... Jhilmil's father... contractor in Udyog Nagar, with whom he had been very close. His stomach churned with nostalgic memories of the past.

He shifted in his seat as his thoughts tugged his mind in two directions–whether to lay bare his past before Jharna or remain aloof from her family.

"Sir..." Jharna's voice broke his thoughts.

No, now he could not hide these feelings any longer, he finally decided after shaking off the clouds in his mind. "When do you want to go?" He asked at last. "And where's your grandfather hospitalized?"

"He is in the civil hospital." Jharna replied. "The only train available now leaves late tonight. But I can't reach there before tomorrow morning as it is a slow train."

"That's a long time," Rohit thought. She should be with her family at the earliest. And he needed to be with her during this period of distress.

He rose from his seat. "Ah! I have to meet a vendor of our company there. Let's go together by car. It's only a three-hour drive."

"Sir, but I don't want to bother you."

"It's no problem at all. Now, get ready and I'll pick you up from your hostel in an hour."

The furrows on Jharna's face smoothed. "Thank you," she said and left hurriedly.

As Jharna left, he went over to the glazed window of the office and looked blankly at the silhouetted horizon. By offering to accompany Jharna, he had taken a deep plunge into the labyrinths of past and he was not sure what his trip to Bilaspur would lead to. Let destiny decide it, he thought finally.

***

"I hope you have brought an extra car with driver, as I informed you on the phone," Rohit asked the vendor's agent who had come to meet him at the Bilaspur hotel. "Please ask the chauffeur to take this young lady to the civil hospital. The car will remain at her disposal as long as she desires," he added pointing to Jharna.

On second thought, he turned to Jharna. "Give me the address of hospital where your grandfather is admitted. I'd like to meet him tomorrow morning."

As she slipped a hurriedly scribbled paper to Rohit and moved toward the car, Rohit noticed the quizzical expression on her face. Was she wondering why he had gone out of the way in accompanying her and whether that gesture indicated that he had some past connection with her grandfather?

Let her make her guesses. Soon, the layers of truth will get unfolded anyway.

***

Next morning, Jharna was grim as she looked out the window of the hospital ward that opened to a small car park near a green patch where some children were playing. She fondly reminisced about the love showered upon her by her grandfather since her childhood. Having lost her father when she was just five, it was *Baba* who had proxied for her father in bringing her up. Now, even he was on the death bed.

Last evening, when she had entered the hospital ward, she had found her grandfather gasping for breath intermittently. "Maa, what do the doctors say?" She had asked, hugging her mother.

She had tightened on the inside and tears had flooded her eyes as her mother had said amid sobs, "They say it is the last stage of lung cancer."

Ramesar was sleeping peacefully, but looking at his emaciated face, sunken cheeks and deep wrinkles, Jharna could guess that the situation was really bad.

The train of her thoughts broke as she heard a car screeching to a halt in the parking lot. Looking intently, she saw Rohit alighting from the car.

She rushed toward her mother who sat somberly by the side of patient's bed. "My boss has come to visit Baba. I just saw him in the hospital compound."

Her mother wiped the wetness on her cheeks. "Oh god!" She muttered covering her head with her *saree*. "It's is so untidy here."

Jharna touched her mother's shoulders and looked for a chair. "Never mind, maa, this is a hospital."

A nurse approached her mother. "Please let him rest for some time. If you come aside, I'll speak to you about the dosage of medicines."

***

As her mother followed the nurse to the far corner of the ward, Jharna walked to the entrance of the ward and saw Rohit approaching. "Thanks for coming, sir," she said. "This way please."

He whispered as Jharna offered a chair, "No, I'm okay. How is he now?"

The patient coughed slightly and opened his eyes slowly. Rohit bent forward and looked at him warmly.

"Who is there?" Ramesar asked feebly.

Rohit held the patient's frail hands. "I'm Rohit."

Ramesar's eyes contracted and he tried to rise on his elbow. "Rohit? Do I know you?" He muttered and opened his eyes wide. "Your voice seems to be a bit familiar. By any chance, are you Rohit from Udyog Nagar?"

She noticed Rohit's eyes moistening as he swallowed hard and said shakily, "Yes." Her eyes narrowed. How do the two know each other?

As Rohit supported the patient's shoulders to position him in a reclining position on the bed, she saw her mother approaching clutching *Baba*'s medical file. But she suddenly stilled and then leaned against a pillar in a dazed state, her eyes riveted on Rohit.

Jharna's mouth gaped wide and her hands went up impulsively to cover it. "Ah! Seems my mother also knows Rohit. It's so mysterious." Confounding riddles swayed her mind as she turned to look at her mother and Rohit in turns.

***

Rohit's eyes had also moved toward the woman approaching from a distance towards the patient bed, when he was distracted by Ramesar's distressed voice. "We're meeting after twenty years. I wish we could have met earlier. But that's destiny. Jharna had said her boss would be coming to visit me. And I could not imagine that you're her boss." He stopped as his body shook with bouts of coughing.

Rohit massaged his back for a while and helped him take a few sips of water. But he turned as he heard Ramesar saying in a raised voice, "Jhilmil, why are you standing away? Come here. Rohit has come...our Rohit."

Hearing Jhilmil's name, his heart missed a beat. He was dazed momentarily with his vision blurred with moisture, but he managed to sneak a glance at her. *Ah! She looks the same, excepting that she has some grey hair and looks exhausted, though there is still a faint glow on her face. It's so sad that I am meeting her again in these sad circumstances.*

His mind was flooded with nostalgia as Jhilmil straightened the *saree*, and stepped forward. Her eyes welled up and then she burst into tears, as she folded her hands to greet Rohit. "How are you?" She said, her voice choking.

Before he could answer, a doctor, his grey hair ruffled, followed by two juniors came over. He saw the reports and his expression turned grave as he pulled down the lower lids of patient's eyes. "Hmm," he said stone-faced and started walking away.

Rohit followed the doctor in the corridor and talked to him about Ramesar's latest health status. Jhilmil also joined them. "The patient's condition–well, he appears to be at the terminal stage. The rest is in God's hands," the doctor said, raising his hand to the sky. "He has been insisting that he be allowed to go home. So, we will discharge him today. You can continue the treatment at home."

Rohit looked at Jhilmil. She nodded. But no words were exchanged.

***

Rohit arranged the ambulance and the patient was moved to his house.

After chatting for some time and humoring him, Rohit got up and patted Ramesar's hand. "I'd leave now and try to come again tomorrow."

Ramesar clasped his hand. "Thank you for coming..." he said weakly, but broke off as he started wheezing. After a few seconds of laboured breathing, he resumed, "Please wait for few minutes...I want to show you something."

He looked toward Jhilmil and said, "Please get my small box from the almirah." Jhilmil brought the old, rusted box and placed it on a stool near her father's bed.

Ramesar's voice faltered. "Jhilmil, Jharna, I want to speak to Rohit in privacy for a few minutes."

As the two women walked out, Ramesar turned slowly on his bed and with trembling fingers opened the latch of his box and pulled out a few faded papers, neatly folded.

He held two papers in his hand. "Rohit, I want to shed off my guilt before I die. So, I want to disclose to you something very confidential..." He broke off as a wheezing bout overtook him again.

Then, he slowly related the events of over twenty two years back when he had been forced by the factory chief to move out of Udyog Nagar with his family. He was also regretful that he himself had been instrumental in stopping all communication between Jhilmil and Rohit by stopping his daughter's letters from being posted.

He lifted his trembling hand with the letters towards Rohit.

"There are just two that somehow remained with me. I want to give these to you, though I know it's meaningless now. At least, it'll clear my conscience, before I leave this world."

Goosebumps rose in Rohit's body and he covered his face in his hands, as the man talked in halting voice.

"Just have a look at the letters. Jhilmil loved you like the mythological Radha loved Krishna," Ramesar continued, as his moisture-clad eyelids closed. "You can read these at home."

Rohit sat speechless, bolts of pain piercing his heart while Ramesar's lips moved again. "I forced her to marry a man against her wishes. But her husband died after a few years of marriage. Jharna was just about five at that time."

His voice was becoming incoherent. "These are my last moments. Please take care of both of them, after my death. Will you?"

Rohit's hand shook as he took the letters and put them in his pocket. "Don't worry. You will live for many more years. Tomorrow, I'll get you shifted to another private hospital where a team of specialists will operate upon you to remove the tumor. After that, everything will be okay."

As he finished, he saw Ramesar closing his eyes and going to sleep.

He tip-toed out of the room towards the two women standing in the corner and said, "He is sleeping. I'll leave now. Please keep me informed about his health. I think we should move him to a specialty hospital tomorrow for an operation."

Jhilmil didn't raise her head and she kept staring at her toes, while Rohit continued, "Don't worry. God willing, he will live. I'll try my best to save him."

"Thank you," Jhilmil said meekly.

Jharna saw Rohit off at the gate. "Sir, you have been of so much help. How would I have handled all this without you?"

On his way to the hotel, Rohit's mind was flustered. Why was Jhilmil so silent? Besides her grief over her father's severe illness, there appeared to be shades of pain and sadness lurking in her eyes whenever he looked at her. Was it because she was angry she had not received any response to the letters she had written to him? Was it because of her helplessness; or was it something else?

***

Rohit proceeded directly to his hotel room. With wavering hands he took out the two letters, bearing the dates of twenty two years back, from his pocket. The first one read:

"Rohit,

Destiny has taken me far away from you. In the last two years, you brought a lot of transformation in me, from being a little teenager to a mature woman. It was a meeting of souls. Please don't forget me...ever, wherever you are.

"I could not express these feelings to you for two reasons. First, because I don't belong to the same social strata as you and I couldn't withstand an immediate rejection.

"Second, because I am a shy person by nature and I had been waiting for the moment when I could see the feelings of reciprocal love in your eyes.

"I'm not sure whether we'll ever meet again. But I'll live the rest of my life in the aura of my infinite love for you.

"Yours forever,

"Jhilmil."

Rohit wiped his eyes and placed the letter aside. He picked up the second letter hesitatingly as his mind debated whether he should open it or not as it may deepen his scars further.

Finally, he read it:

"Rohit,

"I didn't get your reply to my last letter. Either you've not received it or you've decided to ignore it.

"This world is like a full circle. Perhaps, we'll meet some day. Till that time, I'll survive on the memories of our meetings under the banyan tree, near the brooks and in the school, which had ushered in a new spirit in me and transformed my life.

"Goodbye,

"Yours forever

"Jhilmil."

He had a prickly pain smoldering down to his stomach as he moved to the balcony of his hotel room. So, it was the Chief who had villainously planned the ouster of Ramesar and Jhilmil from the factory. Why did Jhilmil not express her sentiments to him when they had been meeting frequently? Why did she remain silent when he met her and sent a message to her through Barli? Had he done injustice to her and hurt her?

A ring on his phone interrupted his thoughts. It was Jharna's call.

There were no words, only sobbing on the other end. A current of grief went through his spine.

"Sir, Baba is no more." He heard the words amid sobs from the other end.

"Oh god! I'm reaching there soon," he said and dashed out.

***

After the final rites were over, Rohit sat somberly in Jharna's house. He had learnt that after their separation, Jhilmil had graduated and started her own school for poor children. A book of her poems had been published. That was a continuation of what they had planned at Udyog Nagar. She had kept her part of the promise, but destiny had prevented him from sharing those moments with her.

Restless, he got up and paced back and forth the verandah, with his hands clasped behind him. What to do next? He had made a promise to the dying man, who had so far been a great support to the family that he would take care of Jhilmil and Jharna. Should he stay on and offer help to them? Would he be misunderstood if he did that?

His fingers brushed his hair as perplexing thoughts ran through his mind, when he saw Jharna approaching with a cup of tea.

"Sir, thank you for all the help."

Rohit took a sip of tea. "No need to say that. What I did was my duty."

Jharna sat with her eyes downcast. Her lips moved but she didn't speak.

"It seems you want to say something, but are hesitating," Rohit said softly.

Jharna shifted in her seat. "You're right. I want to talk to you on a personal matter. I have to fulfill a promise I made to grandfather a few moments before his death."

"A promise?" He repeated, narrowing his eyebrows. Another promise?

"He told me things I didn't know earlier," she started.

After wiping her face, she went on, "You may feel it odd but this is the time when I need to share with you all that grandfather said about your relationship with my mother and the circumstances leading to your separation."

Rohit raised his eyes and looked around anxiously to check if Jhilmil too was around, as Jharna continued. "I know it is an intrusion on your and my mother's privacy, but I feel I should honour the words of a dying person."

Rohit's head was tilted to one side and he averted Jharna's eyes. "Okay, carry on," he said feebly.

"He told me you were friendly with my mother, about setting up a school with my mother and then leaving for the USA many years back...also some letters written by her to you...of course, which you never ...."

She broke off abruptly and looked down rubbing her hands.

Rohit's eyes were downcast. Jharna knows the whole story now. It would be good if she unloads her mind off anything else.

Soon, he shifted, and his gaze was now fixed on her. "Yes, what you say is true. But there seems to be something more in your mind that you want to speak about."

"You're right. I want that both you and my mother share some memories of the past or at least exchange a few words, before you leave," she pleaded.

Rohit had himself been yearning to spend some time with Jhilmil but he was not sure what would come out of that, excepting that it would create heart-burning for both. But looking at Jharna's expectant expressions, he yielded. "Okay, as you say."

"Please wait while I call her here."

***

"My mother has suffered so much. She hasn't spoken a word or eaten anything since Baba's death. Perhaps, meeting Rohit may unburden her of her distress," Jharna thought as she stepped to her mother's room.

"Maa, Rohit is our guest. It'd be good if you spend some time with him before he leaves," she said holding her mother's hand.

"Okay," Jhilmil said after a few thoughtful moments. "But wait for a few minutes. I'll return soon."

Later, Jharna led her mother to meet Rohit in the other room. "I'll make arrangements for dinner and join you in a few minutes," she said, her eyes misty. She closed the door slowly. But through a small aperture in the door he saw her mother speaking to Rohit. Low, interrupted, sobbing filled the room.

***

Rohit put on a faint smile as Jhilmil entered the room with a small book and sat a little distance away from him on the settee.

A lump clogged his throat. But soon, he composed himself. "I'm sorry about your father, but it was destined this way," he started.

Jhilmil tried to muffle her sobs mingled with intermittent coughs with the corner of her *saree*. "Yes, but it is a big loss to me," she said with a great effort. "I am thankful to you for giving a good job to Jharna and also for coming all the way here to help us."

Rohit raised his arm hesitantly to place a consoling hand on her shoulder, but retracted it. "That's no problem. And you needn't worry in future, either. I will do whatever I can."

He wanted earnestly that she come close to him, rest her head on his chest and unburden herself. But she didn't make a move. Instead, she picked up the book that she had kept on the settee and passed it to him. "This is my book of poems that I wrote during all these years. It is for you," she began with a dry smile but stopped suddenly.

Rohit had just turned to look at the cover page of the book, when his eyes caught sight of Jhilmil's body shaking, her head on the backrest. After a few seconds, her face contorted and she shuddered violently.

"Jharna, come here! Quick, call the doctor!" Rohit shouted. He tried to get closer to hold Jhilmil. But before he could touch her she coughed heavily and spat out blood that spewed on her *saree* and the floor. Instantaneously, her eyes grew black and swollen, her lower body slipped to the ground and her head dropped in Rohit's lap.

Jharna rushed in. "Maa, get up," she cried.

"My Rohit is back," Jhilmil mumbled weakly. "I'll be okay now."

***

The doctor pronounced Jhilmil dead within minutes of his arrival.

As Jharna cried and cried with tears gushing out, Rohit turned to the doctor grimly. "How did this happen all of a sudden?"

What the doctor said was startling. "You seem to be a family friend, but perhaps you or for that matter even Jharna don't know that it is not a sudden death. Jhilmil has been under my treatment for tuberculosis for the last two months but unfortunately, she came to me very late, when it had already advanced to the last stage. It seems she had been afflicted by disease for several years, caused by continued mental stress, but she had been neglecting it."

Ratan Kaul

Shrapnels of pain pierced Rohit's heart and he cried. So, the glow on her face that he had noticed when he saw her in the hospital was not a real 'glow' but the redness typical of a TB patient.

He fondly clutched the book given by Jhilmil. He found, when he returned to his hotel, that all the poems depicted the days they had spent together many years earlier.

***

EPILOGUE

A year had passed since Rohit adopted Jharna as a daughter and they moved to their sprawling new bungalow.

On a winter Sunday, he was playing a video game in his study while Jharna was busy setting the up a canopy in the lawn. "Papa, Let's have our lunch here in the open today," she announced loudly.

"I'm on the last level of 'Mercenaries'. Will join in five minutes," he replied. Soon, he walked down the stairs with a paper in his hand and a smile playing on his lips. "Jharna, read this print-out of an email I received a few minutes back."

A glow kindled her face as she read the mail.

"Dad,

"Seems, you've forgotten me. Of course, it is a natural consequence of my misdeeds. But now, I'm out of rehab and I've got back to the mainstream. I've left USA, leaving behind my old memories, and with the help of Uncle Tony, entered Leeds University in England for an undergrad course. I have also joined a band, "Dazzle" that is the buzz of the town here.

"I learnt that mom has started her new life with Doctor Ganesh and Annie has married Mike. They are not in touch with me. Perhaps, you've also settled down with something new. I am the only one left all alone.

"Please forgive me and meet me.

"Dad, I love you. Miss you a lot.

"Samrat

P.S. Can I come to India and spend time with you during my vacation?"

"Wow, that's great news, papa."

Rohit placed his arm on her shoulder. "You've always been complaining that you didn't have a brother. So, here is one for you. I'll ask him to spend the Christmas vacation with us."

"Thanks," she said hugging her father. "Let me lay the table now."

"Is this the beginning of another journey…another circle of life?" He wondered, as Jharna walked to the kitchen.

Reflecting on his past, he conjured up the image of a fortune wheel. The wheel turns and he becomes an engineer. More turns of the wheel and Jhilmil and Sunita come in his life. Facing the vicissitudes of his journey, he finally comes back to his roots. Every change is a turn of a wheel, for good or for ill, but it is not in his hands…someone else governs the circling of fate.

Jharna's voice snapped his thoughts. "Oh! I forgot to give you these red berries, that I and our maid picked from the forest near our house. I hope you'd like them." she placed a small basket before him and left.

As he picked up a berry and smelt it, bitter-sweet nostalgia over took him. He and Jhilmil had endearing moments while they munched the red jungle berries sitting on the stone slabs in the forest near the factory. He regretted momentarily that he didn't do more to find Jhilmil.

Perhaps he also didn't make the best of his marriage with Sunita.

But, he had at last achieved the kind of family he always wanted, even if it was a surrogate family. Even his son was returning to him.

Jharna was back soon with a tray. "Papa, here's sweet-corn soup for you."

"She is the most precious jewel in my life," Rohit thought as he looked up at Jharna.

A small smile worked up gradually on his face as he dipped his spoon into the bowl.

Life had come a full circle for him.

***

www.ingramcontent.com/pod-product-compliance
Lightning Source LLC
Chambersburg PA
CBHW022036240626
47154CB00007B/2435